CASTLES IN THE AIR

FELICE STEVENS

DEDICATION

To my family, now and for always.

ACKNOWLEDGMENTS

Thanks to my editor, Keren Reed, for always pointing me in the right direction. To Hope and Jess from Flat Earth Editing, for making my books shine. Thanks to Dianne from Lyrical Lines for the eagle eyes. And thanks to Reese for the magic and fairy dust to give me covers I couldn't even dream up in my head.

To my readers, thank you as always for making this the best damn job in the world.

And to Ash, for showing me the way.

PROLOGUE

RYAN

Ryan had never felt so hopeless. Garrett was married and gone forever. They'd been divorced for almost three years, and the announcement in the newspaper hadn't come as a complete surprise, but still…

He sighed and tossed aside his phone. Time to get his ass in gear. Now that his license was suspended and he couldn't practice law, he needed a job. Remi had been a stand-up guy to lend him money to get his life back together, but Ryan needed to repay him, and that required a job with a steady paycheck.

The loan agreement sat on his nightstand—he kept the papers there as a daily reminder of how far he'd fallen. But there was something else. He picked up the second page and studied the sprawling signature of the attorney and witness to the agreement. He ran his fingers over the name. Logan's signature was as bold and arrogant as he was.

Logan Silver.

How long had it been since their shocking hookup at

the Marquee—one year? Two?

He couldn't recall—time flew when you were getting high and drunk enough to escape everything you'd lost.

Sex with Garrett had been sweet and about giving each other pleasure, but Logan was a force. Hard. Demanding. Needy.

Ryan had never felt so thoroughly *owned* by another man. The marks left on his body had lasted for days, and he'd relished their soreness.

They'd run into each other at bar association meetings and events, and they'd danced around the sizzling attraction between them. Divorced and spiraling, it had taken a night fueled by too much alcohol and God knew what else for him to lay his desire bare.

Maybe deep down Ryan had hoped something might grow between them, but that had been nothing more than wishful thinking from a one-night stand. Their connection had burned hot and bright that evening, in the shadows of the Marquee, but it had obviously meant nothing to Logan other than another hookup. Not surprising, since the man possessed the killer trifecta: stunning looks, crackling-sharp intelligence, and money to burn. Logan Silver could have whomever he wanted, so why would that be a washed-up, messy failure of a man?

It sure as hell wouldn't be him, Ryan Matson, who'd clawed his way up to the summit of the mountain, and instead of planting that flag of ownership and beating his chest with his enormous accomplishment, chose to throw it in the air, and then watched as it all fell to the ground and shattered into a million pieces that could never be made whole.

Upon the receipt of the letter informing him he'd been suspended from the practice of law, his dreams of success lay smashed to bits. Where once he'd been number one on everyone's lips, he was now a pariah. No one called to check up on him or just to say hello. None of his former colleagues, not his party friends, nor the clubbers he hung out with to get high.

He should've known. People only wanted a winner.

And Logan Silver wasn't a man to hang out with losers. He was at the top of his game. The man dined at the finest restaurants, wore the most elegant clothes, and rubbed elbows with the elite—the best of the best. Ryan no longer fit into that category, and he wondered what Logan had thought, reading Ryan's name on the loan agreement. He knew. It was what he saw every day reflected in the mirror.

Loser.

"The man is out of your league. Get over it."

He grunted and forced himself to get out of bed.

"Time to figure out how to make some money. They say pride goes before the fall, and man, you fell on your ass big-time. Get up and get moving."

Something would work out. It had to.

* * *

A month later, he was pushing a mop along the marble floor at the Sheraton hotel in Manhattan. Desperation had made him seek out jobs he would've never considered only five years earlier, but when the money Remi had lent him started to shrink at an alarming rate, he no longer had the luxury of choice. He hadn't even begun to think about repaying him—another albatross around his neck—but he knew he'd have to make an attempt, even if it was only a hundred dollars a month. Something to show good faith, because he was already behind on payments and while he doubted Remi would come after him, Ryan didn't want to end up owing him for the rest of his life.

With drugs on his arrest record, his selection of jobs was meager. The law might say it protected you, but Ryan knew that was a big, fat farce. Employers had a way of finding out your ugly past. A job working as a janitor in the hotel came along, and as he'd had no other opportunities, he took it.

He tried to keep away from booze and drugs, but it was damn hard, and with no one to talk to or give a damn if he lived or died, he'd indulge. After his shift ended, he'd sometimes party with a coworker and get high or have a few shots of vodka in the morning to get him through the misery of a day spent cleaning toilets. It steadied him. With the walls closing in and the beast of fear and loneliness crawling inside him, getting high was the only way to beat back that devil.

He was getting better, though. Not every day found him reaching for the bottle, and he planned to eventually wean himself completely.

Soon.

His manager, Luis, called him over.

"Ryan, make sure you go to the men's room in the lobby and clean out the trash and replace the toilet paper and soaps; then go do the ballrooms on the second floor."

"I was planning to, as soon as I finished the floors here." He tried to keep a pleasant face, but Luis rode him hard, especially once he'd found out his history as a disgraced attorney.

"Make it quick. We have a group coming in for a conference—some of your old *compadres*."

His stomach bottomed out. "What're you talking about?"

Luis sneered. "You know. *Lawyers.*"

Pretending nonchalance, he shrugged. "I doubt I know anyone. There are a million lawyers in New York City. I'd better get going."

He hurried off, leaving Luis frowning. *Stupid fucker.* Luis loved belittling him and telling him his fancy law degree didn't mean anything anymore. He was right about that, though.

As he passed through the lobby, he glanced at the events

board. The digital sign flashed with the names of all the groups meeting that day. Sure enough, the New York State Bar Contract Law Subcommittee was in Ballroom A.

"Good thing I don't know anyone."

Feeling more secure, he completed mopping the floor and, after loading a cart with supplies, stopped by the lobby bathroom before taking the service elevator to the second floor. A flood of suits meandered about, and to his dismay, he did see a few faces he recognized, so he put his head down and pushed his cart to the bathroom. Once inside, he cleaned the stalls and restocked everything.

As he opened the door to leave, a man smacked right into him. "Sorry," Ryan said with an apologetic smile that died the moment he made eye contact.

Shit. Shit. Shit.

Logan's face froze with shock as his stunned gaze swept over him. "Ryan?"

In his uniform, carrying a bag of garbage in one hand and cleaning supplies in the other, there was no mistaking him for anything other than an employee. Flushing hot with humiliation, Ryan, without answering, pushed past Logan, dumped the items into the cart, and took off for the service elevator. He breathed a sigh of relief when Logan didn't come after him.

Why would he? Imagine me with Logan now. What a joke.

But he couldn't forget the hungry kisses they'd shared in the back of the club, the feel of Logan's hands on his naked skin.…The memory of the lusty encounter made him dizzy. The regret of his fall from grace tasted all the more bitter now that he'd seen Logan standing before him in his Italian business suit, fresh white shirt, and heavy silk tie. Ryan had made his choices and now had to live with them.

Those days are gone. The sooner you realize it, the better.

At six he clocked off his shift and picked up a fast-food

burger on his way home. He entered his tiny apartment, kicked off his sneakers, and opened the bag. It wasn't a healthy diet, but it was cheap and tasty, and Ryan took a refreshing sip of soda. In his former life, on a hard day, he'd get high at a club and end up passed out somewhere… with someone.

Some vodka he'd bought over the weekend and stashed under the sink awaited. He imagined clutching the cool bottle, the icy liquid sliding down his throat, the sweet oblivion of alcohol burning through his blood, his problems drifting away in a white mist of nothingness.

The dumbfounded expression on Logan's face came to mind, and he pictured the pitying looks sent his way after he ran off. His stomach curdled, and his jaw hardened. He wouldn't let his embarrassment drive him to get drunk. Ryan closed his eyes, breathing deeply, willing himself to ignore the alcohol's siren call.

Not this time, motherfucker.

The urge passed, and he exhaled. Maybe there was hope for him yet. He could resist. Proud of his strength, he popped some fries into his mouth. He could do this. He *would*.

Someone knocked, but he ignored it. He'd learned long ago not to fall for that game. Open the door if you weren't expecting someone, and you got robbed or worse. He'd just taken a big bite of his cheeseburger when the knocking turned to pounding, and a voice joined in.

"Ryan. Open the door. It's me. Logan."

Fuck.

He swallowed and crossed the room to stand by the door, but he didn't open it. "Logan, who?"

"Not funny. Open up. Now."

Ryan hated to admit it, but that bossy, demanding tone was a bit of a turn-on. That, and remembering how Logan had gotten them both off in public at that club. Ryan wiped his sweaty hands on his jeans, undid the locks, and turned the knob. An unsmiling Logan faced him.

"Okay. I opened it. Now you saw me." He pushed to shut the door, but Logan wasn't having any of that and shoved hard against it, sending him back several steps.

"Don't be an asshole." Logan strode inside. "What the hell is going on with you?"

Ryan glared at him. "I'm trying to eat my dinner. That's what."

Logan glanced at the table and wrinkled his nose. "Since when do you eat that shit?"

"Since I've been suspended from the bar, lost my job, and can't afford Per Se and Jean-Georges anymore," he spat out. "If you've come here to deride me for losing my license and working cleaning bathrooms, have at it." He opened his arms wide. "I'm an easy target. I'll save you the trouble. I fucked up, and I'm getting what I deserve. I know. I was a shit husband and dumb as hell to get sucked into the life."

Logan raised a brow and crossed his arms. "Yeah, I think that about covers it. But from where I stand, you're also lucky as hell."

Ryan snorted. "Yeah, lucky me. I didn't have to clean up someone's piss or vomit today."

"Don't whine about your problems to me." Logan grabbed his arms and shook him. "You are so fucking lucky Remi is a nice guy and gave you a second chance. I told him he was crazy."

"You would."

"I've known him for years. And yeah, I wouldn't want him to get mixed up with someone who's high and drunk all the time. He's not only a client. He's my friend."

"Well, bully for him," Ryan said bitterly. "Remi's got it all—money, looks, friends who stick by him, and my husband."

"Ex-husband. They're married."

"I know. I saw the announcement."

Still holding him, Logan's touch gentled. "What's happening with you?"

Ryan tried to laugh, but it sounded more like a sob. "Nothing. I'm just trying to get my life in order."

"I know…I can't imagine it's been easy."

"No. It hasn't. It's been fucking hard. But I've been trying to stay sober since I was released from the hospital."

Logan massaged his shoulders. "Very good. Something to be proud of."

God, that felt good. He hadn't been touched in so long. No need to tell Logan about his occasional slipups. How he couldn't resist getting high after work. He didn't need a lecture. He wanted…goddammit, he wanted Logan's arms around him. He wanted someone to lean on for once. Someone to tell him it would be okay.

"Thank you," he whispered, hanging his head. "It's been isolating, doing it on my own. I go to meetings and have a sponsor I can check in with whenever I want, but still…sometimes I think, why bother? Maybe I should just disappear. No one would notice."

More lies, as he hadn't been to a meeting in weeks. What was the point? Sitting in a room and listening to people talk about their lives and misery wasn't going to help him. He already knew what he'd lost. Lying to Logan was as easy as lying to himself.

Logan tightened his grip. "Don't say that."

He lifted his chin to meet Logan's eyes. "Why not?"

"I would care."

Ryan chuckled. "Come on, Logan. You haven't thought of me in ages."

"That's not true." Logan's gravelly voice softened. "I remember. That night at the Marquee."

Pretending nonchalance, Ryan shrugged, but he hadn't forgotten Logan touching him, or the blinding orgasm his touch had pulled from him. "Yeah, it was a hot hookup."

"It was."

"So? I'm sure you've had plenty."

Logan's grin was wry. "Lately not as many as you might think. And you…you were special."

Ryan snorted, unwilling to fall for Logan's sweet words. "Yeah, sure. I bet you say that to everyone. Were you hoping to come here and get laid? Did you figure I'm so desperate, I'd be ready and willing like I was that night?"

"I don't think you're desperate. I think you're doing what you need to survive, and it's admirable. I just wanted you to know that if you need a friend, I'm here."

Stunned, Ryan stared at him. "You? A friend?"

Logan winced. "I guess I deserve that. But really, Ryan, you weren't exactly trying to connect with me either. I'm not into the hot-and-heavy party scene. I don't do drugs, and I prefer to spend my nights with a companion who'll at least remember whom he had sex with the next morning."

Ryan grimaced. "Okay. So why…why did it happen in the first place? Why did you kiss me at the club?"

Logan's gentle fingers skimmed over his face, and Ryan shivered with desire even as he burned. "I always thought you were sexy as hell. But you were married."

Ryan's heart hammered. "I'm not married anymore."

Logan gripped his chin, and Ryan grew hard. "No, you're not. But you also have a lot on your plate."

"And you don't need someone who doesn't fit in with your lifestyle."

Steely sparks shot from Logan's eyes. "Did I say that?"

"You don't have to. You're gorgeous and rich, and you can have anyone you want. And you do. I won't be a back door for you to dip your wick when you're between those dinners at Jean-Georges. I'm no one's pity fuck."

Logan's mouth met his with brutal intensity, and Ryan moaned and clung to him. Their tongues battled, and Logan sucked and bit his bottom lip. He let Ryan go and held him by the shoulders, fingers digging into the muscle. "I don't pity you, but I won't deny I want you again."

Ryan gathered his fractured wits. "I-I'm not ready to sleep with you. As much as I want to, I have to get my head on straight." God, he was such a good liar. Another kiss, and he'd give Logan everything he wanted. He drew in a shaky breath. "I think it would be a bad idea to have sex with you."

"I respect that." Logan nodded. "But you can always use another friend, right?"

"Party of one, no waiting," Ryan joked. "You'll own the top spot." It wasn't easy to admit. "I don't have any friends left from the past, but it's okay. It—it isn't easy to go it alone, but if that's the only way, then I'll do it. I have to."

"I mean it, Ryan. I'll be there for you. People are allowed to fuck up. It's how they recover from it that shows their true colors."

"I want to," he said with fervor he hadn't admitted to anyone, most of all himself. Maybe this was his turning point. He could do it if he had someone in his corner. "I know I was to blame for losing Garrett. I didn't love him like I should've."

"Was it the money?" Logan challenged him, and he flushed with shame.

"Not at the very beginning, but when I found out how much he had? Yeah, I made sure to lock it up and marry him. But I was wrong. I'm just sorry I hurt him so badly. I said some nasty, stupid things I'm ashamed of. He's a great guy, and he deserved better."

"You're right. Garrett's a sweetheart, and he and Remi are ridiculously happy now. He's better off." Logan pulled him closer. "Just so you know, I wouldn't be so nice if someone fucked me over like that," he rumbled.

"I-I know." Ryan gulped, but that growly, possessive tone did turn him the fuck on. "I'd never do it again. I learned my lesson." His dick throbbed, but he remained resolute and pulled away from Logan. "It might be a while."

"Get yourself straightened out and healthy. That's what matters."

"You're not the same person you were when we hooked up," Ryan mused. "What's changed?"

Grief clouded Logan's eyes. "My father died. And in the hospital, he told me he wished he could know I was settled and happy. I'm forty-four, and seeing all these people in the clubs almost half my age…I don't want to be one of those ridiculous old men they talk about who's always on the hunt. I know the reputation I have, and while it was earned, I don't have to like it. Not anymore."

"No, but it's a pretty drastic turnaround. You got us off in public, in a club."

Logan turned red. "Would you believe it if I said that was the first time for me? But you were so fucking hot, and though I knew you were high, I was so turned-on, I couldn't help myself. Do you resent me for it? If so, I'm sorry."

"I don't resent you," Ryan admitted. "I wasn't so high that I didn't know exactly what I was doing. I wanted you. And I haven't forgotten that night either. But if things end up progressing, I'd want more between us than sex," he said, surprised by his own honesty.

"I understand. You know, I was invited to Remi and Garrett's housewarming, and seeing them so happy and planning a future…it got me thinking. I don't want to be alone anymore. I want one special person to be happy I'm there for them. And have me be their support."

This wasn't the Logan Silver he knew.

Then again, he didn't really know Logan. He barely knew himself.

"I think everyone wants that. Trust me"—his gaze swept over the ratty little studio—"living here is no picnic."

"You don't have to." Logan's distaste for his apartment was so patently obvious, Ryan rolled his eyes.

"Well, it's not like I can afford anything better."

It wasn't often Logan showed uncertainty—not from what Ryan knew of him. But now Logan opened his mouth, chewed the inside of his cheek, and licked his lips. Ryan waited. "I have a second bedroom. Move in with me."

Ryan laughed. "Yeah, right."

"I'm serious. You've said you're not ready for anything beyond friendship, and I'm fine with that. But friends help friends, especially ones in need."

"You can't mean it."

"I don't say things I don't mean, Ryan. Let me help you."

Guilt swirled through him even as he considered Logan's incredibly generous offer. Logan believed he was sober and attempting to put his life together. He had no idea Ryan still used. Maybe this would be the turning point for him. Maybe he could do it.

"Okay. Thanks, Logan. You won't regret it."

CHAPTER ONE

LOGAN

Logan opened the door to the apartment, and his heart sank.

It was dark. Empty.

He called out, "Ryan? Are you home?"

No answer.

"Goddammit," he cursed, tossing his briefcase to the floor. His long stride took him across the living room of his penthouse apartment toward Ryan's bedroom. Floor-to-ceiling windows provided a sweeping vista of the city, but he failed to notice the beauty of the glittering lights. Logan had one thing—one person—on his mind.

"Ryan, where the fuck are you?" Logan muttered, anxiety and anger twisting in his gut and growing with each step.

Maybe Ryan did something drastic. At that alarming thought, Logan slammed open the bedroom door, not knowing whether to be relieved or furious that no one was there. He checked the bathroom. Empty as well.

Fear clawed through his belly, and he strode to his

bedroom, holding out hope Ryan would be there.

He knew what was going on in Ryan's head. Two days earlier, Ryan had received notification from the State Bar that his law license would not be reinstated. Not that Ryan had told him—Logan had come home from an out-of-town business trip and found the crumpled letter next to Ryan's bed, resting beside an empty bottle of vodka.

Ryan was nowhere to be found, and neither was Logan's gold watch or the cash he kept in the drawer of his nightstand. For the past forty-eight hours, Logan had done nothing but wrack his brain, trying to figure out where Ryan might be, and hunt through the city in a fruitless search.

His mind working furiously, Logan sank to his empty bed. It wasn't as if he knew Ryan's old haunts. They'd only had that one night at the Marquee before Ryan's troubles caught up with him. Logan hadn't run in Ryan's circle of hard partying. He'd already seen enough of how the city could chew you up and spit you out if you weren't tough enough. Maybe it was a sure sign he was getting old, but he preferred to think of it as growing wiser.

There was no one from Ryan's former life Logan could call or text; Ryan had told him all his old law-firm associates treated him like a pariah—something Logan could've told him would happen. People loved a winner, but it was much more fun to kick a dog when he was down. He hadn't made any friends at the maintenance job where Logan had run into him five months earlier. Hoping to salvage Ryan's job after he disappeared, Logan had put in a call to the hotel's maintenance office to say Ryan had the flu.

Logan spun the phone around in his hands, staring at the screen. He couldn't lose another person this way; he had to do something…anything. He wracked his brain thinking of the name and number of someone who could possibly help.

It might be a call Ryan would be furious at him for making, but knowing his fragile state, Logan couldn't stand by and watch him destroy everything he'd worked toward in the past year.

"Dex, hi, it's Logan Silver. Ryan Matson's friend?"

"Yeah, hi."

Not the most welcoming of greetings, but Logan didn't need a best friend. He needed to find Ryan. Immediately.

"Uh…Ryan's in trouble. I was hoping you could help." He explained the situation.

Dex sucked in a sharp breath. "Shit. No, I have no clue where he could be. Ryan rarely comes to meetings. I've tried to encourage him, but he's pretty stubborn when he doesn't want to do something."

"True," Logan agreed. "But I thought he was attending regularly?" He'd even picked up Ryan a couple of times after meetings.

"No. If I see him once a month, that's a lot."

Dammit. If Ryan had lied to him about going to meetings, what else was he lying about?

Dex said, "As his sponsor, I've tried to encourage him to talk, suggested we meet for coffee, anything so I could understand him better, but as I'm sure you know, he keeps things pretty close to the vest."

"Fuck," Logan swore, knowing Dex told the truth. Ryan was the type to sit and observe but not speak. Logan could relate. He was the same.

"If he calls or comes to the next meeting, could you let me know?"

"I mean…" Dex seemed to hesitate. "I'm there for Ryan, not to report back to you. And the meetings are confidential."

"He's in trouble, Dex, and I'm afraid he might start using again. I just need to know he's all right."

"Sorry, Logan. Best I can do is try to talk to Ryan, gauge his state of mind and help him, however I can."

"Thanks." *For nothing.* Logan ended the call. Thinking hard, he searched his memory. There was another person at the meetings Ryan had mentioned talking to… He started pacing. What the fuck was his name? Eddie…Eric…no… Emerson. That was it. This Emerson had called Logan a month or so ago, when Ryan had left his phone behind in an AA meeting, and he'd stopped by the apartment to return it. Logan searched through old calls and found the number. Ryan had mentioned Emerson as someone he considered a friend. Emerson understood Ryan's situation. As a transplant from a small town upstate, he'd fallen prey to the temptation of the city. Ten years sober, he was an inspiration to Ryan, and Logan could understand their connection.

"Emerson? It's Logan. Logan Silver."

"Hi."

Logan shifted the phone to his other ear. "I'm calling about Ryan."

"Ryan?" His even-tempered voice turned wary. "What about him?"

"Ryan received notification from the State Bar that they're rejecting his reinstatement appeal. He'd been hoping that the time he's worked at the hotel, and especially after being promoted to maintenance supervisor, would show the committee he'd changed and could be trusted enough to get his license reinstated and practice again."

"Yeah, he was cautiously optimistic."

"I wasn't," Logan said flatly. "I had no desire to squash his dreams, but the reality is, he's never going to practice again. He has two felony counts on his record. That's about as impossible to come back from as death."

"Damn, that's rough. I hope you've been supportive."

"If I knew where he was, I would be. He's gone."

"Gone? What do you mean?"

"What don't you understand?" Logan snapped, on edge.

"I mean, maybe he went for a walk, or he's having dinner with a friend."

Logan restrained himself from throwing the phone across

the room. "No. I was away and came home to an empty bottle. That was two days ago, and I've heard nothing from him. He hasn't been home and hasn't shown up for work. I gave them the excuse that he's got the flu, but fuck, I don't know where to go anymore. In between seeing my clients, I've been spending my time looking for him. I was hoping you might have some ideas."

"And you've tried calling him."

"Obviously." Logan's lips thinned. "He's either turned off his phone or sold it to buy drugs or booze." He slammed his fist on the bed. "I can't believe this. Everything he's worked for, all gone to shit."

"Maybe he just needs some time away to think. He could be staying with a friend."

"Ryan doesn't have any friends. Not anymore."

"Well, I'm his friend, so maybe you don't know as much about him as you think."

Logan thought for a moment. "No. I knew about you. When his shifts ended at work, he'd come straight home, and we'd stay in. On the weekends I'd make sure to be with him."

"Were you doing that because you wanted to be with him, or because you didn't trust him?"

Startled by the insightful question, Logan opened his mouth to argue but then decided it wasn't Emerson's fault he saw right through Logan's behavior. "Maybe a little of both," he admitted. "I mean…I was trying to protect him. It's a natural response. If we'd go out to dinner, he'd be surrounded by people drinking. Going out to clubs was way too much temptation, and frankly, that's not my scene. I was doing it to try and make it easier for him."

"Sometimes a friend thinks they're helping, but what they do is make the person feel as though they can't be without them or they'll fail."

"I'm hardly Ryan's savior."

"That's good, because Ryan doesn't need a savior. He needs someone to believe he can beat this, not a warden to lock him up in a room to keep out all the evils of the world."

"Okay," Logan snapped, his patience frayed to the breaking point. "I get it. I suck, and I was wrong. But right now, I have no idea where he is. He could be in an alley getting high, or he could be hurt…" The possibilities were too gruesome to dwell on.

"Where have you looked?"

"All the bars in midtown toward Hell's Kitchen and the river." He swallowed. "The Lincoln tunnel."

Emerson expelled a harsh breath. "That's where—"

"I know who's there and what goes on. But if he's pawned my watch and used the cash he stole from me to buy whatever shit he's putting into his body, he's going to need more money. Fast. And that's the quickest way."

"But he wasn't there."

Lightheaded from the worry twisting inside him, Logan pressed his fingers to his temple. "No. I showed his picture around, and no one had seen him. If you can think of anyplace else I should look, or if he's ever mentioned anything in your group sessions…I know they're confidential, but—"

"There's a meeting tonight."

A horrible-sounding laugh burst from him. "Yeah, I doubt it, but you never know. Maybe he'll think about what he's going to lose."

"You'd walk away from him when he needs people the most?"

"What Ryan needs is help. And now I see it's more than I can give him. I gotta go. If I find anything, I'll let you know." He ended the call.

In the shower, he stood with his head bowed and let the hot water beat down on his tired muscles. In the two days since he'd come home and found Ryan gone, he'd gotten little sleep, staying out till almost two a.m. both nights, haunting the seedy streets by the Lincoln tunnel, seeing more of the ugly underbelly of the city than he'd cared to imagine existed. It shocked and saddened him to see young men and women peddling their bodies, which made him redouble his efforts to find out if Ryan was on the walk. When no one recognized his picture, Logan had been relieved Ryan wasn't there, yet also scared that he was still out there, alone.

He dressed, knowing it would be another long night of searching a city that was proving once again to be a place where, if someone didn't want to be found, they wouldn't be. His apartment in Tribeca wasn't far from the Marquee. Knowing that club had always been a draw for Ryan, Logan set out into the night.

The scene when he walked through the front door was as he remembered—flashing lights, pounding music, and people. Lots of people. Something he detested. Sweaty faces and damp bodies pressed against him, and he recoiled. As he walked the perimeter, he scanned the people dancing, drinking, and slipping away to the nooks and shadowed corners.

Logan leaned on a post, that evening almost two years earlier washing over him, so fresh he could still smell Ryan's skin and taste his kisses. He closed his eyes, remembering. He'd never let himself go so spectacularly.

Was it his third Scotch or fourth? Who the fuck knew or cared? His father was dead, and he was alone. Even worse, he was lonely. Every lover was the same, every kiss was one of good-bye.

Nothing mattered.

He finished his drink while watching the dancers, Ryan Matson in particular. It was impossible not to notice him—he glittered like gold in a sea of darkness. The man had the face of an angel but a mouth of temptation and pure sin. Sweat glistened on his skin, and he gyrated in time to the pumping beat. For years he'd noticed Ryan at various bar association meetings and events or across the conference table when their firms had represented clients with competing interests. There had been times Logan lost his concentration, too busy focusing on Ryan's lush mouth and blue eyes with lashes so long, they touched his brows. Broad shoulders tapered to a lean, muscled body Logan wanted under him. Over him. He wanted to lick him everywhere.

Now there he was, in his direct line of sight, hips undulating, chest heaving. No longer married, now free for the taking. Wild desire spiraled through Logan, and his dick stiffened.

The song ended, and Ryan and his friends left the dance floor, passing by him. Logan put a hand on Ryan's shoulder.

"Want a drink?"

Hazy blue eyes met his, and Ryan brushed the sweaty blond hair off his brow. The smile he gave Logan was pure devilry.

"Yeah. You wanna buy it for me?"

Logan grabbed his hand, and they walked toward the bar, but halfway there, Logan pushed Ryan up against the wall and kissed him. Moaning, Ryan melted into him and sucked his tongue, rubbing up on him like a cat. Logan's control slipped, and he attacked Ryan's mouth, devouring his lips. He bit and licked, teeth clashing, tongues thrusting until Ryan broke free and lay gasping for air on his shoulder, fingers clutching at his waist.

"Fucking hell. Do it." His hands fumbled with Logan's belt.

"Not here," he growled. Nearly blind with lust, Logan had the sense to pull Ryan down the hall, where they passed other couples who had the same idea. Logan didn't care. He wanted Ryan, and he was going to have him.

In a corner, he pulled Ryan into the shadows and took his mouth in another brutal, possessive kiss. Hearing Ryan's groans and sighs of pleasure spurred him on, and before he knew what he was doing, Logan had his cock out and was unzipping Ryan's pants. He shoved his hand inside Ryan's briefs and caressed his hot dick from root to sticky tip.

"Yeah, do it, come on," Ryan urged, eyes gleaming, lips swollen, red and wet. "Fuck. Do it. Do it now."

Logan took their cocks in his hand and, with Ryan humping him, again plunged his tongue into Ryan's delicious mouth while rubbing their shafts hard and fast. This was going to be quick and dirty. Logan had no clue what had come over him, but he didn't care. Ryan writhed beneath him, and with his face flushed and gasping for air, he was beautiful as his climax hit.

"Oh, fuck me, oh yeah," Ryan choked out and came, spurting sticky liquid over his fingers, and Logan's orgasm burst through him a moment later. They remained pressed together, both of them trembling and breathless, Logan's lips pressed to Ryan's neck. He could've stayed there all night, but voices penetrated his postorgasmic bliss. Frantic at the thought of being caught with his dick out in public, he scrambled away from Ryan, wiped his hands on his shirt tail, and zipped up. Ryan watched him through hooded eyes.

"That was hot." His crooked smile was charming, and Logan had the urge to stroke his cheek.

Instead, he pointed at Ryan's still-open pants. "Better zip up."

Then he walked away.

"Hey, handsome." Logan blinked back to the present. Arms slid around his waist from behind, groping him, and he froze. "Wanna dance?" Hot, wet lips kissed his neck, and questing hands reached for his crotch. "Or we could go somewhere private."

Logan turned and grabbed the stranger's wrist. "Get your hands off me." His warning growl, famous at the law firm, would've set any first-year associate quaking in their shoes, but here, where people's blood beat hot with whatever cocktail—legal or not—they chose to indulge in, Logan's obvious displeasure was met with a laugh.

"Don't be like that." The man was around thirty, his eyes glittering like chips of malachite, catching all the colors of the flashing lights. His perfectly sculpted lips curved in a wicked grin, and he rubbed up on Logan, purring in his ear. "Come with me. Let's get high." His gaze flickered to Logan's hand, which still grasped his wrist. He lifted Logan's hand and licked it. "You like it rough? I wouldn't mind a little discipline from you…" He paused. "Daddy."

Logan didn't know whether to be disgusted or amused, but he released the man. "I'm not going anywhere with you. I'm looking for this man. Have you seen him?" He pulled up a picture of Ryan, and the guy shrugged and nodded.

"Yeah. He was here last night. We got high together. So what?"

At those words, bitterness stole a piece of Logan's soul. "Do you know if he's here tonight or planning to be?"

The man's lips thinned. "Do I look like his personal assistant?" His eyes narrowed. "You a cop? Why're you asking?"

Ignoring the man's question, Logan kept his eye on the entrance, but Pretty Boy was insistent, saying, "He was in pretty bad shape."

"He was? What do you mean?"

"What do you think? Guy was high as a fucking kite. Kept mumbling he was sorry." Pretty Boy shrugged.

"And you just walked away from him?"

"I'm not his fucking mother. If you care so much, why don't *you* know where he is?" He stalked away, disappearing into the sea of bodies.

For the rest of the night, until three a.m., Logan waited, but Ryan never showed up.

CHAPTER TWO

LOGAN

Two days turned into two weeks, and still no Ryan. Logan had been slipping out of the office in between client meetings in a vain attempt to balance his work commitments while searching for Ryan, but enough was enough. Logan gritted his teeth and made a decision. Nothing would be accomplished by damaging the firm's reputation. Time to go back to the office full-time. Ryan had vanished, and Logan had to return to his life.

He owed it to his partners, Oliver Tinsley and Simon Brown, to inform them why he'd been so haphazard and unfocused, and though shocked, they agreed his focus had to be on the law practice. Harming his clients' interests served no purpose.

"What do the police say?" Oliver asked. With a frown, he studied Logan through his black-rimmed glasses.

"They don't care. Once they heard he was a relapsed user, they basically told me he'll be found if he wants to be. I filed a missing person report, and they said they'd keep an eye out, but we know what that means."

"I'm sorry, Logan. I thought Ryan was going to beat it. If there's anything I can do, just ask."

"Thanks, Ollie. I thought so too."

"Why don't you come over for dinner this week? Alexandra and the girls would love to see you. It's been too long. I can't remember the last time we got together."

A gentle rebuke, but one Logan felt in his heart. Along with Simon, Oliver had become a second family to him, and he and his wife had been Logan's rock when his father died.

"I'll see."

Simon was even more sympathetic and walked him to his office, where he closed the door behind him. "I don't know what to say. I know how hard it was for you to open up to anyone. Maybe Ryan's just taking some time by himself to lick his wounds over the disciplinary committee's notification."

A wry smile, the first one since Ryan disappeared, tipped up Logan's lips. "Even you don't believe that, Si, and you're an eternal optimist."

He, Simon, and Oliver had met the first day of law school, and after three years living and working together, decided they meshed in business as well as friendship and set up their own firm upon graduation. It didn't hurt that Simon's family had endless money from hedge funds, and Ollie's was old money from New England. Logan was the scrappy outlier, a scholarship kid from Brooklyn whose father owned a bakery and whose mother had stayed home to take care of him and his brother. What they lacked in money, his parents made up for in their unwavering love and support of their sons.

"Logan…can I ask you something?"

In the middle of scrolling through his emails, hoping to find something from Ryan, Logan met Simon's eyes over the top of the computer screen.

"Yes, sure."

"Now don't get mad at me," Simon began, and Logan snorted.

"Then don't say something that's going to piss me off, how about that?"

"I'm serious. How long do you plan on waiting for him to come back to you?"

The somberness of Simon's voice caught Logan off guard. "I haven't thought about it."

"But I have." Simon braced his arms on Logan's desk, bringing his face only inches away from him. "You're doing it again. The signs are all there. It's not the first time, and I'd hate to see you repeat the same mistakes."

Shit.

"There's nothing about Ryan that remotely resembles anyone else I've known."

"Come on, even you don't believe that. It's Logan Silver to the rescue." Simon's eyes narrowed.

"Leave me alone. I have work to catch up on." He returned to his emails, hopelessly scrolling for a message he knew he wouldn't find.

Simon being Simon, he stayed put. "You're lying."

"The fuck you say." That friendship leeway was being tested to the max, and Logan wasn't happy.

"You know I'll always give you the honest truth. I love you, Logan, and it kills me to see you like this. I can't believe someone so goddamn brilliant in business can be so lost when it comes to his personal life."

"Ryan is different."

"How?" Simon's brow furrowed. "Because from where I'm standing, it's looking like Todd all over again, and it scares me to think you're going to get swallowed up in all that again. You're hurt and breaking apart in front of our eyes, and I'm afraid your pieces might be too shattered to fix this time."

Stomach in knots, Logan winced. "Please don't. I'm

already in a lousy mood."

Ignoring him as he usually did, Simon continued. "Why? Because you know it's true? Someone has to help you get out of that head of yours."

"And you're today's volunteer." Logan's smile was wry. "Come on, Si. Leave it alone. I've spent the past two weeks beating myself up. I don't need you to use me as a punching bag."

Surprising Logan, Simon came around his desk and took him by the shoulders. "And that's the problem. Again. You thinking somehow this is your fault. Why're you so involved in his life? The Logan I know doesn't dive into the deep end of the pool, especially for a man he barely knows."

Logan couldn't say a word because everything Simon said was the truth. And his friend knew it and pressed on. "Or am I wrong? Do you care for Ryan?"

"Of course I care for him. He's sick and he needs help."

"Dumbass. That's not what I mean, and you know it." Simon's gaze was intent yet gentle. "Are you in love with him? Is that the reason you're turning your world upside down?"

As close as Logan was to Oliver and Simon, he kept his personal life private. He'd had his share of one-night stands because he had no patience for anyone else's problems or desire to share his, a requirement for a relationship. At least that was what he witnessed with Oliver and his wife.

But Ryan's story forced him to revisit a part of himself he'd buried so long ago, he'd almost forgotten it existed, and coupled with their undeniable chemistry, he'd let his guard down and become vulnerable. Predictably, in the end, he got kicked in the balls.

"I wanted him to get his life together, so I tried to help him."

A disgusted sound passed Simon's lips. "You're too nice."

Logan burst into laughter. "You're probably the first person who's ever said *that* about me. Usually people are too busy calling me a son of a bitch."

But Simon didn't join in the fun. "You *are* an SOB. In business. In your personal life…I hate to say it, but you're a damn mess."

Easing back in his chair, Logan quirked a brow. "Is that so?"

Simon leaned forward. "Yeah. And I'm not afraid to tell you so. Were you two fucking?"

"Damn, you're crude."

"I'm giving you a taste of that blunt Logan Silver charm you've graced me with for years." Simon paused and pointed a finger at him. "I know you paid for everything, all his expenses, and made sure he stayed away from the wrong influences. You locked the two of you away from the rest of the world. Ollie and I have barely seen you outside of the office."

Logan frowned. "Why can't anyone see I was doing it for his own good?"

"What about your good? Since when are you such a patsy?"

His face flamed. "I'm not."

"Are you forgetting? I know you too well. What did he give you? What was so special about him? The sex?"

"It wasn't like that between us. We weren't sleeping together."

Simon's shocked face would've been funny if it wasn't Logan's life they were talking about.

"What did you say?"

"I'm not repeating myself."

Simon stared at him as if he'd sprouted an extra head on his shoulders. "You…I can't believe you were such a sucker."

"I'm not. I was helping him. I know I was." God, how

pathetic and weak did that sound?

"Are you sure it's not more like he helped himself to your generosity?" Simon shot back. "Because I bet, I just *bet*, he's fucked you over and you're too ashamed to tell us."

"Don't be an idiot." Early in life, he'd learned to master a poker face, but once again, Simon knew him too well.

"Oh, I'm not the idiot. How much did he take?" Simon blanched. "You didn't give him access to your bank accounts, did you? Tell me you didn't."

"No, of course not," he snapped. "But…okay, yeah, he took the cash I kept around the house." He lowered his gaze. "And my watch."

Simon slammed the chair aside. "Your father's watch? The one he got for his anniversary? Goddammit. Logan, I swear…"

"Stop. I know. I refuse to believe he'd sell it. You don't know Ryan. You don't understand where he came from and how hard it's been for him."

"Seriously? You're going to play the pity game?"

It was his turn to get angry. "Si, you come from a world very few people understand. There wasn't a thing ever denied to you. If you saw it and wanted it, you got it."

"We're not talking about me. And that's no excuse for the way he's behaving. You didn't have much growing up, and you turned out halfway decent." A grin broke over his face, and Logan's heart swelled with the love of a friendship they'd stretched to the limits but would never allow to break.

"Ryan didn't even have that. At eighteen he was living on the streets because his family threw him out when he told them he was gay. I can't imagine what that must've been like, can you?"

"No. Of course not. You've never talked about his past."

"I don't really know much. Ryan grew up in a small town in the Midwest—he wouldn't even tell me the name or go into details, so I have no idea the extent of what he's lived through, but I admire him. He worked, went to college, became a lawyer. I know he had it rough."

"You can admire him all you want. He's the ex of Remi Angel's husband, right?" When Logan nodded, Simon went on. "Yeah, I thought so. The one who had a big settlement from an insurance payout, I recall you saying? So he won't tell you where he grew up, he married someone for money, and now he's stolen from you. Maybe he's always been a con man, and you're too blinded by lust to see that."

"Lust has nothing to do with it," Logan growled, hoping his tone would serve as a warning to Simon to stop prying.

"Yeah, sure. I heard what you said, and I'm not buying it. Come on. It's me. You can admit you had a thing for him. I'm not going to tell anyone that the great Logan Silver had a crush on someone. I mean, I'm straight, and even I recognize Ryan's gorgeous. I get the allure."

"There's more to life than sex, you know," Logan grumbled.

"Okay. Who are you, and what have you done with my best friend?"

"Don't you have any clients?" he asked, irritated, and wanting desperately to change the subject.

"Yeah, but I'm more interested in figuring out what the hell happened to the man who used to go through lovers like I eat M&M's."

"Better watch your sugar. You're not as young as you used to be." When Simon opened his mouth, Logan put a hand up. "Please. Stop. I'm serious now. I'm really not in the mood to talk, and I have a thousand emails to get through."

To his great surprise and immense relief, Simon acceded to his request, gave him a hug, then left him alone. Logan closed the door behind him and sat behind his desk, Simon's words playing round and round in his head.

Blinded by lust.

If Simon only knew…Logan sighed. Ryan had lived

with him for five months, and they'd never had sex. They'd circled around each other, Logan finally understanding what it was like to want something and not be able to have it. An occasional kiss was all Ryan had allowed, and though Logan wanted more, he'd always retreated when Ryan stepped away.

"I can't. I'm not ready yet. I'm sorry."

Ryan explained that it was part of his recovery process, that until he felt fully healed and healthy, sex would have to wait.

So Logan had waited. He'd learned to be satisfied without having a physical relationship because he wanted Ryan to become whole again. There were days, too few in number, where Ryan would laugh, his face bright as if his demons had vanished in the wind. Those were the times Logan had been filled with hope.

"I just want you to be happy, Ryan."

Ryan hung his head. "I don't know where I'd be without you. I just hope…I hope you won't get tired of me and my problems. I hate being a burden." He bit his lip.

Logan brushed his lips over Ryan's cheek. "You don't have to worry. I'm not going anywhere."

Instead, it was Ryan who'd walked away without a trace, leaving Logan to pick up the pieces of the life he'd left behind. It wasn't the first time he'd been abandoned, and it was another harsh good-bye. It hurt, more than he cared to admit to Simon and Oliver. Maybe because as he'd grown older, he'd also grown warier of giving away pieces of a heart that had already been broken and bandaged, leaving it weaker but no less able to love.

"Forget about it. You have a business to run."

For the rest of the afternoon, Logan immersed himself in files and paper work. He'd learned long ago to compartmentalize his emotions, and by the end of the day, he had cleared his massive to-do list but walked out with a pounding headache.

"Want to have some dinner?" Simon bounded over, and Logan winced at all that enthusiasm channeled his way.

"No, thanks."

"Come on. What're you going to do, slink around the streets, looking for him? How long is this going to go on?"

"As long as I want," he snapped and stormed out, not saying good-bye to Denise, his receptionist. Unfortunately, his dramatic departure was foiled by the fact that he had to wait in toe-tapping frustration for the elevator, which gave Simon a chance to corner him again.

"Logan, I'm sorry," Simon apologized, and the angry words died on Logan's tongue. "I hate seeing you so…not you. Please, let me help. I want to go with you tonight."

"I'm going home." The elevator opened and he entered, followed by Simon. "I have a massive headache, and I need a night to myself." His stare was pointed. "Myself means alone, Si."

They reached the lobby of their office building, and Logan walked out, on Madison and 53rd, into a warm July night. He searched the crowds with the futile hope of spotting Ryan. Never one to listen, Simon followed him as he walked down the street.

"That's what you say, but I know you better than that. You're going to pop some extra-strength aspirin and venture out to look for him again."

Logan's jaw flexed. *Dammit.* He loved Simon, but he hated being so predictable.

"Have you contacted his ex?"

That stopped him in his tracks. "Garrett? Why would I do that?"

"He bailed Ryan out once, right?" Simon shrugged. "Maybe he'd do it again." Simon stuck out his hand, and a cab rolled to the curb. "Get in. Let's go to your place and figure this shit out."

"I—"

"Do I need to say the magic words? Simon says, let's get in the cab and go home."

"You're lucky I like you." Logan slid into the back of the taxi.

"Nah." Simon patted his cheek. "You love me."

CHAPTER THREE

LOGAN

"Okay, thanks, Garrett."

"Please make sure you let me know if you find him."

Garret was the kind of guy who could still be worried over an ex who'd treated him horribly. Logan had to admire him.

"Yeah, I will, I promise. And same for you, obviously. I appreciate it. Bye." Logan tossed the phone to the couch and watched as Simon returned from answering the door with their dinner.

"You want to split the rolls?"

"Yeah, sure, whatever." Logan rubbed his face.

"How's your headache?" Simon set the bags on the coffee table and sat beside him. He began to rub Logan's shoulders. "You're as tight as a virgin."

Logan laughed. "You always did have a way with words." But he groaned with pleasure. "Damn, that feels good. I haven't had a real massage in ages."

"Well, take the time and book one. Or I might have to charge you."

Logan opened their sushi and handed Simon the chopsticks. "Here. Eat up."

"What did Garrett have to say?"

"Not much." He popped the roll into his mouth and chewed. Garrett had sounded shocked at Logan's news of Ryan's disappearance. Remi had informed Logan when he answered the phone that they hadn't heard from Ryan since he'd paid off the loan. "He and Remi haven't had any contact with Ryan aside from his satisfying the loan."

"Can I ask you something?"

Logan quirked a brow. "Do I have a choice?"

Simon picked up a roll. "How much did you give Ryan to pay off the loan to Remi?" Unblinking, Logan stared at him, and Simon ate his roll and threw down the chopsticks. "The whole shebang, right? Including the interest. Jesus, Logan. I can't…"

"Then don't," he said quietly.

They ate in silence and didn't speak again until Simon had cleared away the plastic trays and returned with a glass of Pinot Noir in each hand. Logan took one from him.

"Thank you." He sipped and let the warmth trickle through him.

"What's next?"

"You go home."

"And you?" Simon raised his brows.

"Me?" He took another sip. "I'm going to take a shower and go to bed."

Simon's dark eyes locked on to his. "I think you're lying to my face, but you're going to do what you want no matter what I say."

"It's like you know me or something." Logan's lips twitched.

"I know you care about Ryan. So much so that it's tying you into knots."

"I care because he tried. He's got a job, and he wants to

climb out of a hole that keeps caving in on him. He doesn't have the support we've always had."

A gentle smile tipped up Simon's lips. "So you'll give it to him, whether he asks for it or not."

He shrugged. "I don't think Ryan knows how to ask for help anymore. It's why I'm helping him now. I called his job and said he was sick and couldn't come to work."

Simon squeezed his shoulder. "You're a good man, Logan."

He smirked. "Don't go soft on me now. Come on. I'll walk you to the door."

True to his word, Logan did shower, but instead of bed, he changed into jeans and a sweatshirt and took off. When he reached the police precinct, anxiety swirled in his stomach, and he leaned against a lamppost to steady his breath. Gazing up at the stars, he wished he were a child again, lying in the park with his brother, daydreaming of building houses out of clouds and living in the sky. Castles in the air. Being older, Todd had always gone first and picked out the biggest and fluffiest clouds, but Logan had never minded. He'd worshiped Todd and followed him until Todd went to high school and met a whole new group of friends. Their game had ended because Todd became more interested in snow than clouds. His eyes burned.

Oh, Todd. What the hell went wrong? I should've tried harder, told Mom and Dad earlier. I'm sorry I failed you.

Several loops around the block settled his racing nerves, and he went into the station. The desk sergeant punched something into the computer and shook his head.

"Nothing's come up, Mr. Silver, but you can talk to the detective on the case, if you'd like. He's on shift tonight."

"I would, thanks."

"Take a seat, and he'll be out in a few."

He settled into an uncomfortable plastic chair and scrolled through his phone, figuring he'd be there for a while, but he didn't have long to wait.

"Mr. Silver?" He glanced up to see a slightly rumpled man with a gold shield clipped to his slacks. "I'm Detective Foster."

They shook hands. "I'd like to know what's happening on the Ryan Matson disappearance."

Foster huffed out a sigh. "Come with me, but I'm afraid it's going to be a short and uneventful visit for you." He was escorted to a room and sat on one side of a long metal table. "Coffee or water?"

"No, I'm fine, thanks."

The detective took a seat across from him. In his late thirties or early forties, Detective Foster looked as if he'd had more nights he'd like to forget than remember. His jaw was rough with late-night stubble, and his thick dark hair gleamed in the overhead light. A small scar bisected his upper lip, and his hands were large and powerful. The strong nose fit a handsome, craggy face. Thoughtful blue eyes regarded him.

"You and Mr. Matson were…close?"

Logan's lips thinned. "He lived with me."

"All right. And you say he walked out of the house after receiving a disappointing letter about his law license? Do you know what it said?"

"Yes. Ryan had a drug problem. He was arrested and disbarred."

Foster's tense shoulders relaxed. "Okay, that matches up with what I found in my investigation."

Logan's hackles rose. "Did you think I'd come here and lie to you?"

A surprisingly charming smile lit Foster's face. "Nah. Of course not. No one ever lies to the police, right?"

Logan chuckled, his anger receding. "Yeah, that was stupid of me. But I'm an attorney, an officer of the court." At Foster's arch of a brow, Logan conceded. "All right.

Enough. I, personally, don't lie."

"Better. Okay, back to Mr. Matson. So you came home and found him gone?"

"Don't you have all this already?" Logan demanded, annoyed as hell that he had to reiterate everything. "I gave all the info on the missing person report."

"I know. Humor me. I didn't take the initial report." Foster waited.

Logan recounted every detail he could think of. "And that's it. I've been everywhere I thought he might be, in addition to places I'd hoped not to find him. I spoke to his ex, who hasn't heard from him either."

Foster set his pen on the table, still regarding him with those intent blue eyes. "Have you ever thought that he's gone because he'd rather be in that life than out of it? People who don't want to be found, usually aren't."

"Obviously. But Ryan was sober. He was happy…" The words died on his lips. Thinking about what Ryan's sponsor had said, that Ryan had rarely come to meetings, maybe he'd been lied to all along and was wrong about everything.

"Happy people don't run away, Mr. Silver." Foster read through his notes. "What about hospitals?"

"I called around but found no one matching his description."

"What credit cards does he have?"

"None. Ryan had to declare bankruptcy, so he doesn't have any—only a debit card. I don't have access to his statements."

Foster sighed and tapped his pen. "Have you checked outside the city? He used to live in Brooklyn, correct?"

Logan blinked. "Yeah. I-I didn't think of that. I'm not familiar with Brooklyn at all, and I wouldn't begin to know where to look for him."

Foster cracked a smile. "Lucky for you, I do. I'll widen the search there and see what I can come up with. But I'll say it again, even though you might not want to hear it. If he wanted you to know where he was, you would."

Tired of hearing that refrain, Logan lashed out. "Not if he's injured or dead." He rubbed his face. "I just need to know he's alive, and if he wants help, that I'm still here to give it." Foster remained silent, and Logan, unused to apologizing, realized he'd been rude as fuck. "I'm sorry. I didn't mean to take it out on you. I'm extremely frustrated."

"I understand. And trust me, I've heard worse."

"I'm sure. Can I ask you, what *have* you done since I filed the report?"

Foster met his gaze with unflinching honesty. "Mr. Silver, my partner and I have two homicides and three attempted murders we're investigating. And those are the new cases this week for just the two of us. I'm not going to sugarcoat it for you by lying and telling you that your runaway friend is at the top of our list."

Logan bristled but kept his mouth shut. He didn't have to like it, but he understood.

"We'll increase our canvassing for Mr. Matson and speak to people he knew in his past. Aside from you, who else was he close to?"

"No one, except a guy from his addiction counseling group, Emerson Hogan. I think I gave you his number."

Foster checked. "Yeah, I have it. We spoke on the phone, but it can't hurt to pay him a visit." He closed the file, and Logan knew the meeting was over. There was little else the detective could do.

"I appreciate you taking the time to speak with me. I know you're busy."

"We're always busy, Mr. Silver. Crime never takes a holiday. We'll be in touch."

"Thanks."

Logan walked out into the cool evening and meandered for several blocks, unwilling to sit at home and stare at the walls, wondering, again, what more he could've done to help Ryan. He spied a diner, and once inside, found a corner booth and ordered a coffee and piece of pie.

"What kind, honey?" The waitress glanced over her shoulder at the glass case in the front. "We got apple, cherry, banana cream, and my personal favorite, lemon meringue. Sweet and a little sour." She cackled. "Like me."

Logan grinned. "Well, since I'm more sour than sweet, I'll take the lemon meringue."

"You got it, honey. You want ice cream on the side?"

"No, I think the pie alone is enough of a sugar rush."

"Coming right up." She strolled away.

He sipped his coffee and ran over the events of the night. He doubted his meeting with the detective would lead to anything.

When a plate with a huge piece of pie was plunked down in front of him, he widened his eyes. "That's a lot of pie."

"You look like you need it, honey. Pie can always solve any problem." She patted a plump midsection. "Ask me how I know."

"You may be right," he admitted and slid a large forkful into his mouth.

"A nice-lookin' guy like you, in this crappy place on a Friday night? You got girl problems?"

The tangy pie exploded with flavor, and he chewed and swallowed before meeting her eyes with a half grin. "More like boy problems."

Her eyes danced. "Yeah? I shoulda known."

That set him off laughing. "And why's that?"

"You're too put together. All the best-dressed guys who come here are gay." She put a hand on her hip. "So what'd he do? Cheat on you? He's gotta be a dope."

His smile faded. "No. He and I…it's complicated. But it wasn't cheating. He just…left."

"Donna," the man behind the register yelled. "You got

an order waiting. Quit your yakking."

She rolled her eyes. "He thinks he's funny."

"I don't want to get you in trouble." Logan frowned, but Donna winked.

"Don't you worry. That ain't about to happen. He's married to me. I'll be right back. But lemme say one thing. Anyone who walks out on a guy like you, he ain't right in the head. He needs a shrink."

Logan took another piece of pie and chewed, thinking about what she said. A shrink, huh? Maybe Donna was right. Logan pulled out his phone.

"Emerson? It's Logan Silver again."

"Hi." He sounded strained and cautious. "What do you want? Why are you calling me? I already told you what I know. Or don't."

Emerson spoke so fast, Logan's head spun. "Ryan is still missing. I'd like to know if you heard from him since we last talked."

"Why would I call you? Ryan's a grown man who makes his own decisions. I can't stay on the phone. I have things to do."

What the heck was going on with this guy?

"Wait. Do you know if Ryan was seeing a psychologist or a therapist?"

"I don't think…should I be sharing that with you? His medical records are confidential, aren't they?"

Stunned, Logan stared at the phone in his hand for a moment. "Are you serious? I'm trying to find Ryan, and you're worried about HIPPA? I'm not interested in what was said, but if he did have a therapist, maybe he might have some insight into where Ryan could be."

"I just don't think I can violate Ryan's privacy like that. I have to go."

He held a dead phone in his hand. "Shit," he swore and stared off into space. Why was Emerson so jumpy?

He tried calling Dex, the sponsor, but it went to voice mail, and without leaving a message, he disconnected the call in frustration.

"Something wrong with the pie?"

"Hm?"

Donna stood in front of him. "You're not eating, and I know the pie's gotta be good. I make 'em myself."

"Yeah, uh, sure, it's great. I just have a lot on my mind. Just the check, please."

Donna slapped the receipt on the table. "Here ya go. And don't worry. He'll come back."

Logan handed her a twenty. "Keep the change. And I'm glad you're so certain."

"Thanks." She tucked the bill into her apron pocket. "Listen, I been around the block a coupla times. Guy like you—good-lookin', fancy clothes, and not a snob? That's hard to find. I bet he's younger than you too. He's not thinking. Sometimes you gotta lose what you got to find yourself."

Logan couldn't help smiling. "How do you know I'm not a snob?" God knew he'd been called a lot worse.

She pointed at the dingy diner. "Look where ya are. Ya think you're gonna find the *crème de la crème* comin' in here? Even if my pies are the best. Plus, you talked to me and didn't brush me off like those snoots in suits normally do."

Donna reminded him of his mother—plainspoken and no-nonsense. "Thanks, Donna." He patted her shoulder, and as he left, she called out to him.

"Bring him here next time. I'll set him straight aboutcha."

Logan raised a hand in acknowledgment, and once outside, decided to walk the half mile home and hunched his shoulders against the sudden brisk wind. Would Ryan have a place to sleep?

With each step, loneliness and pain welled up inside him. How did life get to this point, where he was the only one left of the four people who used to sit at the kitchen table, laughing at Dad's silly knock-knock jokes, while he and Todd would pretend-argue over who'd get the juicy end piece of Mom's roast beef?

He let himself into his apartment and sat in the darkness, staring out the window at the twinkling lights of the city. Somewhere out there, Ryan walked alone, convinced he wasn't good enough or worth Logan's time. Something didn't sit right about Emerson Hogan, and Logan decided it was time to pay the man a visit.

CHAPTER FOUR

LOGAN

Having picked up Ryan in the past, Logan knew where to go and waited in front of the church for the meeting to break up. He searched every departing person's face as they exited, but Ryan's wasn't among them. And neither was Emerson. When it was apparent that the last person had left and Emerson hadn't appeared, Logan knew his trip had been another exercise in futility.

"Dammit," he swore, leaning against a parked car.

Unwilling to leave, he decided to check for stragglers and walked inside. He'd struck out with Emerson, but maybe Dex was there? Following the signs pointing to the room, Logan poked his head around a half-open door and found a very good-looking man in his midforties, sitting on a folding chair, talking on his phone. A smile lit his face.

"Yeah, I'm coming home now....I remember. Jeremy said he and Blake will be there about seven....I love you too. Bye."

Logan rapped his knuckles on the door, and the man gazed at him with a quizzical face, brows pinched together over startling blue eyes.

"Can I help you?"

"I was looking for Dex? Are you him?"

"No, Dex is on vacation." The man stood. "I'm Dr. Noah Strauss. I'm taking over for Dex while he's away."

"I spoke to Dex a few days ago, and he didn't say anything about going anywhere. Where did he go?"

"And you are?"

"Logan Silver."

Strauss's brows drew together "Okay, Mr. Silver. Does Dex normally check in with you when he goes away? And I have no idea where he is, though I can't imagine why you'd think I'd tell you his itinerary even if I did."

At the quirk of Strauss's lips, lending an amused expression to his handsome face, Logan's cheeks grew hot with embarrassment, which put him in a bad temper. "No," he snapped, more testy than usual, especially to a stranger, but his nerves had been on edge since Ryan's disappearance. "Of course not. But I've been trying to locate a good friend who's been missing for two weeks, and since I'd spoken with Dex about trying to find him and he knew how concerned I was, I thought he'd have the common courtesy to let me know. That's all. Thanks."

He turned on his heel and strode out of the room and the church. Footsteps pounded behind him, but he continued on, head down.

"Excuse me, excuse me, could you wait a moment?" someone called out to him.

Logan peered over his shoulder to see Strauss running after him. Having little desire to talk to him or anyone, he continued to put one foot in front of the other. Unfortunately, the man was in good shape and easily caught up to him. "I'd like to know more about the man you said is missing."

"Why?" Logan asked, stopping. "I don't see the point."

"Well," Strauss said, "you seem very upset, and you look

like you could use someone to talk to. I'm a psychologist."

Now Strauss had his interest. "You are? Listen, can we talk?"

Strauss's lips twitched. "In case you don't remember, I'm the one who chased after you."

"Yeah, okay, you're right." Logan glanced around West Broadway and pointed across the street to the Smyth Tribeca hotel. "How about we go inside for a drink?"

Strauss nodded. "Just let me call my husband to let him know I'm going to be late."

They crossed the street, and Strauss spoke on the phone as they entered the lobby.

"Hey, babe. I have to talk to someone after the meeting, so I'll be a little late… Oh, he is, huh?" Strauss's eyes twinkled. "Listen, tell my brother he can wait an extra half hour to eat. He's so healthy, give him one of those juices Gino's always selling on television. That'll hold him for a little while." He chuckled, his face soft. "Yeah. Be home as soon as I can… Me too." He tucked the phone into his jacket pocket, and Logan held open the door to the Galerie Bar. He chose a plush seat at a tiny table in the rear.

When they'd settled with their drinks, Strauss tipped his chin. "Tell me, Mr. Silver, what am I doing here? Who is missing?"

Logan sipped his Pinot Noir, contemplating the jewel tone of the wine in the stemless glass. "I have a friend. He suffers from addiction. He claimed he'd been sober but I'm beginning to think that wasn't true. As we know, it's so very easy to fall prey to its wiles, and it takes a lot of strength to beat the habit. A drug is a damn seductive mistress."

Understanding filled Strauss's eyes. "I'm sorry to hear that. And yes, I know. The need consumes you until you can think of nothing else."

"Agreed. Ryan's had a very rough life. Abandoned by his family when he was a teenager, he fought his way through life and went to college and law school. He's really tried to make something of himself. Unfortunately, he's had slipups along the way."

"Slipups? Do you mean relapses?"

Logan steepled his fingers under his chin. "Ryan was beguiled by living the high life in the city. He met his husband, Garrett, freshman year at college. Garrett had a very large settlement from a lawsuit, and Ryan claimed he loved him but admitted the money was a big part of the reason he married him."

Noah's handsome features clouded. "And that money made it easy for Ryan to fall into the life of drugs again."

"If he ever left. I suspect Ryan might've been using when he and Garrett were together, but in school he kept it under wraps. From what I've learned, Garrett was vehemently opposed to any kind of drug use, and Ryan knew it. Having access to Garrett's fortune, plus the fast-paced environment he lived in…Ryan worked in entertainment law, and it's part of the lifestyle to go to dinners and clubs to wine and dine prospective clients. Once you've been addicted, it doesn't take much to send you running to the comfort of what you've always known. He fell into the partying at his law firm and got drawn deeper and deeper into trouble—drugs, booze, all-night clubbing…eventually he and his husband divorced."

"May I ask you something?"

"Yeah, sure." Logan took a sip of his Pinot Noir.

"The knowledge you have of substance abuse, that seems pretty intimate. Were you ever in treatment yourself?"

His throat closed, making it painful to swallow. Or breathe.

"No. I…" He faltered, fingernails digging into the wooden tabletop. Logan had to take a minute to release the tension gathered in his chest. "I don't do drugs. I never have. But back to Ryan…at the end, he was out of control, and it caught up to him. He was arrested and disbarred."

Strauss's jaw dropped. "Oh, damn. That's brutal. My husband's a lawyer, and I know how serious that is."

"It shattered him. He overdosed and wound up in the hospital, beaten half to death." The pain of what Ryan had gone through swept through Logan as sharply as if it had been his own.

Noah hitched his chair closer. "I can see why you're concerned for his safety—you're being a good friend. Anyone who's experienced so many setbacks in such a short period of time and already had a problem with drugs is in a precarious position. Was he able to get his license reinstated?"

"No. His career is over," Logan stated dispassionately, staring over Strauss's shoulder. "I wasn't surprised when the disciplinary committee refused to reinstate him, but Ryan must've believed he'd rehabilitated himself by staying out of trouble and finding employment as a hotel maintenance supervisor. He dived back into the bottle when he received the letter denying his application and walked out on me. I-I feel guilty I wasn't there to support him, but I was out of town for a business meeting." His lips twisted in a grimace. "Of course that's when he received the news, and he was all alone."

"You're together?"

Something about Dr. Noah Strauss's calm, nonjudgmental demeanor made him easy to talk to, and Logan, despite being extremely private, was willing to discuss the intricacies of his tangled relationship with Ryan. He took another sip of wine.

"No…I'm not sure what we are. I don't know what drew me to Ryan." Logan smiled faintly. "Well, yes, I do. I can admit to superficiality. He's extremely good-looking, and I've always been physically attracted to him. I kept away when he was married, but after his divorce, we hooked up in a club. It shocked the hell out of me because I'm not that type of person." He sneaked a look at Strauss, who caught his eye. "Seriously. I don't know what came over me."

Strauss's lips curved upward. "Before I received my PhD, I was a fashion model." His expression was frank. "I've seen it all, trust me. Lust, coupled with alcohol and other stimulants, can blind people to their surroundings."

It didn't surprise him. Dr. Strauss was extremely handsome, but Logan didn't miss the thin scars on his face, almost, but not quite, artfully camouflaged by scruff. He wondered if that had ended his career. It did nothing to diminish his startling good looks, but having had many clients in the entertainment field, Logan knew the price put on perfection and the lengths people would go to stay on top.

"You obviously know more about the club scene than I do. Well, over a year later, I came face-to-face with Ryan again, but this time under much different circumstances." He recounted Ryan's humiliation over Logan's discovery of him working as a janitor in a hotel.

"I can understand his embarrassment. Especially in front of a colleague."

"I couldn't care less what he does. Considering some of the secret lives many people have outside of work, no one has the right to judge anyone. I encouraged him to work hard, remain sober, and knowing his environment wasn't the most conducive to that lifestyle, I offered to let him move in with me. All I wanted was for him to get clean and have a fresh start. We're not personally involved."

"That's a pretty unusual response—taking someone into your home who's a virtual stranger. I'd say that's being pretty personally involved. Sex doesn't always have to play a part in a relationship."

That tension returned, and Logan gripped his glass. "I couldn't stand to see the way he was living—a dingy one-room apartment in a neighborhood where drug deals were as common as pigeons and roaches. Ryan needed to know he was worth supporting, and I have the means."

Strauss clasped his hands. "Understood, and I'm not saying what you did was wrong because I can tell it was done with the best of intentions, but do you see it from Ryan's point of view?"

"I'm not trying to be his savior, if that's what you're insinuating." Why couldn't anyone see he was doing this for Ryan's own good? His hackles rose.

Strauss smiled. "Whether knowingly or not, that is exactly who you are to him. As Ryan sees it, you're rich and powerful and have everything you want. You're also older, I'm assuming?"

"Not by that much, but yes."

"So you swooped in and took over everything in his life he had to worry about, giving him a soft place to land. Do you have him paying rent or any living expenses?"

"N-no. I mean…my condo is paid for, and I'm not going to ask him to chip in for monthly expenses like electric and food. That's petty. Besides, after taxes, he doesn't make anywhere near what I make. Why would I?"

"To give him a sense of self-worth."

"He knows I don't care about those things. I only want him to have a clear and easy path to get back on his feet." Growing uncomfortable under Strauss's unblinking scrutiny, Logan drank some more wine. "But I'm guessing I did it wrong?"

"Your intentions were good; please don't get upset. It's natural to want to protect someone when you see them crumbling. But once again, it comes down to this point"—Strauss paused—"why are you doing this? You say you're not in a relationship, yet all the signs point to the actions of someone who cares deeply."

"No, we aren't. Aside from that one encounter in the club, we've barely had any physical contact."

"It's odd from an outsider's perspective for someone to do all this out of a sense of altruism or the simple goodness of his heart."

"I…I care. I don't like seeing someone as bright and alive as I once knew Ryan to be, throw his life away."

"Because…?" Strauss's opened-ended question unnerved Logan. Usually, he was the one asking the probing questions, but Strauss, with his kind and gentle manner, had managed to burrow under Logan's skin. He didn't like it, but he appreciated that Strauss had put off his evening plans to listen to him, and Logan felt he owed him something.

"I've had experience with someone suffering from addiction. It's ugly, and I wanted to help Ryan. It's the least I could do." As always, any mention of the past left him an emotional wreck, and Logan struggled to keep his composure. His fingers tightened around his glass, and a quick uptick of his lips was the best he could muster. "I'd better not hold you up. It sounded like you have guests for dinner."

Noah didn't take the bait. "It's just my brother and his husband. They can wait. Oren will entertain them until I get home. I think being here with you is more important." A gentle smile warmed his face. "You sound like you could use someone to talk to."

"Me?" As much as Logan respected this virtual stranger's compassion and willingness to sit and listen to him, he was nowhere near ready to unburden his fractured soul. "I'm fine…good. My main concern is finding Ryan." He narrowed his eyes. "Oren." He thought for a moment. "That's an unusual name. What type of law does he specialize in?"

"Mostly family law and some corporate. He works for the firm Davis and Frank. They're pretty small, so you might not have heard of them."

For the first time that night, Logan's laughter was sincere. "Oh, trust me. I've heard of Ash Davis. He's a brilliant attorney." Asher Davis's sexual prowess was also legendary, but Logan didn't want to speak ill of someone

Strauss considered a friend. Besides, Logan was no angel—he had his own less than stellar reputation of bedding and forgetting.

"True, and he's also a very good friend of ours. Oren's worked for him going on five years now."

"Interesting. I know he's very involved with charity work for LGBTQ youth."

"Yes. He and his husband, along with their circle of friends, run a clinic." Noah dug into his pocket, pulled out his wallet, and extracted a card. "This is it. Home Away From Home. Aside from providing medical help during the day, they have a twenty-four-hour, seven-days-a-week phone line, where volunteers talk to people grappling with mental health and substance abuse issues. Oren and I help out."

Logan studied the card. "I had no idea this existed," he mused. "I wish…well, it doesn't matter anymore." Grief surged through him, the pain in his heart an unbearable raw wound that had never fully healed after losing Todd. Logan shouldered the burden of his failure every day, and it bled into all aspects of his life.

"You lost someone close to you to drugs, didn't you, Mr. Silver?"

The words of the card blurred before his eyes. "Yes," he whispered. "And when I did, I lost part of myself as well."

CHAPTER FIVE

RYAN

"You didn't say anything, did you?" In bed, Ryan propped himself up on an elbow and searched Emerson's face. It took a liar to recognize one, and Ryan would know if Emerson tried to bullshit him.

"No, of course not. I told Logan I had no idea where you were." Disapproval radiated from the man standing over him. "But I really don't like lying to people. Especially Dex. You could've let me tell him, at least. It's his job to help people recovering from addiction."

But even as Emerson spoke, Ryan set his jaw. "I have to do this myself. You don't understand."

Three weeks had passed since life had crashed around Ryan for what seemed like the hundredth time. How many more failures was he supposed to accept before listening to the obvious?

There was no place for someone like him. He'd learned that when his parents had thrown him out and told him not to come back. Now, almost forty, he was right where he'd started: alone, homeless, and jobless, all the bridges he'd worked hard to build burned to a crisp.

"What I understand, after being almost ten years clean, is that it is imperative you have professional help. And a good support system behind you. From what you've told me, Logan helped you."

"He gave me everything," Ryan said slowly.

"So you said, but I'm still not seeing why you'd walk out on someone who wants to give you everything."

"I don't want to talk about it." He flipped off the covers. "Can you help me? I need to shower, and I'm a little shaky this morning."

Immediately, Emerson held out a hand, and Ryan took it, rising slowly to his feet. He swayed a bit, and when the dizziness passed, he let go. "Thanks."

He'd been clean for fourteen days. Three hundred and thirty-six hours of his body waging a war against itself. After receiving that letter, he'd spent several days wandering aimlessly, getting high at night with random people at the Marquee. Maybe in his secret heart, he'd hoped Logan would show up to save him again, but he hadn't, and Ryan ended up alone and broken, walking through the dark, desolate streets. At one point he'd passed by Logan's building and hesitated, knowing he could go upstairs and Logan would be there with anything and everything he might want.

He'd turned and walked away, farther downtown, past the 9/11 Memorial and up to City Hall Park, where he'd sat on a bench, staring at the Brooklyn Bridge rising high in front of him.

It would have been easy to walk into the water and let it take him away to nothingness. But something deep inside him had rebelled at that idea, and he'd wound up on Emerson's doorstep, asking for help.

The incessant craving licking through his bloodstream hadn't fully diminished, and he yearned for the oblivion only a good high could give him, but the tiny bit of clarity he still possessed gave him the strength to resist. The days had been brutal, but Emerson had allowed him to do it his way, and so with only the two of them in a cabin somewhere in the Catskills, he'd sweated and screamed, writhing on the bed, begging Emerson to give him one tiny hit of something, anything to make the agonizing pain go away. Violent nightmares assaulted him every time he closed his eyes, leaving him unable to rest.

Ryan knew this was his last chance. If he didn't beat the beast of his addiction this time, he would lose himself forever. During the times when his mind cleared, he'd walk through the forest behind the cabin, scraping his fingertips across the rough bark of the trees, dipping his toes into the cold water of the stream half a mile from the cabin. Wanting to feel the pulse of the world. Needing to become part of the elements of life.

Ignoring the cool dampness after a recent rain, he'd lain among the rocks and wet dirt and breathed in the fresh earthy scent of the forest surrounding him. The rich blue sky soared high above, a vivid backdrop for the trees with their leaf-filled branches reaching upward, and Ryan pictured his body melting into the carpet of mud and twigs, becoming one with the ground. Would anyone miss him or notice he was gone?

Garrett was married and happy without him. Logan didn't need him except as a project to take care of.

No one gave a damn if he lived. Or died.

He should care.

Did he?

Emerson had listened to everything he said and allowed him to make his choices. Logan too had given him that choice, but Ryan had been so afraid he'd overstep and cross a line. Logan had kept telling Ryan how well he was doing. How proud he was Ryan had come so far.

All the well-meaning people telling him how brave and strong he was for getting help…

An utter crock of shit.

He wasn't brave. He was a scared, snively creature, too weak to withstand the slightest disappointment. Like being told he'd never practice law again. It had been easy to order a bottle of vodka, have it delivered, and sink into nothingness.

Logan would have never allowed him to suffer through the agony of withdrawal, listening to his screams, watching him shiver and shake as he detoxed. Logan would've wrapped him in silk to smooth his way, like he always had. It was another reason he'd continued to get high while they were together—his body was the only thing of his own he could control. Logan had made it all so damn easy by doing everything for him, even before Ryan asked.

Not any longer. Ryan didn't want peace and calm. A painless ride out of addiction meant it would slip from his memory, become forgettable. He wanted to suffer, wanted the agony. Even the beating he'd taken that had landed him in the hospital hadn't left enough of an impact, as he'd been too wasted to remember anything but the first punch.

He needed each and every excruciating detail of his withdrawal etched like a scar on his heart and mind so he'd never, ever want to go through it again.

So now, with his head still a bit fuzzy and his body weak, Ryan walked to the bathroom while Emerson waited across the room.

"Proud of you, Ry. It's a big step. A week from now, you'll start feeling like your old self again."

He didn't answer and turned on the shower taps, grateful for the hot water streaming over him. "My old self? That's a joke. Who'd want to be that fucked-up mess?" He washed his hair and stayed under the spray, feeling almost human. He finished and stepped out of the stall. The mirror reflected what he already knew from touching his body—he'd lost muscle mass, and his ribs stuck out. A far cry from the gym rat he'd been years earlier, residing at the top of the leaderboard in his spin class.

He wrapped a towel around his waist and returned to the bedroom. Emerson had left him alone, and he was grateful to be able to get dressed on his own. He slipped into his briefs and sweats, and found Emerson in the kitchen, cooking breakfast. For the first time in memory, he had an appetite.

"I can make you something." Emerson nodded to the counter. "There's eggs and bacon and sausage."

His stomach growled. At the beginning of his marriage, when he'd been relatively sober, he'd loved to cook Sunday morning breakfast for them. Creating meals had been a source of comfort, and he itched to recover that peace of mind.

"I'll do it."

Brows raised high, Emerson nodded. "I'll be out of your way in a second. There's coffee in the pot if you want."

He poured a cup, and while he waited for Emerson to be done, chopped up an onion and pepper and peeled potatoes. It felt good to be using his hands again, and though they were slightly shaky, he didn't cut a finger off. Emerson gave way at the stove, and he proceeded to make his favorite—home fries, then scrambled eggs with two strips of bacon.

"Damn, Ry. That looks amazing, and it smells even better."

Pride surged through him at Emerson's words. "Thanks. I haven't made breakfast in years, but I got the urge. Living at Logan's, every meal, even breakfast, was ordered in, unless we had bagels."

"You didn't cook for him? Man, he was a fool. Those home fries look like the bomb."

"Have some. I made a ton." Without waiting for Emerson's response, he piled some on the man's plate. "And no, Logan isn't the type for home-cooked meals. He's the king of ordering in and making restaurant reservations. I bet the man has never had a home-cooked meal in his life." Imagining Logan sitting around a table in a cozy kitchen and eating a family dinner almost brought a smile to his face.

With a full plate in front of him, he attacked the food, relishing each bite, almost as much for the fact that he'd made it on his own as for being hungry. Emerson picked up a strip of bacon and crunched half of it, then set it on the plate.

"Can I ask you something?"

Ryan finished chewing. "Yeah, sure. What is it?"

"What's the deal with you two?"

"Deal?" His brows scrunched together.

Emerson nodded. "Yeah. I mean…you know Logan's worried about you. He's called me at least four times since you walked out." Frown lines scored his face. "I didn't like lying. He seems like he cares."

Ryan's stomach flipped, and he set the coffee mug on the table instead of drinking it. "Why are you asking me this?"

"Because you've been with me for almost two weeks now, and I think after cleaning up your piss and vomit, I can ask a simple question. I know you live with him, but are you two lovers?"

Lovers. Such a strange word to describe what Logan meant to him. Lovers implied a level of intimacy, and Ryan wasn't sure Logan had ever allowed anyone to see beyond the glittering facade of perfection he wove around himself. The physical was the easy part—willing lips and hands, kissing and stroking, bodies swelling with desire.

But their hearts? Neither of them allowed the other inside those empty spaces.

"No. We aren't lovers. We hooked up once, a long time ago, but that was the only time. I don't know…" He fumbled for words, and Emerson jumped in.

"It's okay. It's none of my business. I only asked because Logan is so relentless in trying to locate you. Most people don't really go out of their way unless they care."

Ryan bit into a strip of bacon. "I'm sure he cares, but not in that way. Logan Silver isn't the type to get emotionally involved with people."

"What about you?"

His brows pulled together. "Me? What about me?"

"Are you in love with him?" Emerson asked, his voice as careful and patient as if he were speaking to a child.

Good thing Ryan wasn't eating or drinking anything, as he would've spewed it across the table and ruined Emerson's shirt. "In love with Logan?" Aware of Emerson's steady gaze, Ryan gathered his shaky wits. "Why would you say something so ridiculous? I can barely get out of bed on my own these days. The last thing I'm thinking about is sex or being involved with someone. Now, can I finish my breakfast in peace?"

"Sure. I don't want to upset you."

After the dishes were loaded into the dishwasher, Ryan laced his sneakers. "I'm going for a walk. I'm feeling antsy cooped up here." The weight of the log ceiling pushed on him, and he felt closed in by the walls of the cabin. He couldn't breathe. He needed space.

"I'll come with you."

Ryan directed a half smile at him. "I'm not going to get high, if that's what you're worried about. I know how badly I screwed up and disappointed everyone who tried to help me."

"How so? I'm here for you. Dex would be happy to help with whatever you need, and Logan is waiting for you to contact him. People care about you, Ryan. You can let us in. At least let Logan know you're alive."

Ryan hardened his jaw. "So he can come in and save the day? Again? No. This has to be on my own. I fucked myself over. I'm sure my job has already replaced me. So that's all my hard work down the toilet."

Emerson surprised him with a grin. "Well, about that… Logan told them you have the flu and you'll be out for a while."

"Of course he did," Ryan said bitterly. "Logan Silver to the rescue once again."

"He's just trying to make things easier for you. Maybe send him a quick text? He's really worried about you."

"Fine." Ryan picked up his phone and sent Logan a message.

I'm alive. I know you want to help, but please let me do what I need to do, alone.

"There. Done."

Feeling no better than he did before, he stomped over to the door and flung it open. "When is everyone going to realize I don't need to be taken care of?" He stormed away and took off running behind the cabin and into the woods, until he was surrounded by nothing but trees and the smell of earth. He found a tumble of rocks, sat against their hard edges, and let the angry tears fall. How long could he go through life, letting other people clean up after him? He was thirty-eight years old, yet as helpless as a baby.

Maybe having his childhood ripped from beneath him had left him without the ability to make good decisions. He'd always been living on the edge of survival. He needed to live on his own and be responsible for himself. Even prior to moving in with Logan, Remi's loan had smoothed the way for him to get his feet back under him. What he needed was to figure out who the hell he was. At his age, it was time.

Twigs cracked, and he huffed out a sigh. Of course Emerson would follow him. He remained silent and closed his eyes.

"You okay?"

Ryan didn't answer.

Emerson cleared his throat. "Look, I know you want to do this on your own, but you have a better chance of recovery if you speak to someone on a regular basis."

At those words, he opened his eyes. "I had that. With Dex and the group and with you whenever we'd hang out. It didn't stop me from reaching for the bottle when I got the letter from the disciplinary committee."

Emerson stood his ground. "Yeah. But you didn't come to meetings that often, and you hid the true extent of your problem and that you'd been using for so long."

Ryan's smile was wry. "I'm a great faker."

But Emerson remained somber. "Which is why I want you to try something new. What would you say about seeing a psychologist? Someone who specializes in the queer community and has worked with people suffering from addiction."

Ryan blinked. "I wasn't aware there was such a specific degree."

"I don't know about his degree exactly, but Noah is a psychologist who works with at-risk queer youth at a center in Brooklyn. He's studied the effects of long-term addiction from childhood to adulthood. I spoke with him a few days ago, and he said he'd love to talk to you."

Ryan highly doubted anyone would love to talk to him about his life. No one needed that much ugly. "I appreciate it, but first of all, I can't afford a psychologist. Even if I don't get fired, my insurance doesn't cover mental health. Second, if I don't have my job, then my main priority is finding a new one and a place to live."

"You're not going home?"

He met Emerson's eyes. "Logan's apartment was never home to me."

CHAPTER SIX

RYAN

All good things must come to an end, and Ryan found himself back in the city. Emerson had to return home and to his job, and Ryan could hardly argue with the man. First thing on his list was showing up at his job and hoping they'd understand.

Alisa, the hotel maintenance manager, was less than sympathetic. "Your boyfriend called the office and said you had the flu. That's a week at the most. But three weeks? And no doctor's note? C'mon, man."

"He's not my boyfriend, but aside from that, it wasn't the flu. I-I had a relapse and started using and drinking again. But I'm two weeks clean and hoping you'll give me another chance." He met her gaze unflinchingly, and for a moment he thought he spied sympathy in Alisa's big brown eyes. But then she reverted to her usual, businesslike self.

"Sorry, Ryan. We had to fill your position."

He sucked in air. "So that's it. I'm out."

"That's it, yeah. I appreciate that you told me the truth,

but I need someone reliable."

He'd said he didn't want easy, and he was getting his wish. While Emerson had offered his couch to sleep on as long as he needed it, Ryan had counted on the job to enable him to find an apartment. Now, with nothing to his name but the clothes he'd taken with him, the best he could do was live in a shelter. The place of last resort. He knew what happened there, so no way.

He shivered and touched the inside of his jacket pocket, feeling the cool metal links.

Logan's watch.

After reading the letter from the disciplinary committee and downing the bottle of vodka, he'd still had enough brain cells working and remembered where Logan kept his stash of house money and his father's gold watch. In his altered-mind state, he'd had no qualms about grabbing it all. The money had dwindled to half, and Ryan knew from the weight of the watch that he could get a hefty amount for it. He stroked the smooth bezel.

"Where did you get that relic? I didn't know they still had watches you had to wind." With a laugh, Ryan sat next to Logan on the bed.

Logan faced him with an unreadable expression. "It was my father's. My mother gave it to him on their twenty-fifth anniversary. The night before he died, he gave it to me."

"Oh." Another life experience he couldn't relate to. "I'm sorry. I didn't know. Is it real gold?"

"Yes." Logan put it on his wrist. "I don't wear it because it's too valuable." He took it off and placed it in the nightstand drawer.

"Why don't you sell it, then?" Ryan asked, and Logan stared at him as if he'd committed murder.

"Are you kidding me? It was my father's."

"Oh, yeah. Sorry."

In truth, Ryan didn't understand. He hadn't seen his

father in over twenty years and barely remembered him. Family meant little to him when he'd been so easily disposed of for being gay.

Did he feel like a shit for stealing it?

Yes.

He had to get it back to Logan, but he was too chicken to face him. For now, he kept it zipped up inside his jacket and walked the streets of the city, looking for a job. He'd filled out application after application, knowing full well for the most part he wouldn't hear from them once they read his answer to the question, "Have you ever been convicted of a felony?" But he applied to other hotels and even as a legal secretary to half a dozen firms, hoping someone might overlook his record. Knowing they wouldn't as soon as they googled his name.

By three in the afternoon, he'd had enough. He'd been out since nine in the morning and needed to rest. He'd returned to Emerson's apartment and settled on the couch to watch some mindless television, when Emerson walked out of his bedroom.

"Oh, good. I'm glad you're here."

"Why?" Ryan drank half his can of club soda.

"I want you to come with me. I'm going to that center in Red Hook to help on their hotline."

Ryan tensed. "I don't want to meet that doctor. I already told you, I can't afford to pay for therapy."

Emerson lowered into the chair opposite him. "I know. But I'm not talking about you meeting Noah, although he might be there tonight, I'm not sure. This is to help your immediate situation."

And despite his initial protest, Ryan was curious. "What situation?"

"A job. Their receptionist is leaving, and they need a replacement. I thought you would be good for the job."

"Oh."

"Yeah, oh." Emerson leaned forward. "It's a start, Ry. And the center has resources that can help you with other issues."

Despite his misgivings, Ryan couldn't help but be interested. It was the first real opportunity he'd had. "I thought the place was just for young people." Was he trying to talk himself out of something that had potential because he was scared?

"They offer assistance to people who need it. I think you'd fit in and find you have things in common with the people who run it. Why don't we go and take a look?"

He sat up. "Now?"

Emerson raised a brow. "You have someplace else to be?"

A wry smile curved his lips. "You're funny. I just thought that since it's late in the day, there won't be anyone there."

"No, the center is twenty-four hours, seven days a week because of the hotline. Drew's sister, Dr. Rachel, runs it, and Noah and Tash also donate a significant amount of their time."

"Tash? Who's he?"

"A psychiatrist who helps out."

Ryan narrowed his eyes. "Are you sure this isn't some trick to get me to meet all these random doctors and go into therapy? You know I'm not into listening to these people tell me that my mommy issues led to my problems, and what I should do and how I should feel when they have no clue what I've been through."

"Just keep an open mind. I'm telling you the truth when I say there is a job opening."

Mistrustful was his middle name, but Ryan grabbed his phone. "All right. I'm ready."

"Let's go."

Their car dropped them off in a part of the city Ryan had heard of but never visited when he was married to Garrett and lived in Brooklyn Heights. He followed Emerson into a low-slung building. A sign hung above the door: The Audrey and Maxwell Klein Home Away From Home CLINIC. Ryan wondered who they were and if they were also doctors there to force him into therapy.

The reception area was an open, welcoming space with cheerful prints on the walls. Ryan noted that the updated technology behind the desk was the same as at his old firm.

"Is that where the receptionist would sit?"

"Yeah. You'd be the first face people see when they walk into the center to get help."

That was a bit discomfiting—Ryan was a mess himself. "Not sure I'm the right person to be greeting people."

"Emerson?"

A man in his mid-to-late forties, with pale-green eyes and dark, wavy hair sprinkled with silver, stood in the doorway between the reception area and the hallway. He wore a white doctor's coat and the script on his jacket read: *Dr. Drew*.

"Drew, hi. I'm glad you're still here."

"I thought I heard your voice. Come to help out on the hotline?" He directed a friendly smile at Ryan. "Hi. I'm Drew."

"Ryan."

Drew extended a hand, and they shook. "Emerson mentioned he was bringing someone who might be able to take over as our new receptionist. Is it you?"

Ryan shrugged. "I'm not sure yet." Why was he being dickish and ruining his chances at a job? He should be grateful for the opportunity. "I guess I have to see if we mesh."

"How about I show you the space? This would be your desk. You'd greet the people as they come in, see if they have an appointment or if it's an emergency that needs treatment right away. I'm one of the doctors, and Jordan is the other—he's an orthopedist. We also have a dentist on staff—Mike."

Ryan was confused. "I thought this was like a hotline place. Like a therapist's office. Why would people come here instead of going to a hospital?"

"Most people who come here can't afford to go to a hospital. They have no insurance. Some are runaways or don't have legal immigration status and are afraid to give out their personal information. Queer young people often end up on the streets because their families turn them out, and trans people, especially, don't often get the proper quality of care. Here we take care of everyone, regardless of race, gender, or status."

Ryan's head spun. "And you do all that here?"

"We do what we can." Drew sighed. "Obviously, we don't have a full-service hospital, but we can set broken bones, stitch people up, and provide the care we're able to. But you are right in that mental-health services are a huge part of our care. My sister's hotline has at least five people monitoring the calls—licensed psychologists, PhD students, teachers, and addiction specialists. That's all in the back of the clinic."

It was an impressive setup, and Ryan wished there had been something like it when he was an eighteen-year-old living on the streets. He might not've ended up the fucked-up mess he was today.

"I'm assuming you don't lack for patients."

"Unfortunately, no. We try our best." Drew's eyes grew sad, and Ryan could see he truly cared. "But ultimately, the person has to want to be helped. Many are so traumatized, it can feel hopeless at first. They fight us because they're afraid. But we don't give up," he said fiercely. "Everyone is worth saving." He turned hopeful eyes on Ryan. "Do you think you'd like to work here with us? Emerson told me a little of your story."

Ryan stiffened. "He did?" Shame burned through him, and he glared at Emerson.

"Nothing personal." Drew reassured him. "Only that you've been out of work for a while, and you need a job. Even if you choose not to work with us, you're free to use our services and talk to someone if you want."

Tension built inside him. "I'm not interested in therapy. But I do need a job. I-I guess I could fill out an application—"

Drew waved a hand at his words. "Eh, we don't stand on ceremony like that here. We just need someone who fits with our mission. You have to have a good attitude and be kind to everyone who comes through the door because you don't know what they've been through."

"I-I can try." His life might be shit, but if all he needed to do to keep this job was to put a smile on his face, he'd figure a way to manage it.

"That's all we can do, right? Trying to do our best is a lot to ask of ourselves sometimes when we feel like the world has let us down, but we should remember there is always someone who needs our help. Someone who has it worse." Drew's voice was calm and peaceful, and he appeared to be so earnest and caring that Ryan's frazzled nerves settled. He couldn't imagine the man raising his voice or getting angry. "Why don't I walk you around the clinic so you can familiarize yourself with the place?"

"Yeah, sure." Ryan nodded. Being with someone like Drew gave him confidence in himself and his ability to succeed. Like maybe he was worthy.

They passed consultation and examination rooms, a break room and supply closets. The clinic was much bigger than it looked from the outside. "Did you start this all by yourself? It must've taken a huge outlay of cash."

"It did, but I had a large insurance settlement, and I wanted to put the money to good use. I'm a plastic surgeon. I couldn't see spending the rest of my life doing nose jobs, breast implants, and tummy tucks. But on top of what I brought in, we get some excellent corporate sponsorships.

My husband's a lawyer, so he's worked out all the legalities. Jordan's husband is in finance, so we get all our advice from him. Plus, their firms make sizable donations." His eyes twinkled. "It helps to keep it all in the family."

"I guess so," Ryan murmured. Everyone here talked about family, but that term remained a foreign concept. How could it not, when his family had turned him out? Alone and rejected by everyone, he'd left town and figured New York was where he could find a home.

He just hadn't counted on what he'd need to do in order to get there.

Drew opened a door. "This is our call center, where my sister runs the hotline. There's always someone here to answer and listen. Sometimes it's Rachel's grad students, or her doctor friends, but many times it's our friends—Dr. Tash and his husband, Brandon, who's a teacher, and Dr. Noah."

In the large room were tables with phones. Three women and two men, headsets on, waved to Drew. A coffee machine and an expensive espresso machine, like they had in coffeehouses, sat on a credenza along the opposite wall, next to an array of snacks. Ryan spotted a large, stainless-steel refrigerator in the corner. Despite his initial misgivings about coming to this center, Ryan couldn't help but be impressed.

"This is a pretty incredible setup."

"Thank you. I'm extremely proud of what we've accomplished. I think you'll find it a good place to work."

One of the men took off his headset and stretched. He rose from his chair, and after taking a bottle of water from the refrigerator, walked over to Drew and him.

"Hey, Drew. Haven't seen you in a while."

"Yeah. Ash was busy with a case, so now that he's finished, we're trying to spend some time together." He smiled at Ryan. "This is Ryan. I'm hoping he's going to join us and take over for Marly at the reception desk."

"Ryan, hi, I'm Noah. Nice to meet you." His blue eyes

were warm.

"Same. I'm looking forward to getting to work." Obviously, this was the doctor Emerson had brought up, and Ryan began to doubt the job was real. Was he being paranoid, or was it a way to get him into therapy?

"Have you been looking long? I can tell you this is a great place to work. You won't find a nicer group of people. They're like your family."

"I hope not, since mine sucked." He laughed, but his weak attempt at humor was met with sympathetic faces.

"I'm sorry," Noah spoke quickly to shut down the awkwardness. "I didn't mean to dredge up bad memories."

"No big deal. I'm fine." Ryan didn't want to say that when all your memories were bad, that was all you could relate to.

"Well, if you ever want to talk, I'm here two nights a week. And you can call me anytime."

"I said I'm fine. I know what you're all trying to do." His temper spiked, and he lashed out at Emerson. "You want me here to keep an eye on me. To make sure I don't start using again and to trick me into therapy. What, you think I'm gonna talk about how my mommy and daddy hated me and that's why I started using? I know it all, and it's not going to work. You're no better than Logan."

He stormed out of the room and ran smack into a tall, blond man exiting one of the offices.

"Ouch." The man rubbed his shoulder where Ryan had banged into him. "Where's the fire?"

Drew, Emerson, and Noah had followed him after his outburst and stood in the doorway to the call center.

"Ryan, come on. It's not what you think," Emerson pleaded.

His steps faltered. He wanted to walk out, but the truth was, if he blew this opportunity, he was back to nothing. He had no options left. Working at the center would give him the stability he needed to find a place to live and get on his feet. Ashamed of his outburst, he rubbed his face and waited for his heart to stop pounding.

"As long as none of you force me into talking to Noah or any other therapist," he mumbled, aware he'd spilled out his private demons to a bunch of strangers.

"I promise," Noah stated, his face solemn. "I didn't mean to upset you and make you uncomfortable. It's just something we tell everyone who works here. If you ever need help, either Tash or I are available to talk. There's no charge."

"Why wouldn't you want to talk to Noah?" the blond man asked, looking puzzled. "He's one of the best therapists in the city, plus he's a really nice guy."

"Not all people believe in therapy. I'm one of them."

"You were like that at one point, remember, Jordy?" Drew said quietly.

The guy grimaced. "Yeah, don't remind me. That whole time of my life is like a bad dream now, a nightmare I was lucky to wake up from. That's not a place I ever want to revisit."

Ryan was curious. Drew had called him Jordy—obviously short for Jordan. He must be the other doctor in the practice, the orthopedist. "What happened to you?" he blurted out, and Jordan's brows arched high in surprise. "Sorry," Ryan apologized. "I didn't mean to pry."

Jordan glanced over to the group standing in the doorway, and a surprisingly light smile tipped up his lips. "Of course you did. You asked. But I brought it up, so it's on me." He opened the door to the room he'd exited. "Come on and sit down, and I'll tell you the story of how I almost killed my career, my friendship with Drew, and myself."

CHAPTER SEVEN

RYAN

At those stunning words, Ryan's jaw dropped. "No, I'm sorry. Really. I shouldn't have said anything. I don't like talking about my personal life, so I don't think I should force you to."

"Don't worry. There's nothing Jordan likes more than talking about himself."

The sarcastic drawl from behind them had Jordan rolling his eyes, while everyone else laughed.

"Very funny, Ash. Don't give up the day job."

A tall man with night-black hair and dancing eyes, pale as moonlight, snickered. "I've been waiting a long time to be able to use that line. I have plenty more stockpiled."

Ryan watched as Ash made a beeline for Drew. "Hey, baby," he murmured and gave him a kiss on the mouth, then wrapped an arm around him. He surmised he was Drew's husband. They settled into each other like pieces of a puzzle.

"Ignore him," Jordan sniffed. "I'll keep it short and ugly. My partner died, and I went into a deep depression. I used pills and drugs to mask my pain. I was spiraling out of control, willing to do anything and everything to keep my friends from finding out how bad it was. As I said, I almost lost my license to practice and my friendship with Drew."

"You almost lost your life, Jordan." Visibly upset, Drew wiped his eyes. "That's what was most important."

"Yeah, well, when you're down in the depths of that snake pit of addiction, you don't think about that. It's like a fire that burns at your insides, and nothing can quench it but what you need and crave to soothe the beast." Jordan's earlier humor had fled. "You're only concerned with chasing the next high and doing what you can to stop the pain. Even if it hurts the people you love most."

God, how he understood every single word.

"How did you stop?" Ryan couldn't help but ask.

Jordan's face lit up. "I met Luke. He brought me out of the darkness."

"It wasn't as simple as Jordan makes it sound," Ash interjected. "We all went through hell and back. You and Luke had a ton of issues to work through."

"You being one of the main ones," Jordan stated grimly.

"I'm not denying that." Ash's eyes grew shiny. "None of us were whole at that point in time. All I'm saying is, you suffered for your recovery. Don't make it sound like a cakewalk or that love set you free."

"Thank you, Ash. I know I couldn't have done it without you all to help me."

Despite the teasing snipes between Ash and Jordan, Ryan could tell there was a deep bond between the two.

Drew stepped to Jordan's side. "Addiction is not an easy hole to climb out of. It takes incredible strength and a will to survive. Luke gave you hope, love, and a reason to walk in the sunlight, but it had to be your choice. In the end, it's a road you have to want to travel, and it can get lonely, even with a village behind you. It wasn't easy to survive after the fire that nearly killed you, but you did it, and we are all so proud of you."

The two men hugged. "And I am so grateful none of you deserted me," Jordan said with a doting smile as he pulled out his phone. "Because I wouldn't have my daughter, Ellie." He showed Ryan a picture of a little girl in a miniature white coat and a stethoscope.

"She's cute."

"Only three and she wants to be just like Daddy," he preened.

"She's a perfect angel except for that fact." Ash smirked. "She'd be better off taking after my brother."

Muttering, Drew raised his gaze to the ceiling. "How many years will I have to endure this?" He poked Ash's shoulder. "Will you knock it off?" He focused on Ryan. "I hope this gives you an idea of how we operate here. We don't hold anyone's past against them if they're trying to move forward." He hugged Jordan. "I could never be whole unless I had my best friend by my side again. Please, think about it, and I hope to see you tomorrow morning."

"Ready to go?" Ash asked Drew. "I promised Esther we'd be there for dinner, and I don't want to be late."

"Let's go. It's brisket night." Drew took his hand. "Night, everyone." They walked down the hallway.

The tension Ryan had been holding broke free, and the words couldn't stop tumbling from his mouth. "I started smoking a little pot at sixteen and then moved on to harder stuff. My parents kicked me out at eighteen when I came out. I-I've had a problem for years," he heard himself say, and Ash and Drew stopped and turned. Jordan remained in the doorway of his office, face grave, eyes intent.

Tears threatened, but Ryan clenched his hands into fists and continued because he believed he'd met people who would listen with understanding hearts and minds. "No one knew. Not my husband when we met in college, nor after we got married. It got worse when I was at my firm. Drugs were plentiful, and booze was always available. Happy hour was every afternoon, and new clients were celebrated with parties at all the best clubs. It was a never-stopping carousel—only it began to spin out of control."

"You're a lawyer?" Ash was clearly surprised.

"Was." His lip curled in a sardonic smile, but the joke was on him. "I was arrested and disbarred." Their faces displayed both shock and sympathy, and Ash was the only one to continue to question him.

"So it was a felony arrest? Have you tried for reinstatement?"

"Yeah. Possession, and I punched the cop. That's what sent me down the rabbit hole. They denied me. And when I saw the letter, I lost it and…"

"Ran right back to the drugs?" Jordan nodded. "I can understand the trigger, especially if you had little to no support."

Ryan didn't correct him. He'd already revealed more than intended, but Noah gazed at him with compassion and concern.

"And how are you now?" Noah questioned. "Have you come to terms with your new life?"

"No," he answered bluntly. "It took me so long and I worked so hard to get where I was, and to know I threw it all away…for nothing. I'm so goddamn stupid and angry all the time. I hate it. I…hate myself for it."

Before he could take another breath, Noah took him by the shoulders. "You know what I see when I look at you? Courage. You've pulled yourself off the edge of the abyss. The strength it takes to make this kind of admission and get clean is unparalleled. I'm in fucking awe of you, and I know everyone here feels the same."

Everyone nodded and murmured their agreement, but it was Jordan whose words meant the most to him. "I understand. Believe me. It wasn't so long ago I was in your position. It pains me to know you don't have the support of family to help you. You can do it—I know you can, but it's easier when you have people who care in your corner."

Noah's fingers tightened on him. "There's no one you can rely on? No one willing to help?" Their eyes met, and there was something there. A connection, but Ryan had no clue why, as they'd never met. "Are you sure?"

He thought of Logan and his willingness to give him everything and make life easy. But it hadn't worked, and Ryan knew he couldn't return.

"No. No one. Only Emerson. I don't know what I would've done without him."

Emerson said, "For the past few weeks, I've been helping Ryan get clean. We were upstate, but I needed to go back to work. He's done amazingly well, and I know he's ready. That's why I thought if he could work here—it would be a start on the road to recovery. You guys helped me."

"I went to meetings on and off," Ryan admitted, "but I still had slipups when the reality of how badly I screwed up my life got to me. The minute I got that letter from the disciplinary committee, I grabbed a bottle." He hung his head. "It was all for nothing."

"Not true." Noah was quick to correct him. "You know you can do it, but your problem runs deeper than a weekly meeting. I know you're very insistent that you're not into therapy, but it can truly help you."

"I agree," Jordan added. "And trust me, I was the first to think I could handle it on my own. Don't let your ego get in the way of your recovery." He glared at Ash, who raised his brows.

"What? I didn't say anything."

"I know, but I was waiting for a comment about my ego."

"Well"—Ash grinned—"since you brought it up…" Those gleaming, silvery eyes connected with Ryan's, and he almost flinched at their intensity. "I'll be blunt, Ryan.

You fucked up and have no one but yourself to blame."

"Ash…" Drew yanked at his arm, but Ryan stopped him.

"It's fine. He's right, and this is exactly what I need to hear. Not people stroking me and telling me how great I am."

Approval shone from Ash's face. "Good. Because while I'm glad you're sober now, you need to get to the bottom of why you keep screwing up your life. I presume you had a job after your disbarment?"

"Yeah. Maintenance supervisor for a hotel. I lost it, so now I'm in the hole again. Plus, I need a place to live."

"Why?" Noah's brow wrinkled. "What happened to the apartment you were in?"

"Nothing. But I can't live there again." No way would he bring Logan into this. His life, his problem. Besides, those bridges he'd burned? Logan's was a hellfire. "Finding an apartment or even a room somewhere until I save up enough is my first priority. I've been sleeping on Emerson's sofa, but I can't keep living like that. It's not fair to him."

"I don't mind, Ry."

"But I do." Emerson was fast becoming another soft landing for him, and it would be too easy to fall back into that comfort. "I need independence, and if it's fucking hard, then that's what it has to be. So," he appealed to Drew, "if you still want to hire me after everything I've said tonight, I'd like to work here."

"I'm good with it." Drew nodded to Jordan. "How about you?"

"Works for me. And if you want tough love, I'm here to give it. First thing you should know is the drug cabinets are monitored with a security camera, so if you think you can break in and grab a quick fix, you can't. I know all the tricks."

Ryan winced but stood his ground. "I get it. And I appreciate your honesty."

"If you're going to work here, you'll get used to it. I'll

be happy to call you out if I see you slip up." Jordan leveled a glacial stare at him. "And I'll know. Trust me."

"I won't fuck up."

"It's not the first time you've made that promise, is it?" Ash asked, his jaw as granitelike as Jordan's, in contrast to his husband Drew's gentle face. "Why should we believe you now?"

Ryan appreciated the hard-hitting, no-bullshit approach, a true contrast to Logan's soft-as-a-feather stroking.

"Because I have everything to lose."

"You can start tomorrow," Drew said. "Be here before nine so you can go through the setup."

"Thank you. I will."

Noah's face shone with approval. "I'm thrilled for you, Ryan. I think this is the start of something special."

Feeling guilty over his flat-out refusal to accept Noah's help, Ryan held out his hand. "I appreciate your offer, you know, to talk and everything, but I think this is the right way for me."

Noah continued to make his pitch. "It doesn't always have to be either or. Circumstances change. I want you to know that I'm here for you. And if you don't feel comfortable talking with me, Tash is a psychiatrist as well. He's the doctor who helped Jordan. We just want you to succeed and be healthy again. I have to go back to the help line, but I hope to see you soon."

Too overcome to speak, Ryan ducked his head to hide the tears that threatened. *Healthy again* implied there was a time when he hadn't abused his body, but that was a distant memory. Twenty years of using on and off had taken their toll. One of the reasons he usually kept away from mirrors. It frightened him to know how badly he'd treated the body he'd been given.

Along with the other men, he walked out past the reception area and trailed his hand along the desk where he'd be sitting. "I'll see you tomorrow. And thanks for the opportunity."

"See you in the morning," Drew called out. He and Ash got into a car waiting for them at the curb, leaving Jordan with him and Emerson.

"I appreciate you sharing your story, Jordan. I know it was hugely personal, but it helped me see that I really can do this."

Jordan faced him with a frown. "I think you can, but don't do it for anyone other than yourself. You have to be hungry to want a fresh start."

"I did, but I forgot what real hardship was like. I didn't think the ground would hit me so hard when I fell."

"Getting high is like sailing through puffy white clouds." Jordan barked out a laugh. "Becoming sober feels like you're being struck by lightning over and over, and even when you're okay, every once in a while you get that electric shock to remind you it only takes one misstep to send you spiraling into that rabbit hole of destruction." His eyes narrowed. "Family can coddle you and be the worst enablers. It took me nearly getting beaten to death to learn my lesson."

To see a man like Jordan, whose arrogant set to his shoulders and tilt of his brow hinted that he came from money and privilege, no one would ever guess he'd wallowed in the filth of addiction. But that was the thing—it could hit anyone, from anywhere.

"I don't have anyone other than myself to do this for. I have no contact with my family. I worked a couple of years before going to college on scholarship and work study, but meeting Garrett my first week helped. He had money from a legal settlement, and I thought I had it made once we were married. We've been divorced for a few years now and basically don't speak. Something else I screwed up badly."

He knew how it sounded—like he'd been a gold digger out only for what Garrett could do for him. It pained him to admit they'd be right. Garrett never worried about money, and he'd paid for everything—Ryan's law school, the apartment they lived in after they were married, and any trips they took. Garrett had lavished presents on him, including the sportscar he'd given him for his thirtieth birthday. The one he'd crashed and totaled in the Hamptons. Ryan had found the sweetest guy in the world and fucked it up by abusing his trust.

"I'll bet. But that's the past, and you can't change it. What you have now is a future solely in your control." A car pulled up to the curb. "That's my ride. I'll see you tomorrow."

Ryan stood on the sidewalk, watching the taillights of the black car fade into the distance. Instead of feeling defeated, with a burden too heavy to bear, Ryan's spirits were invigorated. Finally, he had something in his life with meaning. A purpose.

"You're coming home with me, right? I know you said you can't do it forever, but until you have an apartment of your own, you know you're welcome to my couch."

"Thanks. I feel bad for imposing on you."

"I told you I don't mind, Ry. That's what friends do." Emerson squeezed his arm.

"Thanks. I appreciate everything you've done for me. I just want to be able to stand on my own again."

"I'll call a car."

It only took twenty minutes to make it to Emerson's apartment in Gowanus, and Ryan was surprised to find himself hungry. "How about I make some dinner. Pasta?"

"Sounds good to me."

He puttered about the kitchen, enjoying creating a sauce and chopping vegetables. Emerson went through his mail and answered some emails.

"Pasta's ready."

Emerson joined him at the gleaming quartz kitchen

island. When Emerson had offered Ryan a place to stay, he'd thought the quiet man who dressed in worn jeans and T-shirts rented a small, dingy apartment and he'd be sleeping on a lumpy couch. Instead, Emerson lived in a super-modern high-rise, the bright apartment outfitted with all the bells and whistles and the comfiest sofa bed. He'd since learned that Emerson was a software specialist and made in the mid-six figures. One thing Ryan could be sure of was that people surprised him every day.

They ate, and Emerson kept shooting him looks until he set his fork on the plate. "So you'll take the job?"

Ryan finished his last piece of pasta and wiped his face with a napkin. "Yes. And I-I'm sorry for being so difficult. Thanks for thinking of me. You were right. It seems like a great place to work."

"It's okay. You're my friend."

"And you're mine. I appreciate your putting your life on hold and helping me. Hopefully, I'll be out of your hair soon enough and you can get your life back to normal."

Without responding, Emerson took their plates to the dishwasher and started it running. "I enjoy having you here. In case you haven't guessed, I don't have many friends. I lost most of them when I started drinking, and I'm not exactly mister social."

"I'm sorry. People don't like to stay when it gets messy."

"Your friend Logan isn't like that."

"Logan never saw me when I was in a really bad way. And I doubt I can call him a friend. I blew that one, big-time."

Emerson's brows pulled together. "You never know. I always feel if people care enough, they'll stay for the hard times."

There was little doubt in his mind that Logan was happy to be a savior, but why would he want to see the ugly side of addiction? The screams and cries of withdrawal. The mental torture where Ryan swore his skin was on fire, eating him alive from the inside out. The paranoia, thinking every sound was someone coming to kill him.

Logan was a Prince Charming, living in a castle where nothing touched him that wasn't of his own choosing. Only perfection lived there. Ryan wasn't perfect, and his jagged, broken pieces wouldn't ever match seamlessly with Logan's smooth edges.

"How about we watch some TV?"

Ryan washed his hands and wiped up the surface of the kitchen island. "Yeah. Okay, for a little bit. Then I'd better get to sleep early. I don't want to be late."

Emerson made popcorn and chose a movie. They sat side by side, watching something Ryan couldn't pay attention to, as his mind was too busy thinking about the new job. He also wondered what Logan was doing. Most likely he'd moved on. A man like Logan Silver didn't wait for anyone, especially a messed-up thief like him. He shifted and sighed. The guilt of Logan's watch weighed on him heavily, knowing he'd taken something so sentimental. So meaningful. He'd hurt Logan, the one person who'd tried to help him.

As if reading his mind, Emerson said, "Just so you know, I meant what I said, upstate and here. You can stay as long as you want. It's nice to have someone to hang out with in the evenings."

Their conversations had been so focused on him and his problems, Ryan didn't know much about Emerson.

"I don't want to get in the way of your life either. Don't think you have to babysit me."

"I don't. But I work from home a lot, and it's nice to know there's someone else here." Emerson's eyes twinkled. "It was you or a puppy."

"At least I'm house-trained."

"I just want you on your feet again. I have a big space, and I really do consider you a friend."

Ryan wasn't sure he'd ever had a real friend or people

who cared about him simply for who he was. Once his parents kicked him out, he'd moved from house to house, hoping someone would let him stay on their couch, but none of the parents said yes. Even the people in his firm had turned their backs on him when he got into trouble. They were all the same.

"I appreciate that. And I know I haven't made it easy for you. If you want to bring someone home, you know, like a date, I can always make myself scarce."

Face bright red, Emerson hung his head. "I-I don't date. I'm asexual, and when guys find out I'm not into having sex, they don't bother with me. I've never had a real relationship."

Surprised, Ryan sought to reassure Emerson. "Then they're missing out on a great person." Shiny-eyed, Emerson gave him a brief smile, and Ryan wondered why Emerson had started drinking. A conversation for another day, as Emerson refocused on the movie, but Ryan wanted him to know he wasn't about to disappear on him as well. "When I start making money again, I'll reimburse you for everything. Including letting me stay here. But no matter what, I'll never forget how you stepped up for me. How you took me in and were my friend."

"No, you don't have to. But…"

"But what?" he urged.

"If you want to make dinner for us at night, that would be great. That pasta was delicious."

Ryan laughed—a real laugh—for what felt like the first time in forever. "You got yourself a deal."

CHAPTER EIGHT

LOGAN

It had been over two months since he'd last seen Ryan, and though he'd returned to work full-time, Logan hadn't stopped thinking about him. That one text he'd received from Ryan more than a month ago, saying he was alive, did little to soothe his worries. Yes, he was happy Ryan had contacted him, but it was like tasting a delicious dish only to have it snatched away. Where was he? What was he doing to survive? Logan had questions.

He'd always known it was possible to fade into the blackness of the city—after all, eight million people and a maze of buildings, houses, and subway tunnels made it a veritable treasure trove of hiding places.

Not one to be put off, Logan decided to show up at the church again and wait for the AA meeting to end. A long shot for sure, but what else did he have these days? His inability to help Ryan gnawed at his bones. When the meeting broke, he scanned the faces of the men and women exiting the building. He spied Emerson and stepped in his path.

"Hi, Emerson."

The man's brows flew up, and a flush crept over his cheeks. "Uh, h-hi. Logan, right?"

"Yeah." Not that he gave a shit, but Emerson appeared to be the type to pee in his pants if he became too agitated. Logan could be nice. If he tried hard enough. "I went to your apartment to talk to you a few weeks ago, but you weren't there."

"I-I was away."

Something seemed off, but he couldn't put his finger on it. Yet. Maybe if he talked to Emerson long enough, he'd find out.

"How have you been?"

"F-fine. I guess." He blinked. "Uh, Ryan wasn't at the meeting." Emerson was as nervous and jumpy as a deer caught in headlights.

"I know. I was hoping you and I could talk. You know, maybe put our heads together."

"I-I don't know. I have to be somewhere…" Emerson fumbled with his jacket sleeve, as if to look at a watch, but Logan put a hand on his arm.

"Please. I could really use your help." He gazed deep into Emerson's eyes and smiled. "Please."

He heard the sharp intake of Emerson's breath. Logan had zero remorse for using the weapons in his arsenal, in this case flirting and charisma, to get what or whom he wanted.

Ryan.

"Okay." Emerson nodded, and Logan took his arm. Damp heat radiated from Emerson, and Logan forced himself not to grimace.

"How about the Smyth across the street?" He waited, and Emerson blinked rapidly.

"Y-yeah. Sure."

They were seated, and Emerson removed his jacket. Patches of sweat stained his armpits. Logan continued to stare at him, and Emerson shifted in his chair, clearly uneasy being his bug under the microscope.

"You're a good person, Emerson. I can tell."

"I don't know about that."

"I do. You're kind and caring. I know you're concerned about Ryan."

The server came by, and Emerson ducked his head. "Just a soda—Coke, please."

"I'll have a club soda," Logan added.

"You don't have to abstain because of me."

"I don't want to make you uncomfortable. How about something to eat? It's late, and you must be hungry."

"Thank you, but I can't. It's one of the nights I'm on the help line at the center. My roommate makes us dinner when we get home." Emerson shrugged. He drank more of his soda.

Logan peered at him through lowered lashes and decided to press.

"Tell me about the center you work at."

Interestingly enough, Emerson avoided the question with one of his own. "Have you heard from Ryan at all?"

That took Logan by surprise. "I got a brief text a few weeks back, which didn't tell me much, so I'm still worried. Have you?" he asked pointedly.

"Uh, no. Maybe he's left the city. You know, new life and all that." Finished with his soda, he crunched the leftover ice cubes. "I should really get going."

"To your help line?"

"Uh, yeah. It's in Brooklyn, and it takes a while to get there."

That triggered a memory of him sitting in this very same hotel bar with a doctor…Logan couldn't remember his name but did recall he was a former model. He had his card in his wallet. The man was a psychologist who worked at a center where they helped people. Parts of the puzzle began to click, but he needed more.

"Why do you think Ryan's left the city?" Logan wondered if Emerson was deliberately hiding something from him. "Did you hear something?" An almost frightened expression crossed Emerson's face, and Logan, never one to be denied, went for the kill. "Tell me."

Emerson's brows flew up, and he stuttered, "N-no, just that, I mean…it's been a while, and if he wanted you to know where he was…wouldn't he tell you?" He jumped out of his seat. "I have to go," he flung over his shoulder as he fled.

Unwilling to wait for the server to get their check, Logan tossed out a few bills to more than cover the cost plus a hefty tip, and followed Emerson. He watched the man get into a cab, and he grabbed one of his own from the line of taxis waiting outside.

"Follow that cab. He's going to Brooklyn."

"I don't like going to Brooklyn," the cabbie grumbled.

"Ask me if I care. Just drive and don't lose him. There's an extra hundred off the meter for you."

"Yeah?" The cabbie met his eyes. "Okay. I follow."

"I bet you like Brooklyn now." Logan's smile was grim, and he settled into the seat. With the usual bridge traffic, it took almost half an hour to arrive at…

"Where the fuck are we?" Logan muttered as he peered out of the windows.

"Red Hook. Not so good around here. Don't take out your money. Except for the hundred you owe me. See? Whoever you were following got out of the cab. He's going into that building." He held out his hand.

Logan gave him the fare plus the extra hundred. "Thanks."

"No problem."

He watched the cab speed away, then walked to the building. *Home Away From Home Clinic.* Color him intrigued. Logan pushed open the door and walked inside. A man in his late forties, in a button-down and slacks, glanced up from the front desk. His brow furrowed, but from behind his glasses, his eyes looked kind.

"Can I help you?"

Damn. What the hell was he supposed to say? "I, uh, I heard there was a help line, and—"

"Do you need help?"

The weight of grief and guilt sat heavily on his shoulders, and to his horror, his throat tightened and he could barely respond. "I'm not…no. But I know…" He put a hand to his eyes and gave the man his back.

Fucking hell. Would it ever stop hurting?

The man came from behind the desk and put a hand on his shoulder. "Come sit."

Like a child, Logan allowed himself to be led to the row of chairs in the waiting room and sat. "I'm sorry. I'm not usually this emotional."

The man's smile was gentle. "You can be anything you like here. I'm Dr. Tash Weber, one of the psychiatrists here at the center. Did you come because you're in crisis? Do you need help?"

Logan barked out a pitiful laugh. "Don't we all?" He shook off the doctor's hand. "I'm fine, thanks. Really." At Weber's dubious expression, he offered, "I've had people close to me suffer from addiction problems."

"I can see that it's affected you as well."

"From only a few sentences?" The words tumbled out before Logan realized what he'd said. Embarrassed, he ran a hand through his hair. "I'm sorry. I didn't come here to talk about me."

"Don't apologize. Do you have anyone you can talk to—a therapist or a doctor?"

"No," Logan said abruptly. "Like I told you, I'm not here about me."

"I see." Weber gazed at him, eyes serious and thoughtful,

but Logan felt probed to his soul. He squirmed a bit, a foreign concept to him. "Why are you here, then?"

He had to think fast because he couldn't come out and say, *Well, I suspected that someone who ran away from me might work here, so I followed his friend from their addiction recovery meeting.*

That didn't sound creepy or stalkerish at all, did it?

Surprisingly enough, Weber's calm presence had him revealing far more than he'd intended. Maybe he sensed the doctor was the nonjudgmental type.

"A little over two months ago, a friend who was living in my apartment received bad news that caused him to fall off the wagon. He then ran away, and I haven't heard from him since. I'm very worried for his safety. I've looked for him everywhere, but with no luck."

Weber gazed at him steadily. "I'm sorry to hear that. But I'm still not seeing the connection."

Logan figured he had nothing left to lose. "I know he and Emerson are friendly, so I followed Emerson here, hoping…I don't know what. Hoping maybe Ryan was here. But I guess that's a ridiculous assumption." He stood. "I'm sorry to have wasted your time."

Something subtle shifted in Weber's face. Maybe someone less perceptive wouldn't have noticed, but Logan did.

"No, not ridiculous at all. When we're desperate enough, we'll look for any clue. Most people connected with the clinic have suffered some kind of sexual or emotional abuse or addiction, so it was a natural assumption. I'm sorry we couldn't help you." Weber rose to his feet.

Sensing Weber itched for him to leave, Logan tried to drag his feet. He wanted to delve deeper into this shift of attitude. "I spoke to a doctor from here. I think I have his card." He dug out his wallet. "Yeah. Noah Strauss."

Weber's face brightened. "Yes. Noah works on the help line. Along with his husband, Oren."

"The lawyer."

"Yes. Do you know him?"

"We've never met, but I know the firm he works for."

"Ash, then."

"Our firms have done business over the years. Divorce, contracts…that sort of thing."

A cool wind blew inside as someone entered the building.

"Logan Silver, to what do we owe the honor and pleasure? Did you decide to cross the bridge to personally talk to me about case we're going to be working on together ? Must be a big fish to get you all the way out here."

Ash Davis's slight Southern drawl drew his attention away from Weber. Ash leaned his broad frame against the doorway, and Logan's lips twitched.

"Hello, Ash. No, that's not why I'm here. I'd hoped maybe someone I knew worked here, but it was a silly thought."

Weber extended his hand to Logan. "It was nice to talk to you. Don't be a stranger." They shook, and then, to Logan's surprise, Weber hugged Ash. "See you this weekend? Brandon wants to have all of you over at the house for brunch."

Ash's frown lines smoothed out. "We'll be there."

Dr. Weber disappeared down the hall, leaving Logan alone with Ash, and that silvery gaze pierced him as Ash strode closer and sat by his side. "Care to tell me who you think you might know who maybe works here?"

CHAPTER NINE

LOGAN

"It was silly of me to come. I should get going." Logan pushed up from his seat.

"The Logan Silver I recall didn't do silly." Ash spun his wedding ring around on his finger and tipped his head, but that penetrating stare remained steadfast on Logan's face. "Now, come on. You can talk to me." He grinned. "I don't bite."

Ash was a force to be reckoned with, and Logan decided to give him the condensed version. "I had a good friend I was helping through rough times. I thought he was getting better, that he was okay."

"But he wasn't."

Releasing a long sigh of frustration, Logan shook his head. "No. He received some pretty devastating news—not health-related, but as an attorney, you'll understand. He'd lost his license and was waiting for a letter from the disciplinary committee to reinstate him, but—"

"They turned him down," Ash stated, and Logan cocked his head. Ash shrugged. "I mean, it was obvious from what you said."

"Well, you're correct."

"So, what happened?"

It surprised him that Ash Davis gave a damn. Years ago they'd crossed paths in a divorce settlement, and he'd been all business and a ruthless advocate for his client. This Ash was charming and seemingly invested in Logan's story. The gleam of the gold wedding band caught his eye again. Maybe marriage *had* tamed the savage beast.

"What happened is that Ryan stole over a thousand dollars from me, took my father's gold watch, and disappeared. That was two months ago, and I've heard nothing since except for a brief, vague text."

Ash sucked in a sharp breath. "Shit." He drummed his fingers on the arm of the chair. "You lived together? He was your lover?"

"No. It wasn't like that. I was concerned about him falling back into a life of drugs and alcohol. I didn't want that happening to him. I-I was trying to help."

"How very altruistic of you." Ash raised a skeptical brow, and Logan scowled.

"I'm serious."

Ash's laughter rang out in the small waiting area. "Come on. You're letting a gorgeous guy stay in your apartment, and you're not putting the moves on him? You? Give me a break." Ash's phone buzzed, and he checked it. His eyes grew soft. "I've got to go. My husband is waiting. But if you're really concerned about helping people who need it, why not put up or shut up? Come here and volunteer your time. Tomorrow would be good."

Without waiting for an answer, Ash strode down the hallway.

Finally free to leave, Logan called for a car, and as he stood at the curb, something struck him and his heartbeat rocketed.

How the hell had Ash known Ryan was gorgeous? He wouldn't…unless he'd already met him.

Son of a bitch.

His car stopped in front of the center, and Logan slid inside.

Looks like I'll be coming back tomorrow.

* * *

Simon stormed after him when he announced he was leaving. It was after four on a Friday afternoon, so he hadn't thought it would be a problem.

Obviously, he was mistaken.

"Where are you off to now? Chasing another false lead?"

Logan pressed the elevator button. "No. As a matter of fact, I think I know where he is." Logan explained what happened the night before, and Simon listened and let him finish.

"As crazy as it sounds, you might be right. I'm coming with you."

"What? Why?" Logan brushed him off. "I'm fine. I'll see you Monday." The elevator door opened, and Simon followed him.

"Logan." Simon sounded like a schoolteacher explaining a particularly difficult math problem. "If what you're saying is true, everyone there will be in Ryan's corner. Who's going to be in yours?"

No one. It was second nature for him to be alone, so he didn't question it. But the longer the words lingered in the air, the heavier the weight of his burden felt, and he knew he was lucky to have someone like Simon in his life.

"Thank you. I don't even know if I'm right or…"

"So let's find out."

He sat in the car, quiet and stoic, unbelievably grateful for Simon's presence. They reached the center, and he stood outside on the sidewalk, gathering his thoughts and courage. Simon remained by his side.

"What the hell am I doing? I'm probably wrong. I'm sorry you got dragged out here."

"I'm not complaining. And I'm searching my memory for a time when you had a hunch and were proved wrong." Simon nudged his shoulder. "If I could have anyone defending me in court, it would be you." His gaze flicked to the front door. "Let's go in."

Logan pushed open the door, his eyes immediately focusing on the front desk. His heart slammed in hard, short beats.

"Fuck me," he breathed and stared.

There Ryan sat at the front desk, talking to a young man. He was smiling and looked…at peace. Certainly happier than any day he'd been with Logan in all the time they'd lived together.

"Shit. You were right," Simon murmured. "I can't believe it."

"Thought you said I'm always right." Leaving Simon's side, Logan walked toward the U-shaped desk. Ryan finished with the person he was speaking with and turned to greet him.

"Welc—" The smile on his lips froze, and he turned white. His eyes glowed blue and bright. "Oh."

Trying to remain calm, Logan sauntered the last few steps. "Hi, Ryan. Nice to see you again."

"L-Logan, hi. How—"

"Was your question going to be how I'm doing?" He leaned on the desk, coming almost nose-to-nose with Ryan. So close he could feel him quivering. Smell his fear. "Because I'm doing really, really shitty." He licked his lips. "See, I don't like thinking I'm a fool. Or that I was made to look like one. And I think you know that."

"A fool?" Ryan gulped, his Adam's apple jumping.

"Why? How?"

"Are you serious?" Logan growled. "You ran out on me, with no note, no phone call, nothing for months except some stupid text saying you're alive." His lip curled. "After living with me for months, you didn't think I'd want to know something more? Something about how you were doing? It's like you wanted to wipe me out of your life forever."

Ryan lifted his chin. "Would that be so bad?"

"I can't believe you're even saying this. I took you into my home, gave you everything—"

"Yeah, I know. And I was suffocating."

Suffocating? Is he fucking kidding me?

"And then you stole from me. Or did you forget that in your new and happy life?" Like nails, the words spit from Logan's mouth, and he could see he'd hit his mark when Ryan flinched.

"Ryan? Is everything okay?"

"We're fine." Irritated at being interrupted, Logan barely glanced at the man in the white coat.

"I wasn't asking you. I was talking to Ryan."

Now the man had Logan's full attention. "Who are you, and why are you inserting yourself into my and Ryan's private business?"

The man's glacial eyes hardened, and his jaw set in a hard line. "This is my clinic, and Ryan works here."

"Jordan, it's okay," Ryan soothed. "I can handle it."

"I won't have anyone threatened or intimidated." Jordan moved closer to Ryan, and Logan wondered if they were sleeping together. For some reason that pained his heart.

"Threatened?" Logan sputtered, about to go off on this arrogant asshole. "Are you crazy?"

"Don't use that kind of language here," Jordan snapped, and Logan, about to let loose, felt Simon's hand clamp on his shoulder.

"I think we all need to calm down. If it would be okay

with you, maybe Logan could wait until Ryan finishes work, and then they could talk."

"Who are you?" Jordan asked.

"Simon Brown. I'm one of Logan's law partners."

Jordan joined Ryan behind the desk and pulled him away. He bent his head in close, whispering.

Logan bristled. "Don't try and talk him out of it."

Ignoring him, Jordan continued to murmur in Ryan's ear. Ryan shook his head. "I get off soon. We can talk then if you want to wait."

"I've been waiting for months. I can wait a few minutes more."

He allowed Simon to lead him to the corner of the waiting room, where they sat. Jordan remained by Ryan, as if afraid Logan would snatch him up from behind the desk and run away with him.

"I can't believe he's really here, just living his life. No shame or anything for the way he treated me," Logan said, furious with himself. "And he's obviously found himself another sucker to fall for his sob story."

"You think he was lying about everything from the beginning?"

"No, he was in bad shape. I heard from Remi how badly he was beaten and that he was using again. And I know he had it rough. But look at him. The way he's listening to that guy's every word, like he walks on water or something. They have to be lovers."

"Sounds like you're a little jealous."

His jaw dropped, and he glared at Simon, who remained unfazed. Damn, he must be losing the frosty stare that used to send associates into a frenzy of fear. "I know you didn't just say that to me."

Shit. Simon knows me too well.

"The hell I didn't. Did you forget I know you two hooked up once? In a club? The Logan I've known for over twenty years never did that. You don't even kiss people in public. So for you to get so out of control that you had to have him, means something in Ryan touched you where no one else has. Maybe you don't want to admit it to me. But you need to stop fooling yourself that Ryan's just another guy to you."

He didn't respond and sat, his mind a muddle of incomprehensible thoughts. He couldn't understand if he was angry, hurt, or a combination of both. Whatever this emotion was, Logan didn't like it.

The clinic emptied out until it was only Ryan left out front. He'd shot occasional glances Logan's way but worked steadily, answering calls, intercom messages, and entering information on the computer in front of him. At five thirty, Jordan walked out from the back.

"Okay. I'm finished with my last patient, so we can go into my office and talk."

"You're a doctor?" Logan sat stunned. He hadn't a clue, and Jordan, perhaps enjoying his discomfort, sneered at him.

"Yeah. I told you this was my clinic. I'm the orthopedist here. Follow me."

With Simon at his side, Logan trailed behind Ryan and Jordan, past exam rooms, supply closets, and other offices. Jordan stopped at an open door.

"After you."

They entered and sat around the conference table, but not before Logan spied a lineup of pictures on the credenza behind Jordan's desk. A little girl, from birth through toddler years, with Jordan and another man. Noticing where his attention was drawn, Jordan's entire face softened.

"My little girl, Ellie. She's three."

"You have a child?"

"Yes. Why are you so surprised? Many gay couples have children."

"Couples?"

Jordan rolled his eyes. "Yes. What is with you and the

questions about my personal life? You're here because you're making trouble for Ryan."

"Trouble for Ryan? I've been worried sick for the past two months. I've had the police looking for him—"

"The police?" Jordan's voice rose. "Why would you need the police?"

Logan's lips pressed thin. "He lived in my house for almost six months. I was away on a business trip and came home to find a letter denying his reinstatement to the bar, next to an empty bottle of vodka."

Ryan's cheeks flushed red, but he met Logan's gaze defiantly. "They know my story. I told them everything."

"You did?"

"Yes," Jordan responded smoothly. "And he's getting help."

"That's good. But did he also tell you he stole money from me along with my father's gold watch? Do you know I gave him a hundred thousand dollars to pay off a loan and didn't charge him interest and that he's never attempted to pay me back?"

Ryan pinched his eyes closed, but then straightened his shoulders. "I'm sorry. I-I'll get you the money."

"You know what really hurt the most?" Logan continued as if Ryan hadn't spoken. "You didn't want my help? That's fine. But it didn't even occur to you that I'd want to be there for you after the news? That I'd be concerned for your state of mind, your mental health? You just walked out of my life and disappeared, like I didn't matter one damn bit."

"That's not the way it happened," Ryan protested. "It was humiliating, and to have to tell you…I just couldn't."

"But you could take my money and the one thing that mattered the most to me and vanish, leaving me sick to death with worry, thinking you were out there, alone and in trouble. Doing God knows what to stay alive. Maybe you were even dead. I didn't give a damn whether or not you ever got your license back. I only wanted you to get well. I thought we were friends, but I guess I was wrong because a friend won't leave in a time of crisis. You want to be with them, so they can help you when you need it most."

Simon put a hand on his shoulder to comfort him, but it had the opposite effect. It made him grow sick with anger that poured through him like poison.

"I'm thrilled you've got a new life, Ryan. Now you can stay the hell out of mine."

He stormed out of the office and the clinic and called for a car.

CHAPTER TEN

RYAN

Stunned and somewhat shaken, Ryan sat quiet, Logan's harsh words still echoing in the air.

Jordan bent over to whisper in his ear. "Are you okay?"

Ryan nodded, but truthfully, he wasn't. Not one damn bit. Seeing Logan had been more painful than he'd imagined.

Simon, who'd remained seated, stood and pinned him with frank eyes. "Maybe Logan didn't handle it right by overprotecting you, but he didn't deserve the way you treated him. Old habits are hard to break, and he had the best of intentions. Logan never meant to hurt you. Can you say the same?"

He walked out, and Ryan dropped his head into his hands. Jordan pushed his chair away, and Ryan felt the weight of his disapproving stare.

"Well, that didn't work out as planned. Do you know what Logan's friend meant when he mentioned old habits?"

"No. Not a clue." Ryan too wondered what Simon meant, but he'd left before he could find out.

"Did Logan ever have an addiction problem?"

"No. Impossible. He's way too strong."

"Do you think I'm weak?" Jordan asked, a smile lifting the corner of his lips.

"No, of course not. You're anything but."

"And yet I was an addict. You see the point I'm trying to make? Maybe he is the way he is because he knows firsthand how you're feeling."

Doubtful, Ryan shrugged. "I don't know. Maybe."

"And that part about you stealing from him, the money and his father's watch"—Jordan's icy blue eyes fixed on him—"is that true?"

Shame coursed through him, his face heated, but recovery meant facing up to his truths, ugly as they might be. "Yeah. I-I was drunk and had to leave as soon as I could. I knew Logan had house money he kept in a drawer by his bed, so I grabbed it. I saw the watch, and I wasn't thinking, just knew it was gold and worth a lot, so I took it too. When I sobered up and realized what I'd done, I kept it safe. I wanted to return it, but…" He shook his head. "I'm disgusted with myself."

"You should give it back. If nothing else, it will give you closure, and Logan will have the thing that matters most to him."

"You're right." He brushed at his eyes. "I'm not a thief. I'd never steal from anyone here."

"I understand. When you're using, your entire personality changes and you do things you'd never imagine yourself capable of, just to chase that next high." Jordan gazed out into the distance, then blinked. "But that's not who you are."

"No, it's not. I haven't touched anything since I started living at Emerson's, and I don't want to. I'm happy working here, and I feel like even though my contribution is small, I'm part of something bigger that's helping other people."

"That's good. It's a first step. And I'm glad you feel that way. This may not be what you planned for your life, but you've certainly stepped in and stepped up, and you are a huge asset for us."

Strange how a simple compliment could mean so much. Ryan couldn't recall anyone at his old firm ever saying, "Good job." The glow of being appreciated settled warm in his chest.

"Thank you. I know I have a lot to learn, but I'm finally beginning to understand what it means to belong."

"You're part of the team. You'll always belong here." Jordan paused. "Have you given any thought to talking to someone? As someone who used to think therapy was for weak people and was bullshit, I'm being honest when I say it can help."

Weighing Jordan's words, Ryan sat motionless, but his mind was busy with a million thoughts, all of them centered around one man.

Logan.

He still desired him with the fire of a thousand suns, but Ryan knew his selfish actions had forfeited any chance of them ever exploring the desire that had simmered between them.

"Ryan? Are you okay?" Jordan's voice penetrated his foggy brain.

"What? Oh, yeah. Therapy. I don't know. Talking about how my parents didn't love me enough isn't really my thing."

Jordan's lip kicked up. "It's more than that. I didn't have parental problems—mine accepted me from day one and were thrilled when Luke and I were married. But what it can do is help you see why you keep making bad choices."

"But I'm not. I'm here, and that's a good choice, isn't it? I'm on the right track now."

"Are you?" Jordan murmured. "I wonder."

Feeling defensive, Ryan struck back. "What? What do you wonder?"

"How did it feel seeing Logan again?"

Caught off guard, Ryan didn't have enough time to clamp down on the heat rushing through him, and his face burned. "What? I'm fine. It wasn't a big deal."

Jordan arched a brow and checked his watch. "I have to leave. You can fool people, Ryan, but do you really want to fool yourself?"

"What does that mean?"

Jordan slipped off his lab coat and reached for his suit jacket. "Think about it. And also ask yourself why you still have Logan's watch. Good night."

Ryan sat in Jordan's office for a while after he'd gone. One thing he'd learned about Jordan was that he loved to speak in riddles, but the man was damn perceptive. Ryan knew what he needed to do.

* * *

Giorgio, the friendliest doorman, was on shift when he entered Logan's high-rise, and he gave Ryan a huge grin.

"Ryan. Where the heck you been?" They bumped fists. "You're looking good."

"Had to get away for a bit. Is he home?"

"Yeah, yeah. Go right on up."

It was easy to pretend happiness, but once he was in the elevator, the nerves took over and he began to sweat. And shake.

Am I making a mistake?

He closed his eyes and did some deep breathing. He didn't need to go into the apartment to return the watch. Everything could be done at the door. Standing in front of Logan's apartment, Ryan felt better that he was solving the last of his problems and he'd have a clean slate.

He rang the bell, the door opened, and a dressed-down Logan stood before him. As sexy as Logan looked in his perfectly fitted suits, seeing him in his gray sweats and a

T-shirt set Ryan's heart thundering.

Meanwhile, Logan stood still, cool as ever. A smile that held little warmth slightly ticked up one corner of his sensuous mouth.

"Returning to the scene of the crime?"

The hot flush of humiliation flooded through him. "I-I wanted to give you back the watch. I didn't sell it. I don't even know why I took it. I was—"

"Not in the hallway, please. Come inside."

When he hesitated, Logan's false smile grew bigger. "Don't worry. After you ran away, I locked up all the valuables."

"Logan, come on," he pleaded.

Logan tipped his head. "I don't conduct my business in hallways. Enter or leave. The choice is yours." Logan waited.

Head held high, Ryan crossed the threshold. He stood in the white-marble foyer, unsure if he should go farther. Logan shut the door, locked it, and walked past him to the living room, where he poured a glass of Scotch. Ryan remained in the foyer.

"Do you plan on shouting your business from all the way over there? If not, come in."

Might as well, since he'd already broken the promise he'd made to himself to stay out of the apartment. He remained standing, though, watching Logan, who stood by the bar.

"To what do I owe this great honor?"

God, he hated that snide tone. He hadn't heard it in so long, he'd forgotten that Logan Silver was considered one of the shrewdest hardasses in the business and didn't get there by being sweet and nice.

"I know I don't deserve it, but can we at least try and be civil?"

"That's a joke coming from a man who stole from me and allowed me to think he was dead."

"I-I had my reasons."

"Which I'd like to hear." Logan finished his drink and set the tumbler on the bar. "You owe me at least that, don't you?"

Ryan hung his head, gathering his strength to talk. "I don't want you to think I didn't appreciate every single thing you did for me. If it wasn't for your encouragement to aim higher, I would've still been in that crappy apartment, working at scrubbing toilets."

"There's nothing wrong with that. It's a necessary job."

"I'm serious. I did appreciate it. But you just made it all so damn easy for me."

Logan stilled, his eyes intent and hard. "And what is the problem? I was helping you. Trying to encourage you. And you took advantage of me."

"I didn't mean it to be like that. But it all came crashing down on me when I got that letter from the disciplinary committee. My life was gone, and I had no way of ever getting it back. Everything hit me at once—my parents, Garrett, and now my livelihood. All gone for good. The house of cards collapsed, and like Humpty Dumpty, I knew I couldn't ever be put back together again. So I took the easy way out, which was to reach for something that would make me feel better."

"I didn't keep any liquor in the house. I respected you and your recovery." Logan poured another splash of Scotch and lifted the glass to his lips. Ryan knew that gesture was meant to show him that Logan had wiped his life clean of him.

Ryan tipped his head toward Logan. "I didn't ask you to do that. I don't want people changing their lives because of me and my problems. The world isn't covered with padding. No one's guaranteed a safe place to land. Anyway"—he pushed his fingers through his hair—"it's New York City. You can get anything you want delivered."

Logan nodded with understanding. "I know. I checked."

Face hot, Ryan continued. "I couldn't stand to be trapped here, waiting for you to come home to tell me everything would be all right. Because it wouldn't be. Ever. I'd lost the one thing I'd gotten on my own. An education. And I threw it all away for the sake of a fucking high." He reached into his pocket, pulled out the watch, and set it on the bar top. "Here's your father's watch. I-I always kept it with me. I knew you treasured it."

"Yet you took it. Knowing how much it meant to me." He picked it up and stroked it gently, then slipped it into his pocket. The coldness faded, replaced by fiery anger. "Did you really hate me? Was I hurting you that badly that you needed to steal the one thing in the world that meant anything to me?"

"No, of course not. I didn't hate you—I don't. I'm sorry," Ryan whispered. "I was so out of it, I didn't know what I was doing."

"Bullshit," Logan snapped, and pointing his finger, advanced on him. "You knew. You knew enough to go where I kept the money. You knew the watch was gold and you could make a quick sale for drugs."

"No, I swear. That's why I never sold it." Trembling, Ryan turned, ready to flee. "I didn't do it to hurt you."

Logan grabbed his arm, his angry face inches from Ryan's. "I tried to help you, and all you did was hurt me. You had people lie to me when I was afraid you were in trouble. I was all over the city looking for you, afraid of what you might do to make money for a score. I badgered the police, let down my partners in meetings, neglected my clients. You made me look like a fool."

Ryan's breath caught, trapped in the intensity of Logan's glittering eyes. "I don't think you're a fool."

The temperature between them rocketed to the boiling point, and Logan's expression turned dark. "I am. Because of this." He leaned in, his lips dangerously close. The tension shimmered in the air between them. Ryan shivered and closed his eyes, yearning to feel Logan's mouth claim his. They'd kissed, but only briefly when he lived with Logan because he'd claimed he wasn't ready. But that was another lie. He knew if he let Logan touch him again, he'd never let him go. He still dreamed about the harsh possessiveness of Logan's touch and burned for him, but that was something he'd keep to himself.

Cursing his name, Logan thrust him away, putting a good five feet between them.

"Thanks for the watch."

"We can work out a payment plan for me to return the money."

"Don't bother. It's not as if I expect you to pay me back." *Bastard.*

But he could hardly be angry. If he was being honest with himself, there was no one else to blame. And he would be damned if he'd owe Logan anything. "I'll do it, don't you worry."

CHAPTER ELEVEN

LOGAN

Simon was waiting for him in his office bright and early Monday morning after a weekend Logan had spent wrestling with the devil. One part of his brain wanted to find Ryan and tell him he was sorry for being such a bastard, but the other side kept yelling at him to leave Ryan alone.

"Last I checked, you have your own office, right next door." Logan scowled at his friend sitting on the long leather sofa. The large window behind his desk provided a gorgeous backdrop of midtown skyscrapers, none of which he appreciated at the moment.

"I know."

"So?" Logan hung up his suit jacket, and coffee in hand, sat behind his desk. "Why are you here? We haven't shared a room since law school, and I'm not about to start again."

"Logan, shut up." Simon sauntered over to stand before him. "Tell me what happened Friday night."

"Excuse me?" He set his cup on the desk and glared.

"It gives me great pleasure to repeat it: shut up. You're babbling about nonsense. Now tell me what happened after you stormed out. I left a few minutes after you, and you were gone."

"I didn't storm out. I walked. Briskly. I can't help it if I have long legs. And nothing happened. I went home."

Logan's direct gaze did little to change the skepticism on Simon's face. "Really?"

"Yes, really. Who are you, my mother?"

"Apparently not, because I know you never lied to her. How did you feel seeing Ryan?"

"You want to know how I feel? Angry. Duped. Stupid."

Simon sighed. "But at least you know he's safe. You can stop worrying."

"Yeah…" He drank some coffee. "I can't believe I was ever worried about him. I'm such a fool. Go ahead. Tell me again."

"You're not a fool. You just take your caring to a higher level, and Ryan didn't want that. Sometimes tough love is the best and only love a person should get."

"Simon's right."

At the sound of Ryan's voice, Logan's hand jerked, and he spilled hot coffee on himself and his desk. "Fuck, *ow*." Simon offered him a tissue. "Like that's going to help," he grumbled but took it anyway.

"Fine. I'll just remove myself from your pissy presence. Maybe you can chill him out." Logan caught Simon giving Ryan's shoulder a reassuring squeeze, and his eyes narrowed. What the hell was that about? Did he actually sympathize with Ryan? Whose friend was he?

"What do you want?"

Ryan took several steps into the office. "I said I'd set up a payment plan for the thousand dollars. Here I am." Hands in his jeans pockets, he stood in front of the desk.

"You're awfully cocky for a thief," Logan drawled and watched Ryan pale, then flush a bright red.

"All right, I deserve that. How do you want to work this

out? I make forty-six thousand a year at the clinic. After taxes, I take home about fifteen hundred every pay period."

Jesus. Logan blinked. That wouldn't even cover a quarter of his monthly expenses. The reality of Ryan's world hit him, and he struggled not to blurt out, "Forget it." Logan folded his arms. "Let me ask you something."

Ryan shifted on his feet. "Okay…"

God, he felt like a complete and utter shit, but if Ryan wanted to be treated like just another guy, then so be it. "Why shouldn't I call the detective who was handling your case and tell him to arrest you for burglary?"

Ryan went still. "I—you could." He tipped his chin up. "If you want to, we can go to the station right now, and I'll turn myself in."

"Goddammit." He smacked the arm of his desk chair and stood up to pace. "I don't want to hurt you, Ryan." This wasn't how it was supposed to be.

"I think you do. You want to hurt me the way you say I hurt you."

"The way I *say*? You don't believe me? Why would I spend months of my life trying to help you stay clean if I didn't care?" He was fuming. "First you say I'm too coddling and overprotective. Now you're saying I want to hurt you. I'm a real shit of a human, aren't I?"

His secretary, Denise, closed the door, but he couldn't even feel embarrassment for raising his voice. He barely felt anything at all.

Ryan frowned. "I don't think that. I know you tried to help me. But what I can't figure out is why. We're not lovers—a few kisses and one hookup barely qualify. So why me?"

"Because I couldn't stand seeing you throw your life away."

"But it's *my* life. For some reason, you made me your project. Like I was someone without the capacity to know what's right for me. And I accepted it all because it was so damn easy. I used you, Logan, and I'm sorry. I allowed you to take control. But I never should've allowed it to happen, in spite of your good intentions."

This wasn't the same Ryan from before. This man was ready to accept responsibility for his mistakes and stand on his own. Logan wasn't sure how to respond, so he remained quiet.

Ryan, on the other hand, had a lot to say. "You wanted to keep me in this bubble where only you and I existed, but I don't want that. I can't fall into the soft landing you're always offering me. It's too easy to always let you make the decisions. It was wrong of me then, and nothing's changed. I don't want you controlling my life."

Logan grew still, Ryan's voice fading into the background.

He was standing next to Todd's hospital bed, the first time he'd OD'd, and Logan was so scared. Strange machines beeping and oxygen hissing. His parents didn't want him to see Todd so sick, but he fought them until they gave in and agreed.

All he wanted was his big brother, not the moody, angry person who never had time for him anymore because he was always out with his friends. Logan was only sixteen, but he knew what they were doing because when Todd came home on the weekend, his eyes were glassy and his breath smelled like beer. One time Todd was out, and Logan sneaked into his room and looked through his drawers. Beneath a pile of underwear, he found it. A plastic baggie full of white powder. He dropped it, recoiling as if he'd get high simply by touching the outside. He made sure to shove it under the boxers, where he found it, and ran out.

Later Logan asked him about the drugs, Todd yelled at him, "I don't have to listen to you, Logan. It's my life. You're my brother. You don't control me. Nobody does."

"If you don't stop taking them, you're gonna die," Logan

screamed in his face, then burst into tears. "I don't want you to die."

"Logan? Logan?" Ryan shook his arm. "Are you even listening to me? Are you all right? You look pale."

"Yeah. I'm fine. You're right. It's your life, not mine, and I shouldn't butt into it. So I won't." He drew on the coldness he'd lived in since Todd had vanished. "We're finished here. You can go."

"Logan, please. It doesn't need to be like this."

"Like what?" He made a vain attempt to form a smile, but it was closer to a grimace.

"We were friends…at least I thought we were."

"Friends?" His laughter traveled the range of brittle to the verge of anger. "I don't think so. Friends don't lie to one another. They don't steal from each other and disappear without any thought or care."

"I do care about you. And I want to pay my debt to you."

"Why? So you can wipe me out of your life?" He advanced on Ryan. "You want to repay me? Okay. What about the money I gave you to pay off your debt to Remi?"

Ryan's eyes widened. "Th-the hundred grand?" He started backing away, toward the door.

"Yes. Did you forget about that? Was I a fool to give it to you without a signed agreement? It's looking like it."

"I'll pay you. For all of it, I promise. Somehow."

"It was never about the money," he murmured when Ryan hit the door. "But I don't forgive."

Ryan's face flamed and their gazes clashed. "What do you want from me?" Ryan breathed and rubbed his face.

Logan almost felt sorry for him. Almost. If Ryan wanted to live in the harsh reality of the world, this was it. He didn't like acting like a bastard, but dammit, he was fucking hurt. "What do you think?"

He wondered if Ryan could tell him, because he sure as hell didn't know.

"I…I'll get you the money. I'll pay you five hundred dollars every two weeks. I don't need much money to live on. Emerson isn't charging me rent."

"You're living with him?"

"Yeah. He's letting me stay until I get my feet under me. Which is going to take longer now, but it's fine." Ryan met his eyes defiantly. "I got myself into this, and I'll find my way out."

"You'll stay with him, yet you couldn't wait to run away from me. Are you two lovers?" Logan asked and immediately regretted his words. But he waited…

Ryan shoved him. "I don't owe you any explanations. I'll start paying you the money with my next check." He wrenched open the door and walked out.

Each encounter with Ryan left him more frustrated and bewildered. Why the hell did he care who Ryan was sleeping with?

Because you want him and he doesn't want you.

Logan returned to his desk and concentrated on the contracts waiting for him. He'd always prided himself on his single-minded dedication to his work. His clients deserved the best, and that was him. He clicked the newest folder and allowed the first real smile of the day. Remi had signed with a publisher and was writing a memoir—*In a New York Minute: The Story of How I Loved, Lost, and Found Life Again.*

He ran through the contract, red-lined and changed some provisions, then called Remi.

"Hi, Remi, I'm almost done looking over your contract. Are you writing this yourself, or having a ghost?"

"Garrett is helping by cleaning up all the language, but I'm doing this on my own. My story, my words."

"Good for you. I'm looking forward to a signed copy."

"You know it. How're you doing?"

"Hanging in there."

"Did you ever hear from Ryan?"

"Yeah. I finally found him. He's working at an LGBTQ center."

"Really?" Remi sounded both doubtful and surprised.

"Yeah. I think you'd find him a very different person than who he was the last time you saw him."

"I'd hope so, considering he was beaten bloody and coming off an overdose."

Logan winced. "Yeah…I know it wasn't good."

"Is he living with you again?" He'd mentioned in passing that he'd given Ryan a place to stay when he found him living in a squalid one-room studio, and Remi had merely nodded.

"I knew there was more to that than what you let on in your office."

As it turned out, Remi was wrong.

"No, he's staying with a friend."

"Hmm. Why do I feel you're not happy about that? Just how deeply involved with him are you?"

Logan tensed. "Don't be ridiculous. I'm not *involved* at all. I tried to help him, but he played me for a fool. And I'm nobody's fool."

Remi chuckled. "That I know, but lust can make fools of anyone. Wars have been fought over it and because of it."

"Look, I just called you to say that the contract is in order. Just a few minor changes, and I'll be sending it to you later today."

"Yeah, I'm not worried. Why are you so dodgy whenever I bring up Ryan? Frankly, I didn't understand that whole situation you had going on."

"Why do you need to?" Logan snapped.

"Because you're my friend as well as my attorney. And I've never seen you like this."

"Like what?"

"On edge. Angry. Are you concerned about him using again?"

"That's no longer my business. Ryan told me to stay out of his life, and that's what I plan on doing."

"All this has to do with Todd, doesn't it? I know you don't like talking about it—"

"Finally you're right about something. I don't like to talk about it, and I'm not going to. I'll send you the contract in a few. Say hello to Garrett for me. Bye."

And much as he hated being obnoxious to Remi, Logan hung up on his friend's protests. Sitting with his head in his hands, the walls of the office closed in on him. Choked him. He saved the changes to Remi's contract, sent the copy to his secretary, and grabbed his suit jacket off the rack.

Denise sat at her desk outside his office and frowned when he walked out. "Is something wrong? Are you ill?"

Going strong in her early seventies and happily married with four children, three cats, and a husband who adored her, Denise kept his work and personal calendar, handling with a kind yet firm hand overly anxious clients, and the occasional lover who'd gotten it into their head that sleeping with him once meant a lasting relationship. Denise was more than an employee. Logan thought of her as a second mother.

"No. I just…I need to go out for a little while. I won't be reachable, so if anyone calls…" He shrugged.

Sympathetic brown eyes met his, and she flipped her long gray ponytail over her shoulder. "It's been a morning. I understand."

She'd known Ryan was living with him, and he'd confided in her the story of his disappearance, but with all the tumult, he hadn't filled her in on the latest news.

"Thanks. I should be back in the afternoon."

"So Ryan has returned. Is everything okay with you two? Is he home with you now?" She pursed her lips. Logan knew she didn't approve of their living arrangements. In her mind, Ryan had taken advantage of him, and being fiercely protective of Logan, she made her opinions known. Unlike his responses to Simon and Remi, with Denise he kept his piss-poor attitude to himself.

"No. He's decided he prefers to only have a business arrangement between us for the future."

"Everything happens for a reason." Denise's nod was firm, and her face reflected the internal struggle to hold off from saying "I told you so."

"You're right." He gave her a quick smile. "I'll see you later."

He left, and in the elevator called for a car. The ride to Prospect Park took about forty minutes, and the walk to the area he and Todd had called their special place another ten. Sunlight filtered through the trees, and he sat on the ground, lifting his face to its warmth. Propped up against a tumble of rocks, he gazed at the puffs of white clouds drifting across the bright blue sky. People walking past side-eyed him, and Logan knew he was a strange sight—a grown man in a suit, sitting on the ground in the park in the middle of the day.

"Look, Logan, look." Todd pointed upward as he sucked on his lollipop. His lips were stained cherry red. "That's an old man with a beard. It's Merlin the magician. Like Daddy read to us the other night."

Logan reached into the bag of candy and pulled out a Tootsie Roll. Every Saturday he and Todd would walk to the candy store and get a bag of their favorite candy with their allowance money. Their mother would take them to the park, where she would meet her friends and he and Todd could play in the grass.

"Uh-huh. And that's his castle." He didn't really understand much of the story, but he didn't want Todd to think he was a baby. Clouds fluffed out in a rectangle with one long trailing end. "See? There's the tower for the princess."

"What princess? There's no princess in the story," Todd scoffed.

"Maybe it's for the prisoners."

"That makes more sense. They'd fight dragons and then capture the bad guys and put them there."

Logan didn't care if there were dragons, princesses, or knights. All he wanted was for these days to last forever. Just Todd and him with the sun on their faces, laughing.

But like those clouds in the sky, forever was a fleeting moment.

Twenty-eight years had passed since he'd last seen Todd, and while he'd held out hope that Todd had somehow survived, in the dark corners of his heart, Logan knew Todd was dead. The reality was, he'd lost him the first time Todd had gotten high. The sweet-faced big brother who'd always held his hand crossing the street, who'd sit with him at school lunch if no one else would, had turned into a sneering, cold stranger when he entered high school. His once bright-green eyes had become vacant.

To this day, Logan couldn't understand how and why Todd had fallen. He'd been loved by his parents. Logan had adored and looked up to him. Todd had lived in a safe home and wanted for nothing.

And yet…it hadn't been enough. His parents' pleading, Logan's crying…none of it had been enough. Todd had refused any treatment offered, and Logan'd had no idea that when he'd said good night to Todd in the hospital and promised he'd help him through whatever he needed, it would be the last time he'd see his big brother. At some point in the middle of the night, Todd had pulled out his IV, slipped out of the hospital room, and disappeared. The police couldn't find him, and since he was no longer a minor, there wasn't much else they could do.

Dammit, Todd, I'm trying to live, but the hole you left behind is inescapable. It keeps letting all the pain in, and

I don't know how to stop it.

Logan wiped the tears from his face.

Like those castles in the air made of clouds, happiness was an illusion, gone in the whisper of the wind.

CHAPTER TWELVE

RYAN

There was an almost sexual satisfaction in sending Logan the first payment. Initially, he'd thought he wouldn't be able to manage sending him such a large chunk of his paycheck, but Emerson had assured him he was happy to have him stay, and they'd worked out a good system. Ryan didn't even mind sleeping on the sofa bed—it beat the hell out of a shelter or a crappy apartment where he'd share the sheets with bedbugs and other creepy-crawlies.

Two weeks had passed since that ugly scene in Logan's office, and there'd been no word from him. Ryan wasn't certain if he was glad or if he wanted to see Logan if only to show him he could make it without his help. He liked the job, and while it wasn't challenging, he appreciated the routine. Drew, Jordan, and Mike were all great to work with, and he was busy enough during the day that he didn't have time to think about the aching loneliness of his nights. He'd finally agreed to talk to Dr. Weber—*Dr. Tash*, as he insisted on being called—and his first session was scheduled for that evening.

"What made you change your mind?" Emerson asked when Ryan had confided that morning that he'd decided to try counseling.

"I've been having lunch daily with Jordan and Dr. Tash. Jordan's been astonishingly open about his addiction, and he's helped me see that therapy isn't only about revisiting and reliving the problems of your past, but it can assist you with building toward a future you once thought impossible."

Emerson's face lit up. "That's an incredible way of looking at it. And I'm so proud of you for taking your life back."

"Oh, no." Ryan shook his head and made a fist. "I sure as hell don't want that old life I had. That Ryan needs to disappear and never return. I'm starting new."

With his body stronger and his mind growing clearer every day, Ryan didn't regret leaving Logan. Life had become too easy with everything available at his fingertips. Logan had thought he was helping, but the old Ryan had taken advantage of that generosity and had not only abused Logan's trust but sabotaged his own chance at recovery.

At the center, he made a coffee and settled into his seat to input the information of the new cases from the previous day.

"Morning, Ryan," Mike said as he passed by. "How's it going?"

"Great. How're Rachel and Max?"

Mike's eyes lit up, as they did every time anyone mentioned his family. "Doing just fine. Don't forget your appointment later."

Mike was going to clean his teeth and give him an exam—Ryan hadn't seen a dentist in years and was afraid of what he might find, but Mike had assured him there'd be no fee. The center would pick up the cost under his work insurance.

"I won't. Be prepared, though." Embarrassed at how

he'd let his health go, Ryan found it difficult to meet Mike's gaze.

Mike grew somber. "It's okay. I'm not here to pass judgment. We'll get you taken care of. See you at one." He disappeared down the hall, and Ryan resumed his work, greeting the other employees of the clinic as they entered. Jordan walked in with a man Ryan hadn't seen before but recognized from the pictures in the office.

"Ryan, this is my husband, Luke. He wanted to meet you after all he's heard from me."

His brows rose. "Uh, I hope that's a good thing. Nice to meet you."

"Same. Jordan tells me you've mastered the system."

"I'll let you two chat," Jordan said and kissed Luke's cheek. He scooped up the files waiting in his box. "See you later."

"I'm not sure *mastered* is the right word, but it's getting easier." Ryan figured he might as well put it all out there, since it was obvious Luke was there for a reason, other than to say hello to the new receptionist. "What did Jordan want you to talk to me about?"

Luke grinned and rubbed his chin. "Guess we weren't too subtle, huh?"

Ryan caught the same slight drawl in Luke's voice that Ash possessed and recalled that the two were brothers, yet they looked nothing alike.

"It's no big deal. Jordan's help has been what's carried me through this part of my recovery. He told me you gave him tough love when he was going through his problem."

A pained expression crossed Luke's face. "It was a rough time for all of us. Knowing how I felt about drugs, he hid his addiction from me and almost died because of it. It wasn't a matter of tough love. I wasn't going to give up on him, but he had to be the one to make the choice. For himself." Luke made a cup of coffee, took a sip, then leaned on the desk. "He said you had some problems with a friend not fully understanding your position?"

Denial sprang to his lips. "I…it was a little more in depth than that, but I couldn't go on with it like it was."

"It's hard when a partner doesn't understand your needs and isn't supportive."

"Logan wasn't my partner. And it's not that he wasn't supportive. He was, in fact, too supportive, cheering me on when I didn't deserve it—because I was still using drugs and drinking. I was being rewarded for fucking up my life."

"And you felt you needed to be punished instead." Not a question but a statement. Luke's thoughtful but probing expression left him squirming in his seat.

"I don't know. Maybe. I do know I didn't deserve to be told how great I am."

Luke finished his coffee and crumpled up the paper cup. "We all do things we regret. I know I have. Don't beat yourself up about it. You can't change the past. Concern yourself with the future. That's where opportunity waits and what you have control over." Luke grew passionate as he made his point. "There were times when I was a teenager, when I wasn't sure I'd make it to my twenties. Now I'm forty, married, and a father. I love my life and wouldn't change it for anything. I have my daughter, a man I love who loves me, and my brothers. But nothing came easy."

Ryan had heard snippets of conversation about the three brothers and veiled talk of how rough their lives had been, but as a stranger, he didn't feel he had the right to ask questions.

"Nothing good ever does, from what I've seen of life."

"All I can say is this: Don't let 'no' stop you. If you want something, go for it until you get it."

"Is that what you did?" Ryan queried, the need to know too strong.

"No, that would be me," Jordan interjected with a smile.

Ryan's phone rang, and several people walked through the door. "But that's a story for another day. I believe I have a new patient." He walked over to the young person standing at the door, holding their arm in an awkward position. Jordan spoke to them quietly, and they nodded and followed him to the back.

Luke frowned. "Unfortunately, it never ends. No matter how much we try and help. I haven't seen you at the after-school center yet, have I? Lots of times, people from the clinic help out over there as well."

"No. I don't know anything about it."

Luke fished out his wallet from his pocket and handed Ryan a card. "It's in Chelsea. If you ever want to keep busy, stop by. Jordan set it up as a place so kids from all over the city can come after school to study, play computer games, or just hang out. Keeps them off the street and away from the gun violence. We offer tutoring or just somewhere to be safe."

"Sounds great. Thanks."

Luke called for a car. "Listen. I know you think you want to do this alone, but trust me, if you have support and help, accept it. There's nothing wrong with leaning on people. A lot of times we make assumptions, which can put us where we didn't need to be if we'd just taken a moment to realize it's okay to let people in."

Once Luke left, Ryan thought about what he said. Had it been a mistake to push Logan away? It wasn't as if what he'd done was so terrible. Was he being too hard on Logan? It was a question he wrestled with the whole day.

* * *

Ryan had thought it would be awkward to talk to someone he saw on a regular basis, but Dr. Tash was likely the most nonjudgmental person he'd ever met. His kind eyes drew you in, and Ryan unburdened all the ugly pieces he'd thought he'd buried so deep, they'd never be revealed. It felt brutal, and for the third time during their session, Ryan had to stop to blow his nose and wipe his eyes. Once he began talking, the tears, like his words, wouldn't stop.

"I remember wanting to throw up from nerves, waiting for my mother to get my father his beer. He never did anything—she cooked, cleaned, and waited on him. He sat and turned on the football game. My mother stood by the kitchen entrance"—Ryan rubbed his face—"and I told them I was gay. My father stood up, and I backed away, but he came at me. First he spit in my face, then hit me so hard on the side of my head, it banged against the wall and I saw stars."

"And your mother?" Dr. Tash asked quietly.

"She just stood there and let him do it. Never said a word."

"What happened next?"

He clasped his hands. "It's kind of a blur, but he told me to get out. That I disgusted him, and if I wanted to be one of *them*, I should sleep in a barn with the other animals. Next thing I knew, he was tossing my clothes in my face. I grabbed my old duffel bag, shoved whatever I could inside, and left. The last thing I remember is the sound of the lock clicking on the front door as I walked down the steps."

"And you haven't had any contact with them?"

"I tried to come home when he was at work to talk to my mom, but she wouldn't open the door. She just told me to go away."

Shaking his head, Dr. Tash covered his eyes for a moment. "I'm horrified you went through all that."

"It happened over twenty years ago, and most of it has faded from my memory." Ryan shrugged, hating that he lied, but better to keep secret what he'd done to survive. The scars that bound him tightened.

Dr. Tash raised his gaze to meet his. "I understand if you don't want to talk about it. But it could help you."

"How?" he asked, voice trembling. "How could telling you how much I hated myself for living help me now?"

"Because you're still punishing yourself for something that isn't your fault."

Ryan's laughter was bitter. "And the truth will set me free?" He'd been a prisoner of his own mind for longer than he could remember. Mere words wouldn't help him.

Dr. Tash remained solemn. "If you can't share it with me, or someone else you trust, try to find the forgiveness inside yourself."

"I hurt my ex badly. And I hurt Logan."

"Maybe telling them you're sorry will help."

The thought of facing Garrett made him queasy. He'd rather face Logan's wrath. "I'd thought…maybe to talk to Logan. Try to explain why I ran away."

Dr. Tash nodded. "Good. I think it would start you on the right path."

Ryan managed a thin, humorless grin. "Or get me thrown out on my ass. I'm not Logan's favorite person. He won't want to see me. He hates me."

"You'll never know unless you try. I know you and he aren't in a good place, but maybe now that you're more settled, you can talk to each other, and if not become friends, at least end the vitriol between you. Think about it, and maybe our next session you'll be able to tell me that part of your life is settled."

Their session over, Ryan pondered all they'd discussed as he closed his computer and zipped up his jacket. *How do you fix your life after it's been fractured and torn?* Mistake after mistake had piled up, leaving him buried, barely able to breathe.

In the end, he knew Garrett would forgive him because he was that kind of person—sweet, kind, and caring. Plus, he had his new husband and life. Ryan doubted Garrett thought about him at all. The one thing Garrett had always wanted—a home and family—was a foreign concept to Ryan. The best thing Ryan had ever done for Garrett was leave him.

But not Logan. That was another story. They had unfinished business, and Ryan was certain Logan counted the many ways he'd like to hurt Ryan every single day. For a detail-oriented person like Logan, he might have even written out a list. There'd be no forgiveness.

And yet…

Maybe Dr. Tash is right. Get it out of my system for good and put it behind us so we can both move on. Without taking time to think too hard and chicken out, Ryan called for a car, and within forty minutes, found himself in the elevator of Logan's building, on his way up to his apartment. He rang the bell and heard the soft chimes. Footsteps approached, and sudden fear seized him.

What if Logan had someone with him? A bitter taste rose to his tongue. Why did that fill him with pain and anger? There was nothing between them but a cold, empty void.

Maybe this is a mistake.

He could make a break for the fire stairs nearby if he hustled.

Before he could react, Logan stood in front of him, green eyes cool, dark brows raised, the trace of a sardonic smile curving his lips. Resentment radiated off him. "What're you doing here?"

A torrent of words escaped him. "Please don't shut the door in my face. C-can we talk a few minutes? I promise I won't take up your evening. I just—"

"Come in." Mercifully, Logan cut him off. "I don't have plans."

Ryan dutifully followed him. He'd always loved how open the apartment was—each room flowed into the other, with simple, clean furniture. Large, modern art pieces brought splashes of color to the stark white walls, and Ryan recalled Logan's laughter when asked if he'd decorated the place himself.

"Not on your life. I gave my client's wife free rein, and she delivered. Deirdre complained it looked like a cross between a college dorm and a library."

Logan held up a bottle of club soda. "Join me for a drink?"

Figuring it would be good to have something in his hands, Ryan agreed, noting Logan chose to have the sparkling water as well.

"Thanks," he said when Logan handed him the glass.

Surprising him again, Logan settled into the space next to him instead of the chair across the coffee table, and his proximity sent Ryan's confused emotions into a spiral of longing, desire, and fear.

"Now, to what do I owe this honor?"

Ryan took a sip of his water and set it aside. "I came here to apologize."

"What for?" Logan's face reflected his puzzlement. "You already did so for stealing from me, and you made the first payment today—thank you very much, by the way—so I'm not sure what you're talking about."

"I'm not either," he muttered before huffing out a breath. "I…uh…I started seeing a therapist. Today, actually, was my first session. He suggested it might be a good way to get closure if I sat and looked you in the eye, said I'm sorry, and told you why I did what I did."

"And then what?"

Ryan thought a moment. "Well, I guess then we—I mean, I—can move on. I know I hurt you and I sounded ungrateful. But I'm really not. I appreciate everything you did for me."

"Except you couldn't wait to run away when you read the letter."

Ryan hung his head. "I was ashamed and embarrassed." He raised his gaze to meet Logan's. "I didn't want to be a liability."

"That was in your own head. Did I ever give you a reason to think you were?"

Once again, they'd reached that damned impasse, but this time Ryan decided to lay it on the line. "Whether you did or didn't, I felt like a failure. Unworthy. They're my feelings, and that makes them valid."

"Unworthy of what?" Logan's brow wrinkled. "It sounds to me like you've set up a standard to measure against a preconceived idea of how I live or whom I surround myself with."

"Everyone in your life is rich and successful. Of course I'm going to feel less than. How could I not?"

"By not dwelling on what you can't change and who you're not, and becoming who you are. Who you can be." After delivering those startling words, Logan ran his hand through his hair. "Look. I'm not saying I handled it well. In retrospect, maybe I was a little…overprotective. Overbearing, even. I guess I didn't trust you enough."

"Which I proved by running to the bottle the minute I got bad news. I should've talked to you. I owed it to you for everything you did for me." In all the time they'd spent together, right there on this couch, they'd never had a talk so intimate or honest. "I still don't understand why you bothered. I gave you nothing in return."

"You owe me nothing. And you did give me something I needed more than anything."

Logan's face became serene, the harsh lines smoothed, and the hardness around his eyes softened. He looked younger. Vulnerable in a way Ryan had never imagined.

"What?" he asked.

Logan smiled, but wetness gleamed in his eyes. "Redemption."

CHAPTER THIRTEEN

LOGAN

"I don't understand. Why do you need redemption? For what?" Ryan's brows shot upward. "Did you…were you addicted?"

It didn't matter that over a quarter of a century had passed. The vision of Todd lying in the hospital bed remained vivid and fresh. Like the first cut of a knife to smooth, unblemished skin.

"No. Never. But someone I knew was. And it ruined his life." He pinched his eyes shut. "And mine."

A hand gripped his arm. "I'm sorry. Why didn't you ever tell me?"

"Because…it doesn't change anything," Logan said, low and quiet, the words so painful, each like a hot blade thrust into his heart.

"Logan," Ryan breathed, and to Logan's horror, a tear slid down his cheek. Followed by another. Frantic at losing control, he pulled away.

"I'm fine," he bit out, brusque and rough, but he needed that wall of ice.

"Bullshit. Why are you lying?" Ryan still held his arm, and Logan liked it. It had been so long since he'd felt the touch of another, so he sat still and let the warmth of Ryan's hand soak into his skin. Melting the cold surrounding him.

"I'm not. He's gone. It doesn't matter anymore."

"You're wrong."

"Simon told me I'm never wrong."

Apparently, Ryan wasn't in the mood for his joke, because he pushed back. "You are, because everyone matters, whether they're still here or not. At some point they touched your life and made it better."

Despite himself, Logan's lips twitched. "That's very New Age of you. Can I assume that means the therapy is already working? And speaking of, what made you decide to get help? You were so adamant about not talking to anyone, yet now you're spouting their wisdom like it's the gospel."

Ryan shrugged. "I guess because they made me see I didn't have to talk about the past, but could concentrate on creating a future instead. Working at the center has given me a new perspective. I know how lucky I am to have people who really care. Plus, when I stop concentrating on myself all the damn time, I feel better helping people who actually need it."

"You needed it too. Don't deny it."

Ryan's attitude had changed in the time spent away from him. This Ryan had hope in his eyes and renewed confidence, minus the ugly arrogance of the perpetually high Ryan in his heyday of addiction.

"I want to know what's going to happen to me tomorrow and the next day, rather than forget about today and yesterday by getting high." Ryan's gaze was steady. "I'm doing it for me. Not for Jordan, Emerson, or you. I'm the one in control of where I take my next step."

During the time Ryan had lived with him, he'd walked with a shadow on his shoulders. Defeated. Living but not alive. Logan hadn't realized it until now, seeing the light spark in Ryan's eyes. His gorgeous face beamed forth brightness, and Logan recognized it now as a fierce will to live.

"I think you're finally on the right track."

Moving closer, Ryan gripped his arm tighter. "I'm sorry, Logan. I never wanted to hurt you or make you feel like I didn't care. I did." He hesitated. "I do."

Logan's heart hammered. "Present tense?" What the hell was wrong with him? Here he was, old enough to know better, with plenty of lovers under his belt, yet those two words from Ryan left him feeling like a teenager with his stomach doing dips and twirls.

"Present tense, yeah."

"When you vanished, I grew angry and bitter because I felt used. But more than that…I hated the thought of losing you. Never seeing you again. I lived through that once already." He hung his head. "All I knew was that yet again, I failed to protect someone."

"I don't need protection, Logan. I need the truth. I don't mind someone telling me I've fucked up. In fact, I want you to tell me."

Logan carded his fingers through Ryan's hair, the hitch of his breath audible in the stillness of the room. "You fucked up." Ryan's mouth was so close, his lips soft and tender-looking. Logan's tingled with anticipation, and desire pooled deep in his belly.

"I know. I've never denied it. I'm trying to wade through the mess of my personal and professional life."

"Are you lumping me in with everyone else?" Logan murmured. "Calling me a mess? I think I resent that."

Ryan's eyes danced, his lips curved, and Logan imagined the taste of his smile. "I don't think that's possible. There's no one like you."

"Flattery might get you everywhere."

Serious again, Ryan bit his lip. "I didn't come here to seduce you."

"Is that what this is?" Logan asked. "Seduction? It's been so long, I'm out of practice." He released Ryan and put some distance between them. Up close, Ryan was way too tempting, and being celibate for so long, Logan struggled not to push Ryan on his back and kiss him. Visions of their clothes flying in the air and hot, naked bodies made him quiver. "What did you come here for, exactly?"

Face flushed, Ryan pinched the bridge of his nose. "I don't know. I hated being at odds with you and having you think I didn't care about you."

"And do you? Care about me?"

"I lived with you for almost six months, Logan. You took me in, treated me with kindness, and expected nothing in return."

Logan chuckled. "Damn. Who knew I was such a saint?"

Ryan laughed loud and long, and Logan liked hearing that sound. There hadn't been much joy in his life for years.

"Would you like…are you hungry? I haven't ordered dinner yet." Why the hell was he nervous? He and Ryan had eaten countless dinners together.

Maybe so, but then we'd been strangers, sitting across from each other, each too busy hiding, never seeing who the other truly was.

Ryan studied him for a moment. "I would, but will you let me make it?"

"You can cook?" He'd had no idea, but tonight was full of surprises for them both.

"I can. Nothing fancy or restaurant quality, but I make a mean pasta Bolognese or burgers or steaks."

Logan jumped to his feet and swept a hand in front of him. "Step into my kitchen, then. Occasionally I buy food and put it in the refrigerator, only to throw it out a week later." He grinned. "Today is day two, so you're in time."

An hour later, he sat across from Ryan, a sizzling steak on his plate, crispy onions piled high. Between them Ryan placed a salad bowl filled with chunks of artichoke hearts and bright-red cherry tomatoes peeking through fresh green leaves.

Logan sniffed with appreciation. "I'm sorry, but can you tell me why I never knew you could cook like this?" He cut into his steak, the sharp knife slipping like butter through the perfectly pink meat. Logan moaned with pleasure as he chewed. "I could've saved so much money." He licked his lips. "You've officially ruined me for Keens, Cote, and Hawksmoor."

"I wasn't in the right headspace." Ryan helped himself to salad. "It's just something I dabble in. I enjoy it."

"And lucky me, I'm the beneficiary." Logan polished off his entire meal and brought his plate to the dishwasher. "Thank you. This was unexpected and delicious." Ryan stood behind him, holding his plate. Logan plucked it out of his hand and set it on the counter, then slid his fingers through Ryan's hair. "Like this." He settled his mouth over Ryan's, intending the kiss to be brief, but at the touch of Ryan's lips, Logan pulled him close. Their tongues met, and Logan was lost in a blaze of heat. In the distance he heard a plate clatter to the floor but paid no attention to the sound. All that mattered were the hungry, desperate noises coming from Ryan. The clutch of his hands in Logan's shirt. The thrust of a hard dick against his.

Then he was gone, the two of them standing apart, chests heaving, gasping for air. Eyes wide, Ryan took another step away.

"Wait, stop. I-I didn't come to sleep with you."

A bit hurt, Logan gathered his scattered wits. "I don't recall asking you. That was a thank-you kiss." He picked up the dish, which luckily hadn't shattered, and placed it in the dishwasher. "You'll know when, or if, the other happens."

Logan half expected Ryan to walk away, but he stood firm. "I'm not sorry I kissed you. I just don't want to fall into anything too quickly, especially now, when I'm getting my life together. That has to be my main concern."

Funny enough, Logan understood. He recalled the counselor his parents had talked to when Todd was hospitalized telling them, *"Don't pressure him about finishing school, getting a job, or anything else. His recovery must be his priority."*

"I agree. I want you to get better, Ryan. There's no time limit on how long it takes. Let me call you a car, and I'll walk you out."

In the elevator on the way down, Ryan seemed unusually nervous. Before they passed through the front door, Ryan pulled him aside. "I don't expect you to sit around and wait for me to get it together. I understand."

A car pulled up, and Ryan hesitated a moment, then kissed him on the cheek and ran out. Logan remained standing with a hand to his face.

I'm glad one of us does.

* * *

The next morning, Logan sat at his desk, staring at his computer screen. He hadn't slept well, as his mind had kept spinning in a thousand directions after Ryan left. What did Ryan want? What did *he* want? Was he ready to let Ryan into his life again? Could he stand by and let him make mistakes—mistakes that had lost him his brother?

But Ryan was stronger than Todd. He asked for help and actively sought to put his life back on track. Todd had run from responsibility…family…life in general. For years, Logan had searched for Todd with no success. Once he'd left the hospital, it was as if the earth had swallowed him up. Like Ryan, Todd hadn't wanted to be found, and after twenty-eight years, Logan had reluctantly admitted defeat. Todd was gone. Unfortunately, discovering Ryan in dire straits, his first impulse had been to immediately protect him and effectively lock him down to prevent him from disappearing.

"You are such a dumbass," he muttered.

"I thought that was my line." With a smirk and a cup of coffee in hand, Simon strolled into his office.

"You again?" Logan scowled. "What're you doing here?"

"I work here." Simon stood behind the chair opposite him.

"Could've fooled me," Logan sniped. "I thought you merely came to annoy the crap out of me."

"I care about you. And I know what you're going through with Ryan—and that it's because of Todd."

His gaze jerked to Simon's grave face. "I've told you before I don't want to talk about it."

"And how's that working for you? I'll answer that: not so good." Simon leaned forward. "You need to let it out, Logan. If not to me or Oliver, then a therapist or someone else."

"What's the point?" he lashed out. "He's gone."

"Is he?" Simon frowned at him. "I think he's been living inside you like a beast, feeding on your soul."

"Please stop. I have work to do. I appreciate the concern, but it's not helpful."

"Only because you won't let it be." Simon stepped out of the path of his secretary, who marched up to him and folded her arms. "Maybe he'll listen to you."

Despite feeling worn out by the constant hammering at his brain, Logan held up his hands. "Have at it."

Her fierce expression softened. "Oh, Logan, I'm not going to browbeat you."

He managed a chuckle. "I must really look pathetic, then."

"No, honey. Just heartbroken. Simon is right. What

happened with Todd has stolen all your joy. It's why you can't form lasting relationships. And there was nothing you could've done to save him. Trust me. You couldn't have solved Todd's problems. You were a child when it happened."

"He was my big brother. I loved him."

"Of course you did. And he knew it, which was why he tried to hide it from you." She wiped her eyes. "The problem was, he didn't love himself enough."

At this point, it became irrelevant if Denise saw his tears. Grief washed over him like a tidal wave. "He just left. And every night, all I think about is him alone. My parents never recovered. They tried for my sake to cover it up, but I could see the pain in their eyes even when they smiled. I know that's why my mother died of a heart attack. It was more like a broken heart."

"It changed you as well. All that suffering you took on your shoulders, the sorrow over his loss…there are times I don't recognize you anymore."

"I don't recognize myself," he admitted. He could, to Denise.

She circled his desk and took his big hand in her small one. "But somehow Ryan, for all he's put you through—which I still haven't forgiven him for, mind you—managed to be the one man who's touched you. Here." She put a hand over her heart. "And that gives me hope because it shows it's still alive and beating. Waiting for you. You want to be happy again, but most importantly, you *deserve* to be."

Logan didn't trust his voice and had to wait to respond. "I'm not sure I know how. Not anymore."

She squeezed his hand. "I do. And you have people willing to help. Maybe it's Ryan you needed to allow yourself to heal. His brokenness brought out the caring, compassionate man you've tried so hard to forget existed. But you can't, can you? You want to protect him and prevent him from becoming another Todd."

His phone buzzed. Denise reached across and answered. A client had arrived, and Logan wiped the wetness from his face.

"Give me a minute."

Denise replaced the receiver. "Don't worry. It's Jethro Sutton. He's here to review the contract offer from the Crowns. I'll talk to him about his kids."

"Thanks." He slanted her a quick glance. "I'm sorry—"

"Don't you dare," she cut him off, eyes flashing, hands on hips. "You needed this. Fact is, for years, I've been waiting for you to explode. This?" She waved a hand. "This was mild compared to what I expected."

The door closed behind her, but he continued to stare into space, while inside, the pain screamed into the void.

CHAPTER FOURTEEN

RYAN

It was his day off, but at five thirty a.m., Ryan found himself awake. The pull-out couch was comfortable, he had no complaints, and though Emerson working from home made late mornings under the covers almost impossible, that wasn't the reason he was awake at o'dark stupid.

That morning it wasn't Emerson's clicking on the computer that had him sitting at the kitchen island, drinking coffee, staring out the window as the sky brightened from dove gray to blue and the sun rose over the tops of the buildings. The dinner with Logan sat like a thousand-pound weight on his chest, and as many times as he replayed their conversation—and who was he kidding? That possessive, demanding kiss occupied his every thought—he still had no idea if he'd hear from Logan again.

The door to Emerson's bedroom opened, and with his hair sticking up in all directions, blinking and bleary-eyed, he shuffled into the living room. "What the hell are you doing up so early?"

"I could ask you the same," Ryan answered, finished his coffee, and reached for the pot to pour another.

Emerson joined him at the island. "I smelled the coffee. At first I thought I was dreaming; then realized I was awake and came out to see what was going on."

"Coffee can be the subject of many dreams," he joked, but Emerson didn't smile in return.

"You came in pretty late last night." Emerson's statement held underlying questions.

Normally a private person, Ryan nonetheless wanted to give Emerson an explanation, so he met Emerson's gaze frankly. "I was with Logan." Emerson's brows shot high, and Ryan's face grew hot. "It's not what you think."

A slight grin played on Emerson's lips. "How do you know what I'm thinking?" He braced his elbows on the counter. "And go you."

He blew out an exasperated sigh. "See? You're coming to the wrong conclusion. Nothing happened, except we agreed to…I guess start fresh is the best way to put it."

"Starting fresh from what? You've always said there was nothing between the two of you."

"And there wasn't," Ryan said, already weary of explaining. "And isn't. The fact is, Logan and I haven't ever known each other while I was healthy. I was always either high, or drunk, or thinking I could somehow manage to take drugs and drink and still function in society. I'm just learning who I am as this truly sober person I see in the mirror."

"So those meetings you came to…you weren't really off the drugs?" Disappointment clouded Emerson's eyes. "You were lying."

A healthy recovery meant telling the truth. To everyone, but especially to Emerson, who had been unselfish in his friendship. "Yes. I lied to everyone, including myself. I fooled myself into thinking I could do both. But I can't.

Won't. It's not fair to the people around me trying to help, and it's not fair to me. I swear, I haven't had a drink or taken anything since I came to you. For the first time since I was seventeen, I'm completely sober."

"I'm glad to hear that." Emerson poured himself coffee. "What're you going to do today? You're off, right?"

Ryan finished his second cup. "Yeah. I might go to the center Luke and Jordan told me about. The after-school one? I'm curious to check it out and maybe help there." His smile was wry. "They say it's to keep kids off the streets and away from the violence, but it might help me as well, by giving me something to do with my time, aside from getting into trouble."

"Sounds like a plan. I haven't been, but I hear it's a great place."

"After I make breakfast." Ryan chuckled. "How about my famous hash browns with your eggs?"

"*Mmm*." Emerson's face lit up as he rubbed his flat stomach. "I'm ready."

Ryan snorted. "For a skinny guy, you sure love to eat." It might only be six in the morning, but energy buzzed through him. After years of waking up with a fuzzy, numb mind and head-pounding hangovers, feeling energized and anticipating the day was something he'd need to get used to.

He couldn't wait.

* * *

The Keith Hart Community Center took up half the block, and Ryan was more than a little impressed when he pushed open the glass front doors and entered the bustling space. Computers on desks lined one wall, while well-stocked bookshelves rose floor-to-ceiling on the opposite side of the room. There were tables and chairs and a play area with video games set up for kids, and Ryan counted twenty children, in ages ranging from around ten to eighteen.

An older Black woman approached him, her brow furrowed. "May I help you?"

Realizing it must look strange—him, a grown man, entering a space for children—Ryan hastened to explain. "Hi, yes. I'm Ryan Matson. I work at Home Away from Home with Drew, Jordan, and Mike, and they suggested I come here to see the place and if I could help in any way. It's my day off, so I figured I'd check it out."

Relief replaced the woman's guarded expression. "That's wonderful. We can always use an extra set of hands. My name's Wanda, and I help run the center."

A young girl ran up to her, a notebook in her hand. "Miss Wanda. Look at my math homework. I got everything right." She blinked at Ryan. "I'm sorry. I didn't mean to interrupt."

"It's okay, Allie. Good job. I'm so proud of you." Wanda gave her a hug, and Allie beamed, gave him a shy glance, then ran off to her desk. Wanda faced him. "Allie is one of many kids who come here after school because their parents work and can't afford full-time help. We're licensed by the state as a childcare center and have several educators on our staff, as well as volunteers who help out when they can."

"Like Brandon, Dr. Tash's husband?"

Wanda's eyes lit up. "Yes. Brandon is the best. He should be here soon. He tries to come after school lets out. And all the guys from the clinic like to stop by during the week or on weekends to help out." She sighed and cast her eyes upward. "I bless them every day for what they're doing for these kids."

"I wish I could've had something like this growing up."

Her gaze was frank and assessing. "I'm sure. But you made something of yourself, despite the hardships."

"And lost it all." The words tumbled out before he could stop them. "I'm trying to find my way back." Ryan felt it only right to explain his situation. "I-I had a problem with drugs and alcohol, but I'm clean now, and I'm trying to get my life together. The job at the clinic has been a lifesaver."

"It truly can be." Wanda put a hand on his shoulder. "We're all lost at some point. Don't be ashamed of your past. You're here now, and that's what matters. Would you like a little tour?" She stopped. "I'm sorry. I'm getting ahead of myself. Maybe you just stopped in and didn't plan on staying."

The din of chatter rose around him. Ryan had never been a fan of children and had zero desire for kids of his own. Yet something in this place called to him, and he nodded.

"I'd love to stay and help."

"Fabulous." She linked her arm to his. "I'll introduce you to TJ. He's been here about four months—came from Arizona and is a guidance counselor at a junior high school in Brooklyn. Great with the kids." A silver-haired man sat with a teenaged boy at one of the computers. "TJ?" Wanda called out. "Could you spare a minute?"

TJ said something to the boy, gave him a nod and pat on the shoulder, and rose to his feet. At his approach, Ryan noticed he was tall and lean, with hard lines carved into his weathered face. His eyes were a vivid, grassy green, playing in sharp contrast to thick silver hair swept off his brow. Ryan had never met TJ, yet he seemed familiar.

"What can I do for you?"

"This is Ryan. He works at the clinic, and he's here on his day off to help us. I thought maybe you could show him the ropes."

"Wonderful. Welcome aboard." TJ extended his hand, and Ryan took it.

"Thanks. I'm not sure what I can do, but…put me to work." He laughed.

Leaving Wanda behind, he and TJ walked through the space. "Tell me a little about yourself. Wanda said you work at the clinic? I haven't been there yet."

"Yeah. Only for a few weeks." He blew out a breath. "I-I'm in recovery. I was a lawyer."

"Was?" TJ inquired. "What happened?"

Ryan decided on the condensed version. "Probably what you think, or maybe worse. When I came out to my family, they kicked me out. I started using drugs. I made my way to New York City, got a job, went to college, and met my husband."

"You're married?"

"Not any longer." His smile was wry. "I kept my drug use pretty minimal in college and law school, and I could hide it from my husband. It was easier to drink because… it's what you did at college, you know?" He shrugged. "At my law firm, I got into the party scene, and it spiraled out of control. We divorced, and I got worse. Long story short, I was disbarred, and that sent me on a self-destructive path. Lucky for me, I have some good friends who helped me. Now I've been clean for several months, have a job with the clinic, and I'm seeing Dr. Tash as part of my recovery."

Approval shone from TJ's eyes. "That's an amazing survival story. I commend you on your fight, and I understand completely. I'm also a veteran of the drug war—got hooked at fifteen, used for over twenty years and ended up in the hospital. I got clean because I finally decided I was worth saving, and I learned to love myself. Now I'm married, have a child and a great job, giving back to people. It can happen. Not easily, but if you want it badly enough, you can do it. I hope you have a good support system."

Thinking of Emerson, Jordan, and Logan, Ryan knew how lucky he was. "I think I do."

The remainder of the afternoon was spent reshelving books and putting away supplies left scattered throughout the center by the kids. Brandon showed up after five when Ryan was taking a coffee break and joined him at a small table.

"How's it going? Glad to see you here." He gazed at the

children around the room. "Great place, isn't it?"

"It is. I didn't think I'd enjoy spending my afternoon with kids, but it's all been good so far."

Brandon's eyes danced. "They can be a handful. Tash and I babysit Ellie, and she is certainly a child who knows her mind."

"Like Jordan?" Ryan laughed. "He's a typical surgeon. Very opinionated and—"

"Arrogant?" Brandon snickered. "Jordan does think very highly of himself, but he and Luke have a great relationship. Luke doesn't let him get away with any of it. He's quiet but very determined. He had to be, growing up the way we did."

Ryan couldn't help but ask. "You're all brothers, but you don't look at all alike."

Brandon grew somber. "Yeah…we're foster brothers, and none of us had any family. I was the youngest and Ash the oldest. He left when he was around eighteen. Luke and I stayed together for a while then…we left Georgia. It was a very bad time in all our lives—one we don't like to talk about. I'm happy we're all together, and nothing's ever going to come between us again." Brandon pressed his lips together, ending the conversation.

Ryan understood he'd reached a wall, one that Brandon, for all his friendliness, wasn't willing to let him breach. "You're lucky. I was an only child, and I've always been on my own."

"Until now." Brandon's smile was sweet. "Tash tells me you're doing a great job at the clinic. The guys are extremely happy you're working there."

Hearing that his work was valued and appreciated made him happier than he'd imagined. "Thanks. That means a lot."

As they drank their coffee, Ryan's phone buzzed. It was Logan, and his heart raced.

What're you doing for dinner tonight?

He chewed on his lip. *Eating.*

Very cute.

Ryan sent a grinning emoji.

Seriously. How about dinner? I can meet you at my office or your apartment. Whatever you'd like.

Ryan's lips twitched. *Who knew you were such a soft touch?*

I'm pretty hard around you.

Ryan's fingers faltered. *I'm not spending the night.*

Did I ask you to?

Ryan groaned inwardly. Why did he always play into Logan's hands? Logan sent another text.

Come on. Pick wherever you want.

He thought for a moment. *Table 87 on Atlantic Avenue in Brooklyn?*

Pizza? In Brooklyn?

Yeah. You have something against cheese and crossing the bridge?

See you there at 7.

Ryan responded with a pizza-slice emoji and pocketed his phone. He found Brandon's gaze on him.

"Sorry. Just a friend. We're making dinner plans."

"That's nice. A good friend, I'm assuming, from how red your face is."

"I have no idea what we are," he admitted. "We're figuring it out as we go."

Brandon's phone rang. "Sorry, that's Tash. Hey, babe. What's up?"

Moving away to give Brandon privacy, Ryan glanced at his watch. Damn, how had it gotten to be almost dinnertime? He tossed out his empty cup and headed toward Wanda, who was saying good-bye to some of the children with their parents. He waited until they were finished.

"I have to leave, but I wanted to say thank you for letting me stay and work with the kids. I really enjoyed it."

"You sound surprised."

He laughed. "I guess I am. I didn't think I'd mesh with little people, but I was wrong."

"So does that mean we'll be seeing you again?"

He nodded. "Yes. I hope so."

"Good. It was nice meeting you, and whenever you want, you're welcome to come."

"Thanks."

He found TJ next.

"Thanks for all the help. I appreciate it."

"No problem. I hope we'll see you again."

"You definitely will."

* * *

It took several train changes, and he made it to Table 87 with less than five minutes to spare.

And of course Logan was already there, sitting at a table, reading the menu. It gave Ryan a chance to study him from across the room. He was in a charcoal gray business suit with a blue-and-white-striped shirt and blue silk tie. Silver streaked his thick, dark hair which curled at his strong neck. Maybe Logan sensed Ryan's stare because he raised his gaze, those clever, assessing green eyes clashing with his.

A punch of lust hit Ryan in the gut, and his breath caught. *Be strong.*

He waved a hand, then made his way past the other diners to join Logan. "Hi. Hope you weren't waiting long."

"Nope. Just got here a few minutes ago."

Ryan lowered himself into a seat as the server stopped by their table. "Hi, I'm Josh. Can I get you guys something to drink? Beer, wine, or a cocktail?"

"I'll have a ginger ale," Logan said, and Ryan frowned.

"Don't order a soda because of me."

"I'm not. Ever since I was a kid, the only drink I could have with pizza is soda."

Ryan highly doubted it but thought it nice of Logan to respect his sobriety. "I'll have a club soda with lemon."

"Okay, I'll get those for you."

They sat staring at each other until Logan grinned. "You blinked first. I win."

"What? We weren't playing a game. I was just thinking how crazy it is that I'm here with you."

"Why?"

Was Logan being deliberately dense?

"Because…because…I don't know. I never thought I'd have a chance to get my life together."

"I think you can do anything you want. You're stronger than you think."

Face hot, Ryan ducked behind the menu. "Uh, what kind of pizza do you want?"

"Anything but olives. I hate them."

"Don't worry. I do too."

"Finally someone I can relate to. Both my partners insist I have no taste, but I can't stand the taste of them."

"So, regular cheese?" Ryan didn't care which, as long as there was plenty of it.

"We could do mushrooms or pepperoni." Logan, on the other hand, seemed to take pizza ordering as a very important decision. "Or both. Maybe two pies."

"Two?"

"Yeah." Logan's eyes crinkled. "In case we want a snack for later."

Ryan's mouth dried. "I, uh, I'm not sleeping with you."

Logan's fingertips brushed the back of his hand, and the menu he held shook slightly. "Who mentioned sleep?" That low, gravelly voice sent shivers through him. "All kidding aside, I just want to talk and get to know who you really are, Ry. I don't think we've ever done that."

"Considering I'm not even sure, that's probably going to take longer than one night."

A wickedly charming smile tipped Logan's lips. "I'm counting on that."

They ordered a half-pepperoni and half-mushroom pizza. Logan hadn't been kidding when he said he drank soda with his pizza—he drank two more glasses and finished four slices. Ryan ate two, and the server stopped by their table and regarded the leftover slices.

"Do you want to take them home?"

"Yes, please," Logan answered without hesitation.

Ryan wiped his mouth. "Emerson's place is only a few blocks from here. Do you want to come over for a coffee?"

"Not particularly." The server returned with the box and their check. Logan handed him his credit card without even checking, his gaze bright and intent. "Come home with me? You don't have to spend the night, but I'd like to talk without worrying that we're going to be interrupted."

Recalling Logan's possessive, greedy kisses, Ryan's breath grew short and his resolve weakened. "I—okay. For a little while."

Once the receipt was signed, Logan beckoned to him as strode to the exit. "I'm getting a car now. Let's go."

Normally Ryan didn't go for the bossy type, but there was something about Logan's dominance that called to him, and he followed Logan to the street, where their car waited. They remained silent for the ride to Logan's apartment, but once inside, Logan set the pizza on the small entrance table and pressed him up against the door.

"Do you know how crazy you make me?" Warm lips grazed his.

"I think you're about to tell me." Ryan sighed.

"Actions, not words," Logan murmured and cupped his chin. He settled his mouth over Ryan's, and like the other times they'd kissed, Ryan lost himself in Logan's complete domination. Logan's tongue pushed and probed, teasing, and thrusting.

Ryan clutched Logan tight and sank his teeth into his neck, then licked it before pushing Logan off him. "We need to stop."

"Fuck," Logan groaned. "Did you bite me?"

A red spot marked Logan's neck. "*Mm*, yeah. Sorry." He paused. "Not sorry."

Logan nuzzled below his ear and ran his tongue down Ryan's cheek. "I'm not either. It was fucking hot." He kissed Ryan. "I can't even lie and say I didn't mean to attack you." He pushed a hank of sweaty hair off his brow. "Whenever you're near me, I lose my self-control."

As much as he wanted to rip off his clothes and have sex with Logan, Ryan knew it wasn't the right time to take it further. Yet. "I didn't intend for this to happen."

"I know. And that's why it was amazing. The unexpected is always the best." Logan grinned, and Ryan's heart sank, as he knew he had to set boundaries.

"But are you going to be satisfied if I say all I'm ready for now is kissing?"

Frown lines scored Logan's brow. "I already said I'll respect your wishes."

"I know." Ryan dropped his gaze. "I have a hard time saying no to you. That's part of the problem."

"It doesn't have to be." Logan tugged his hand. "Let's sit." A rueful smile flickered over his well-kissed lips. "I do think we need to talk."

Ryan sat beside Logan, and despite the fact that only moments earlier they'd been pawing at each other like wild animals, he was nervous to hear what Logan had to say.

CHAPTER FIFTEEN

LOGAN

He didn't like the hesitation in Ryan's face. Ryan was radiating vulnerability, and Logan was determined to soothe his nerves.

"I don't want you to think I'm only interested in you for sex. I would've thought I proved that already by the arrangement we had before you left."

Wary eyes met his. "Something I still don't understand. Why did you take me in and give me a place to stay without expecting anything in return?"

"I don't recall saying that. I'd hoped you'd learn to trust me and we could see if there was something worth pursuing."

Ryan's expression turned dubious. "That's not going to fly anymore. I know there has to be something else. If you're not going to share it with me, I don't see what we have to talk about."

As always with his past, Logan threw up roadblocks. "I don't know what you're talking about."

"Don't lie to me," Ryan snapped, eyes flashing fire. "I may have lost my license, but I can still tell if something smells when I ask questions. And you stink."

Logan rubbed his face. The time of reckoning had come. If he didn't rip out his guts, Ryan would walk. And in the past months of being alone, Logan realized he wanted Ryan with him more than he wanted to hide the past. Gathering his thoughts, he stared at the floor.

"The person I mentioned before. The one I knew who was addicted. I had a brother. Todd. He was my hero, my best friend growing up. I loved him more than anything. Todd was the first person I told I was gay. I told our parents, and he was by my side from the beginning. But…" He gulped for air, as it was suddenly hard to breathe. "His first year of high school, he got hooked on drugs. He changed completely—only hung out with his friends, became moody and unpredictable. He never had time for me, and if I tried to talk to him, he lashed out."

"I'm sorry," Ryan whispered. "You never said you had a brother."

"I never speak about him. It's too painful. My entire childhood died the day he overdosed." Tears dripped down his face.

"Logan." Ryan gripped his arm. "It's okay."

"No. It'll never be okay." He pulled away from Ryan, hating the pity. "I wanted to help him, I tried to, but he ignored me. Our parents offered him everything—rehab, interventions…but nothing they did worked. He didn't care how much I cried or loved him."

"He died?"

He faced Ryan, whose devasted eyes mirrored the heartache Logan had carried alone for years. "The last time I saw him, he was in the hospital, hooked up to machines. He was so weak, so helpless. I begged him to get help. I didn't care that he'd said he hated me or that I was a pain in the ass. I wanted my brother back. I wanted him to get better. I don't even know if he heard me because he was so out of it."

"I'm sure he heard you and understood," Ryan murmured, but Logan knew those were nothing more than platitudes meant to soothe his soul.

"At some point in the evening, after we went home, he pulled out all the IVs and tubes, walked out of the hospital, and disappeared. My parents tried to find him, but you know better than anyone that if you don't want to be found, you won't be."

"So he could still be alive."

Logan shrugged. "It's doubtful. I hired detectives to look for him, but they came up empty. Todd was using so heavily, I can't imagine how he would survive. That was twenty-eight years ago, and not a day goes by that I don't miss him."

"So when you met me…"

"I saw Todd, all over again. And I couldn't let the same happen to you." He wiped his face. "I refused to let someone who had so much to live for, so much life inside him, throw it all away to sniff junk up his nose. I know I didn't do it the right way, and I should've told you why, but even after all these years, it hurts so damn much to talk about him. I just couldn't."

"It makes sense now." Ryan's soft voice flowed over him, a balm to his wounded soul. "Thank you for sharing your story with me. I'm so sorry that happened to you and your brother. And I understand how he must've felt and why he did what he did."

"You do? Maybe you can explain it to me, then. Because Todd had everything to live for, and he threw it all away," he said bitterly.

"That's your view. But I see it from Todd's side. Drugs made him feel powerful, maybe in control when he didn't have much say in his life. That's what happened with me. Plus, it was a way to help me forget how horrible my life was."

"I know your family turned you out when you were a teenager, but how did you survive?"

Ryan paled. "I should get going," he mumbled, starting to get up, but Logan clamped a hand on his arm.

"Please. I've told you the most devastating thing to happen to me. And I think you know I wouldn't judge you. At least I hope you do."

Ryan stood rigid under his touch, but then, to Logan's relief, he took his seat and stayed. "I haven't told anyone, not even Garrett. When we met, I glossed over my past because it was too ugly for someone like him."

Logan steeled himself for what he knew was not going to be pleasant for Ryan, but he was no one to judge. "I appreciate you telling me what you can." He slid his hand down Ryan's arm and took his hand. "Just so you know, I'm not going anywhere. No matter what you say to me."

Ryan trembled, tears glistening on his lashes. "The first few weeks after my parents threw me out, I crashed in people's garages because my friends closed their doors to me once they found out I was gay. I decided I had to get out of that town for good, but with no money, it was almost impossible." He licked his lips, and Logan's heart broke not only for Ryan, but for all the people like him and his brother who were so desperate, they had no choices left.

"I'm not here to judge you."

Ryan's laugh broke on a sob. "You don't need to. I'm damn good at doing that all on my own. I figured the best place to…do what needed to be done was at the truck stop five miles out on the highway. I just wanted to make enough money to get away. There were always truckers there for the night, looking for sex. So I closed my eyes and let them do what they wanted. Maybe I should've figured out something else because living with the knowledge of what I've done has been like a slow death. It haunts me."

"I'm so sorry. No one should have to go through that."

Logan rubbed Ryan's back and wrapped his arms around him. "But you survived."

"Yeah. I waited until I made enough money to get a bus ticket to New York City. When I got here, I worked at whatever jobs I could get, still getting high when I could because it helped me forget my miserable life. I lived in shelters or sometimes slept in the park, and I spent my time at the library, reading and watching people. I knew the only way to live in the city was to make money, and that meant education. I'd always planned on going to college, so I saved every damn penny I made to go to school. When I had the chance, I took the College Boards and did well enough for a full-ride to a state university. That's when I met Garrett."

"And you thought all your problems were solved."

A deep-red flush covered Ryan's face. "I'm not proud of it. And I did really like him. I know he's a great person. I fucked up."

"He is, and you did. But I think you weren't in a position where you could accept you deserved someone like him, were you?"

Ryan hung his head. "I-I guess not. It's probably why I continued to get high. I figured it was all a dream that could come crashing down at any moment, so I might as well enjoy the ride. And I was right."

Logan touched Ryan's chin so their eyes met. "Are you sure about that? You're sober now, aren't you?"

"Yeah. I have been since I went upstate with Emerson."

"Count every damn day as a win. You can still have that dream." He brushed his lips to Ryan's, whose sigh of pleasure whispered along his face. "And I'd like to be part of it."

"Why? I've hurt you so much. All I've done is take from you."

"Nothing I haven't been willing to give. And I'm not done yet." Logan nuzzled in close. "Stay with me tonight."

Ryan tensed, and Logan kissed his neck. "No pressure, I promise. I just want to wake up with you in the morning."

Ryan's steady, clear gaze probed him. "I'm not your project, Logan. I don't want to be someone you save or rescue."

"When I was young, I had dreams of being a fireman," Logan teased before turning serious. "Ry, look. I don't think of you as a project, and I'm sure as hell no savior. What I see is a person who sounds like he still doesn't know his worth. Some people only find beauty in perfection. I see beauty in the broken. The places where color bleeds outside the lines. Where cracks allow the sunlight to break through, throwing light where only darkness once lived. I want to help you get rid of the darkness."

"It helps to talk to you," Ryan admitted. "And I don't have as many black days as I used to."

"Good. Because I hope to be a friend, standing by your side while you figure it out. I believe in you." Lacing their fingers together, Logan tugged Ryan closer. "Stay the night? Please?" He ran his nose down Ryan's cheek. "I still have all your clothes."

"What? You do?" Ryan stared at him in astonishment. "I figured you'd dumped them as soon as I left."

Logan stared at their entwined fingers. "I planned to, but when it came time to call Goodwill…I couldn't do it. Maybe subconsciously I was always hoping for this moment. Please?"

"I'm still not sure," Ryan said, evidently still vacillating.

"Of what?"

"That you won't try and keep me in that protective bubble. Where it was only you and me and I was completely dependent on you for everything." Ryan frowned, and his brow puckered. "You did it because you didn't trust me."

Logan opened his mouth to deny it but snapped it shut, realizing he didn't want to lie. "You're right. I thought the less temptation the better, so I kept you all to myself, figuring I could shield you. Keep you from the harm waiting out there. I realize now that was the wrong move. I have to let you make your own way, and if that includes you stumbling and falling, then so be it."

Ryan's eyes glowed. "Thank you." He placed an impulsive kiss on Logan's lips and murmured, "And if I do, I won't mind you catching me. Sometimes."

"So you'll stay?" Logan's hopes rose. "I'll make sure you get up early enough to get to work on time."

Ryan nodded. "Okay. I just have to let Emerson know I won't be coming back tonight."

"I'll give you some privacy." Logan bounced up off the couch. "I'll have to get you some towels. Oh, and a new toothbrush. I did toss that."

He crossed the bedroom to the en suite bath and got out everything Ryan would need, including a new toothbrush his dentist had given him on his last visit. To his surprise, Ryan was standing in the middle of the bedroom, a grim expression on his handsome face. Logan's good mood faded.

"Uh-oh. I'm thinking you got an earful from your friend Emerson."

Ryan shrugged. "It's not important."

"If we're going to start over, then neither of us should keep secrets. Tell me. Or"—Logan patted the bed, and Ryan sat beside him—"let me guess. Emerson warned you about me. Said I wouldn't respect what you wanted and would make it all about me. I'd push you to sleep with me, and you'd give in too easily."

From Ryan's red face, Logan surmised he was correct.

"You know what I say? Fuck that. No one needs to know what's going on in our bedroom except the two of us."

"Even your partners?" Ryan pressed him. "Simon especially acts like he's pretty invested in what happens."

Logan's smile was wry. "He is, but Simon's always

had an opinion on my personal life. He's one of my closest friends, so I cut him some slack, but the truth remains that neither he nor Oliver have any influence in what I do outside the office." Logan pinned Ryan with a direct gaze. "The same might be said for your new best friend, Jordan. He has a lot of opinions."

Ryan's skeptical expression cleared. "That he does. And yes, we've grown close because we have a common bond, but that's it. All Jordan and Emerson want is for me to stay clean and sober."

"So do I," Logan said fervently.

"I know. And for the first time, I'm surrounded by people who don't need to get high to be happy. These men have devoted their lives to helping others, and I'm trying to learn from them."

"You're not the same person you were." Logan regarded Ryan with newfound respect. "Something inside you has shifted."

"I think so. When I first started working at the clinic, it was just another job and a way to make money to get on my feet. But every day I see how they make a difference in people's lives, and though I'm only tangentially involved, I feel proud. I look forward to each day now." Ryan gazed downward. "Plus, I can admit I was wrong about not needing help. It's been good talking to Dr. Tash. He makes me feel like I can still accomplish something good."

Logan recalled the soft-spoken man from their meeting at the clinic. "He seems like someone you can trust."

"I think he is."

Logan took Ryan's hand in his. "I hope you know you can trust me too."

"I do, but first, I need to learn to trust myself."

CHAPTER SIXTEEN

RYAN

They might have kissed and flirted, but it felt strange talking to Logan regularly, yet at the same time, it was as natural as breathing. Logan's work commitments prevented them from seeing each other since he'd stayed over, but in an unspoken agreement, they'd taken to randomly texting each other during the day, and FaceTiming occasionally at night. If his phone dinged and it was a text from Logan, Ryan's heart gave a little happy bounce. It might be silly for someone his age, but Ryan imagined that was what a first crush must feel like. He'd never dated when he was a teenager, and with Garrett, he'd approached their relationship in a cold, calculated way, which he now regretted.

Ryan took a bottle of flavored club soda and opened his laptop. The news played in the background, and he scrolled through his emails. He saw an ad for Remi Angel's upcoming memoir, and it reminded him again that he owed Garrett a face-to-face apology.

A FaceTime request came in from Logan, and he hit the

button. "Hi. How was your day?"

Logan made a face and pulled off his tie. "Awful. I just got home. Some bar association dinner, then speeches…you know how it goes." A pang hit Ryan's heart, and it must've shown on his face, as Logan winced. "Shit. I'm sorry. That was cruel. I didn't mean it."

He straightened his shoulders. "No. It's okay. You didn't say it to be malicious. And yeah, I remember." His eyes danced. "Bunch of pompous blowhards. Present company excluded, of course."

Yawning, Logan scratched his head. "You know it. How was your day?"

"Good. I'm really enjoying meeting the people and talking to them. It's an incredible resource for the community. I wish I'd had a place like that to turn to when I was kicked out. They're saving lives."

"I'm glad you've found something so important to you. And you're still talking to Dr. Tash?"

"It means a lot. Much more than the legal contracts I used to work on." He grinned. "No offense. And yeah, I talk to him."

"None taken. I've ended many days at the office with my eyes crossed from staring at the screen too long. Did you have dinner yet?"

"Yeah, some pasta and vegetables. What about you? Did they give you a meal?"

Logan made a gagging sound. "Rubbery chicken and overcooked vegetables. I'm starving." He waggled his brows. "Too bad you're so far away, or I'd try to entice you to come over and cook for me."

Ryan snorted. "Get real. At ten o'clock at night, all I'm ready for is bed."

"Spoilsport." Logan pouted and Ryan snickered, then became serious.

"I was thinking…I need to talk to Garrett. It's time."

Busy stuffing grapes into his mouth, Logan stopped, looking like a chipmunk with his cheeks bulging. "That's good." He chewed. "I agree."

At least that was what Ryan thought Logan said in between chewing, so he continued. "Yeah. It's been too long, and it's hanging over my head. I'm going to text him."

"You want me to come with you? For moral support?"

"That's sweet, but I should do this on my own."

Admiration shone from Logan's eyes. "All right. It'll be okay."

"I think so. Garrett's moved on, and he's happy. This is more for me than him. In fact, I'm going to reach out now and try to set something up."

He sent Garrett a quick message: *Would you be willing to meet me to talk?*

"All right. Let me know how it goes. Talk to you tomorrow."

"Wait," he called out, and Logan cocked his head.

"Something wrong?"

"What are we doing here?"

A cocky grin curved Logan's lips. "Talking?"

"You are so annoying," Ryan groaned. "Come on. You know what I mean. Are we dating?"

"I don't know." Logan propped his chin in his hand. "I've never dated before. You tell me."

Talking to Logan was as frustrating as trying to wiggle into a too-tight pair of jeans. "You're something else. Good night."

Logan wiggled his fingers. "Night. And Ry?"

About to click off, he paused. "Yeah?"

"Sweet dreams."

With a wink, Logan ended the FaceTime, and Ryan shut the computer. After that kiss they'd shared, his dreams had been anything but sweet. He couldn't stop imagining Logan naked and touching him. Kissing him. There were times he woke up from dreams so vividly erotic, he hoped Emerson didn't hear his moans as he finished himself off. In all honesty, not seeing Logan these past weeks was for the best. It wouldn't take much to persuade Ryan to fall into bed with him, and he was determined to remain steadfast in his refusal. For now.

But God, the nights were lonely. He'd listen as the men at the clinic talked about their husbands and families, and an ache would rise inside him. Wanting that peace and sense of place with someone. Knowing he was going home to a sofa bed and another night of staring at the television, thinking about Logan.

As it was, his showers were fast becoming his favorite part of the day. It was where he fantasized about Logan. He might've been flying high the night of their hookup at the Marquee, but that kiss they'd shared a few weeks back had been with a clear mind and a heart open and yearning. He'd forgotten the pleasure of another man's touch. His lips tingled at the memory.

Desire slammed through him, and his breathing grew short. No one had ever turned him on like Logan Silver. Ryan left his phone and computer on the couch, went into the bathroom, stripped quickly, and turned on the taps. With the steamy water cascading over his head, Ryan poured the slippery shower gel into his palm and gripped his aching cock. He pictured Logan on his knees, dark head bobbing up and down, swallowing his cock. Those full lips and that slick tongue licking him, cocky mouth stuffed full as he sucked his shaft and those long fingers played with his ass.

Ryan's eyelids fluttered, his vision blurred, and he groaned as he jerked off harder and harder. Legs spread for balance, his hips rolled and he came, spurting hot and heavy between his fingers.

"Fuck." Chest heaving, Ryan needed a moment to gather his wits and braced his hands on the tiled wall. He turned off the tap, dried himself, and dressed in sweat pants and a T-shirt.

He'd just sat on the couch when the door to Emerson's bedroom opened, and he poked his head out. "Are you finished?"

"Yeah, why?" Heat rushed through him. Had Emerson heard him in the shower?

"Just wanted to get a snack, but I didn't want to disturb you when you were talking to Logan."

Ryan's brow furrowed. "You don't have to stay in your room. This is your apartment."

Emerson grabbed a bag of chips off the counter and opened a can of soda from the refrigerator. "I know, but I wanted to give you some privacy." He put the chips on the coffee table between them and sat across from Ryan. "You two seem to be getting along better now."

"We are. Both of us have changed."

"I understand you have, but how has he?" Emerson crunched some chips.

Ryan took a few seconds to respond. "I think he's finally willing to let me do this my way, regardless of right or wrong as he sees it."

"That's good." Emerson shifted in his chair. "Are you going to move back in with him?"

"No. I need to find my own way and do this myself. I can't spend my life on your couch, but I'm not going to live with Logan again."

"Oh, good." Emerson sounded relieved. "I mean, I want you to have independence, but I really do like having you here."

Ryan felt sorry for Emerson, who rarely left the apartment aside from his sobriety meetings. Even if Ryan suggested a walk or going out shopping, Emerson made an excuse to stay inside. "I'm happy to stay as long as you want me to, but eventually I'll move into my own place, once I have enough money saved and job stability."

Looking forlorn, like a kicked puppy, Emerson shrugged. "Yeah, I know."

His phone buzzed, and his nerves zipped. The text was from Garrett.

Hi. Sure. I'm willing to talk. I can meet you any day after school, starting at 4:30.

Ryan's heart hammered. He was going to do this. He had to.

I don't get off work until 5:30, but I'm in Brooklyn. We could meet near you.

Sounds good. I'll let you know when and where.

"Bad news?" Emerson inquired.

"No. Just the opposite." As he explained, Emerson's eyes grew wide.

"Wow. Are you nervous?"

Was he? Ryan thought for a moment. "I'm not worried about Garrett forgiving me. Knowing him, he'll be happy I'm getting my life together. But I did hurt him badly, so I want to get it right."

"You will."

* * *

Several days later, Ryan walked into a coffee shop on Livingston Street in downtown Brooklyn and spotted Garrett sitting in a booth with a cup of coffee before him. Ignoring the flutter of fear in his chest, he crossed the restaurant to join him.

"Hi."

Garrett glanced up, and there was no anger in his eyes. They were as gentle as ever. "Hi, come and sit."

He slid into the bench seat. "Thanks for agreeing to see me. I know you didn't have to, especially the way I've treated you."

"I'm not here to hold a grudge. I don't think that serves any purpose."

"Thanks."

An awkward silence fell over them. Incredible to think they'd been married and spent over a decade together, and now Garrett was almost a stranger to him.

A server appeared, holding a pot of coffee, and after he filled their cups, Ryan ordered a corn muffin.

"So, uh, I've been clean now—totally clean—for over four months. For the first time since I was sixteen."

Garrett's brows shot high. "So in college…"

"Yeah." He nodded and slid his hands around the coffee cup, soaking in the warmth. "Even when I was in college, law school, every day, I was either drinking or taking something. I'm sorry I lied. I know it was a big trigger for you, and that it was a mistake, but I couldn't tell you."

"Because?" Garrett prodded, and Ryan flushed with shame.

"Because I didn't want to lose you. I did like you in the beginning, but…can I tell you the truth? You might end up hating me after, but I feel I have to be honest."

Garrett met his eyes with steely determination. "Then tell me."

"I never really loved you. I liked you a lot, but I wasn't in love with you." His voice dropped to a near whisper. "I asked you to marry me because I found out about your trust fund."

"I know. I figured that out after the divorce, and I'm not angry with you anymore."

"Yeah?" He sniffled and breathed deep, hoping to settle his galloping heart. "You're way too nice. I'm not sure I could be if I were in your shoes."

"I'm not a saint. I am pissed you used me and that I was too dumb to see it—"

"Not dumb," Ryan interjected. "You're anything but. I

took advantage of your good nature and the fact that I was your first."

Garrett blushed, but his gaze remained steady. "I wasn't for you, though, right? Even though you said we were virgins together? You lied to me about that too."

He sighed. "Yeah, but only because the others who came before you were business. If you know what I mean."

Garrett paled, and his jaw dropped. "Ry…I-I…"

A fresh wave of humiliation crashed over him. "Don't," he snapped, then gentled his tone. None of this was Garrett's fault. Maybe, if Ryan dug deep enough, he could justify it wasn't his either, but he wasn't there to give himself absolution. "Sorry. I didn't mean to yell at you. I just can't stand pity. And no, I'm not going to get into it. It's my past, and it's going to stay that way. I had my reasons at the time, but…anyway, I didn't come here to make excuses for myself. I wanted to tell you how sorry I was for lying to you and marrying you for the wrong reasons. I'm sorry for the hateful things I said about you being Jewish. I was wrong, and I'm trying to become a better person now. You're a great guy, and Remi is lucky to have you."

At the mention of Remi's name, a sweet smile curved Garrett's lips. "Both Remi and I are lucky to have each other. As for everything else, I'm glad you've gotten help and you're clean and sober. I don't hate you, but I was angry for a very long time. What I learned is that it's not productive to hold on to that kind of anger because it kept me in a dark place and I couldn't move forward. Once I let it go, I was free."

"I envy you." Ryan couldn't imagine he'd ever be free from his past.

"Don't measure your happiness in life against anyone else's. That's a trap. I haven't seen you in a long time, but I can tell you're not the same person I used to know."

"How?" Funny, but Ryan felt the same as always on the inside. Unworthy of love, still uncertain where he stood in the world. All he'd done. All he'd lost.

"Your eyes. They're calm. When we were together, you were skittish, always looking around—past me, through me. Never at me. Like you were searching for something better. Now you're quiet. Your eyes are bright and light you up from within." Garrett finished his coffee. "I have to get home, but I'm glad we talked. I wish you only the best, Ryan. I hope you find happiness." He put a five-dollar bill on the table and left.

Ryan wondered if he'd ever see Garrett again. Watching him walk away was like closing the door on part of himself that no longer existed. But if that was the truth, who was he?

Alone. That's what you are, and that's what you always will be.

He sat for a few minutes, picking at his muffin, and his phone rang. Logan's number popped up on the screen.

"Hey."

"How'd it go? I figured I'd wait an hour to call you."

Warmth rushed through him. Maybe he was wrong, and he wasn't really alone.

"Better than expected. Or maybe not since I figured Garrett wouldn't hold a grudge."

"And you got to say everything you wanted to?"

"Yeah. And Garrett appreciated it."

"Want to meet for dinner?"

Much as he'd like to see Logan, he had little desire to go into the city and rehash the meeting. "I'm kind of tired. Rain check?"

"Are you sure you're okay?"

"Yeah. But the thought of sitting in a restaurant and making small talk gives me hives. I'm going to go home and pick up something on the way. I'll catch up with you tomorrow."

"All right." Logan sounded doubtful, but Ryan ended the call and paid his bill.

Like he told Logan he'd do, he stopped at his favorite takeout place for some scallion pancakes, an egg roll, and chicken in garlic sauce.

Emerson had already eaten by the time he arrived home, and was busy playing a video game. Ryan sat at the island and unpacked his meal.

"No worries about kissing anyone tonight," Emerson remarked.

"Want a scallion pancake? There's a bunch." He crunched on his egg roll.

"No thanks. I had a burger and fries already."

Ryan drank some water and watched Emerson blow shit up on the sixty-five-inch screen. The egg roll and scallion pancakes filled him up, as his stomach was still in knots from his meeting with Garrett, and he stood in the kitchen, debating whether to eat the chicken or save it for his lunch the next day, when the buzzer sounded.

"Are you expecting a delivery?" he called out over the sound of explosions.

Emerson shook his head, and Ryan hit the button to answer. "Hello?"

"Logan Silver to see you, Ryan," the doorman said.

Logan? Here? "Okay, send him up, thanks."

Figuring he needed to let Emerson know, Ryan tapped him on the shoulder, and the controller went flying.

"Sorry. Just wanted to let you know Logan's here. I didn't know he was coming."

"Uh, okay." Emerson saved his game and shut down the box. "I'll be out of your way in a sec."

"You don't have to leave. It's your apartment," Ryan started, but Emerson had already disappeared into his bedroom. The doorbell rang, and Ryan answered it. Logan leaned against the wall and held up a bag.

"I brought dinner." A charming, wicked grin tipped his lips.

"What? Why didn't you tell me you were coming?"

Logan sauntered inside. "I decided spur-of-the-moment. I'm alone, and you're alone, and that's stupid."

Ryan chuckled. "It is? I bought dinner—chicken and garlic sauce. I just finished the scallion pancakes and egg roll."

"Looks like we're on the same wavelength. I brought dumplings and spareribs." He set the bag on the kitchen island.

Ryan's nerves tingled at the glint in Logan's eyes. "Why are you really here?"

"Because I've heard the Chinese food is better on this side of the river?" Logan joked, but then his smile faded. "Seriously? I knew that meeting with Garrett was weighing on your mind, and I didn't think you should be alone."

In an instant, he was on the defensive. "Did you think I'd be so upset I might slip?"

Logan grabbed his arms and held him tight. "No. I care. And I thought you might need a friend to talk to."

"Oh." Feeling foolish, Ryan rested his cheek on Logan's. "Thank you. I'm not used to having someone to lean on."

"Now you do."

Three simple worlds that, as it turned out, weren't so simple after all. They could change his world.

CHAPTER SEVENTEEN

LOGAN

"Look at you, all dolled up. Where are you going?" Smirking, Simon leaned against his door, watching him as he slipped on his suit jacket.

Knowing he was being baited, Logan made a face. "Dinner and a play."

"With Ryan?"

"Yes." If he'd hoped Simon would be satisfied with his answer, he was wrong.

"So you two are getting serious?"

His patience worn thin, Logan snapped. "I'm seriously annoyed at being interrogated. It's dinner and a play, not a wedding. Now if you've got nothing else to say, I have to leave."

As he brushed past Simon, he found his arm gripped, and he stopped, raised his brows, and removed Simon's hand. "Don't do that again, please."

"Wait. I'm sorry. I didn't mean to tease you."

Unsmiling, he met Simon's eyes. "Yes, you did. I'm glad

you think my personal life is fodder for you to make jokes. You know, you nagged at me to stop looking for Ryan when he was missing. When he showed up, you didn't trust his motives and warned me to keep my distance. You've been after me for years to have a steady relationship, and here I am, trying to figure it out, and you're still coming after me. What the hell do you want?"

"I don't want anything except for you to be happy."

"Who the fuck is happy? You?" He laughed bitterly. "I don't see you settling down. You told your father to shove his opinions about your personal life up his ass, and you have a different woman with you every time I see you at an event. Before you stick your nose in my bed, check yourself."

Simon paled but stood his ground. "You're not me. I have my reasons."

"So do I. And I'm not you is right. So let me do what I want."

He pushed past Simon and hit the button for the elevator.

The car ride gave his anger a chance to cool. He'd make up with Simon in the morning. He didn't want to let his bad mood ruin the evening, especially with him and Ryan just beginning to get on the same wavelength.

The car pulled up in front of the Richard Rodgers Theatre on 46th Street, and he spied Ryan's golden head in the crowd milling about, waiting to see *Hamilton*. As always when he saw Ryan, his heart did funny things in his chest. Seeing him bright-eyed and gaining weight, making healthy choices, was bittersweet for Logan. Happy as he was for Ryan, the lingering sadness would never leave him that his brother hadn't taken the help offered.

He stood unnoticed for the time being, watching Ryan scroll on his phone. Why this man above all others? Logan had never lacked for bed partners. He enjoyed men and occasionally a woman in his bed, but over the years he'd retreated more and more, preferring solitude to faking it.

Desire had faded into the background of a life he'd kept on mute.

Until Ryan.

Who, at that moment, glanced up from his phone and smiled, blue eyes lighting up, meeting his gaze over the heads of people passing by. A wellspring of happiness rose within him, and a grin, wide and silly, spread across his face as he rushed to Ryan's side.

"Hi. Sorry I'm late."

"You're not."

He hesitated, then kissed Ryan's cheek. "I'm glad we could do this. I'm sorry I've been unreachable these past few days. Suddenly everyone wanted to renegotiate their contracts, and I had to make my hours fit their schedules to meet the ones who are playing and in the middle of road trips."

"Don't worry. I understand. And you're here now. That's what matters. Want to go in and sit?"

Hand in hand, they joined the line at the entrance and were shown to their seats. They settled in with their playbill, and Ryan scanned the crowded theater.

"I haven't been to a play in…forever." Ryan's bright eyes dimmed. "Garrett used to love going, but I'd always make excuses and he'd end up taking his grandmother."

"I haven't had the time either, but I thought it would be a nice change from a movie or simply dinner." Logan held out his hand.

Ryan looked down and took it, sliding their fingers together. "It is. But I'm enjoying all our time together, no matter what we do."

They shared a smile.

The lights dimmed, and Logan became so engrossed in the play, he was surprised how fast the time flew. The lights flicked on for intermission. It had been a long time since he'd been able to put the rest of the world on hold for an uninterrupted hour of pure entertainment. People got to their feet, and he knew they were going to the bar for drinks.

"Do you want something—a soda or water?" he asked Ryan.

"No, I'm good, but you can. I won't mind. I've said it already—you don't have to change your lifestyle to suit mine."

"I already have." He leaned in close, inhaling the scent of Ryan's skin. "I'm here with you and enjoying every single second of it."

The play was good, but his real pleasure was watching Ryan. Using the cover of darkness in the theater, Logan paid attention to how Ryan concentrated on the stage, laughed at the jokes, and sang along to the most popular songs that even Logan knew.

The lights came up and people filed out of the theater, but he sat and waited, unwilling to break the magic. Ryan smoothed the playbill. "Thank you for taking me here." A small, almost sad smile broke free from his lips. "It's one of the first times in a long time I've felt part of something."

Logan squeezed his hand. "If we don't leave, they might lock us in here. Come back to mine?"

Ryan studied his face. "Okay. For a little while."

Logan frowned but didn't say anything. It wasn't the time for it, but once they reached his apartment, he poured them both some sparkling water and pointed at the couch.

"Let's sit. Why're you so hesitant about spending time alone with me?"

Ryan flushed. "I'm still not ready to have sex. I can't give you an exact date when I will be, so I'll understand if you walk."

He put a hand on Ryan's shoulder. "I'm not pressuring you."

"So you're going to be fine with us continuing like this? I can't imagine someone like you waiting for me to get myself together. You never have before."

Someone like you.

Those words hit him hard in the heart, and not in a positive way. Despite everything he'd said and done, doubt remained in Ryan's eyes and the tense set of his jaw.

"Let me tell you a story. My father told me that when he first saw my mother at a dance, it was as if everyone else around him ceased to exist. Other girls he'd dated faded into oblivion. He might've been a little bit of the bad boy—smoked cigarettes, cut school. But all that changed when he met my mother. He stopped hanging out with the troublemakers, began to study, and turned his life around."

"That's a sweet story, but I don't see what that has to do with you and me."

Maybe he wasn't as good with his words as he'd thought, because he was having so much damn trouble explaining himself. Or maybe for the first time, his words came from the heart, not glibly rolling off his tongue.

"I'm not saying either of us has to be 'good enough' for the other, but my story proves that people can change. My father did. You did. And so can I."

"I don't want you to change."

"Maybe I do." Logan clasped his hands and stared at the floor. "My father dying made me realize how alone I was. I could disappear tomorrow, and aside from the few people in my office, who would really notice or care?"

"That's silly," Ryan protested. "You have plenty of people who care."

"I can name them on one hand. But I'm not looking for pity."

"What are you looking for?"

"You here with me." Logan pulled him close. "I come home, and you're not here, and I don't like it."

"You could get a puppy."

"You could not be ridiculous. I miss you, Ryan."

Ryan smiled against his cheek. "Why? I wasn't your lover, and I was a pretty terrible roommate."

"Because I like having you here. With me. And I think it's silly for you to be sleeping on a crappy couch when I have a perfectly good second bedroom available."

"It's not a crappy couch," Ryan protested, eyes dancing. "Emerson spent a lot of money on it."

Ignoring Ryan's attempt at a joke, Logan continued to make his point. "How much are you paying Emerson? It's not going to be like before. I'll charge you what you pay him, and we'll split the utilities." Uncharacteristically nervous, he clasped and unclasped his hands. "This time… this time will be different. You're sober and on a true road to recovery, and I…" He hesitated. "I'm not sure what I'm doing."

"Letting me in?" Ryan said, placing a hand over his. "Showing me who Logan Silver could be if he allowed himself to feel?"

He felt something. A driving need to have Ryan in his life. "I'm not sure even I know who that is, but I think you're the one who can help me discover it. If you move in, I want to see if it takes us to the next step."

"You mean lovers."

"Yes. I'm not that altruistic. I want you. And I think you want me too, but I understand you have a list of things to work on before that comes to pass."

"I do…but don't think you're not on that list." His eyes twinkled. "Maybe not number one…"

The fact that Ryan didn't automatically say no gave Logan hope, and he leaned in to press a kiss to Ryan's lips. "I'm okay with that…for now."

A line bisected Ryan's brow. "You're actually serious? You want me to move in again?"

"Why not? You can have your own bedroom, your own bathroom—"

"What about my freedom?" Ryan crossed his arms, and Logan recognized the steely determination in those incredible blue eyes. This wasn't the broken, desperate man of months ago. "Do I get that too?"

"Meaning?"

"To come and go as I please without explanation. If I want friends over, I can have them. If I want to go out, I don't need to check in with you. I need trust. Something you admitted you lacked in me."

"You want trust? How about the fact that I'm trusting you with something I've never given anyone else?"

"Which is…?"

"Myself."

CHAPTER EIGHTEEN

RYAN

"So you're telling him tonight?"

Ryan was FaceTiming with Logan at the clinic. "Yeah." The prospect of hurting Emerson wasn't something he looked forward to, yet he couldn't put his life on hold much longer. "Why do I feel like a shit?"

"Because you're a nice guy. If it were me, I would've been out of there the night after we decided."

"Meaning you're not as nice as me?" Ryan teased.

"It means I want what I want." Logan's husky, possessive growl sent a thrill through Ryan. "And that's you, here with me. It's time, Ryan."

"I want that too." He was stronger, and Logan was less hovering and watchful. Time to stop denying the growing awareness between him and Logan. It wasn't going to be the same as last time. There'd never been a lack of physical desire between them, but his drug use had set up a barrier he'd refused to allow Logan to breach. Now, with his mind and body clear, he could see a future.

It had taken two weeks of discussions with Logan about

boundaries and expectations, but in the end, Ryan decided to do what was best for him, though he knew he'd meet with some resistance. But when he and Emerson sat together after dinner that evening, Emerson surprised him with the vehemence of his disapproval.

"I can't *believe* you're doing this."

"Emerson, I'm telling you, it's not what you think."

Ryan had already packed up his meager belongings to move to Logan's, but explaining his decision to Emerson was proving harder than he thought.

"What am I thinking?" Uncharacteristically fired up, Emerson glared at him. "Come *on*, Ryan. What's it been— three or four months, and *poof*, you're back together and living with him? I thought you were smart. He's going to say and do whatever he can to get you."

Growing annoyed with Emerson acting as though he were a brainless fool and treating him like a child, Ryan reined in his temper and took a deep breath before replying.

"You know Logan and I have spent a lot of time together these past months. I know him much better than I did when I first accepted his offer to move in. That was a foolish decision. This one isn't. I'm going to be the adult here and not go off on you, so I can explain why you're wrong. One. We aren't 'back together' as you think because we never *were* together the last time I stayed with him. Two. Not that I have to tell you this, but I'm staying in his second bedroom, not sleeping with him." Exasperated from explaining himself, he held up his fingers. "And three, what the hell do you mean, *get me*? No one can get me. And Logan isn't who you think he is."

"So he's not the arrogant, obnoxious, rich lawyer who has an answer for everything and can twist your words until you don't know what you're saying?"

Despite the reality of Emerson's frustration, Ryan's lips twitched at his pretty accurate description of Logan's character. "Well, yeah. He can be arrogant and obnoxious. And part of a lawyer's trade is to fit the narrative to what they want the public to see and hear. But that's not how it is between us. Logan is more than a smirk and a fancy suit." He hitched his seat closer. "Emerson, please. I can't get into the specifics, but Logan and I have had long, *long* talks. We've opened up to each other like never before, and I understand what he did and why."

"Which is what?"

Ryan's stare was pointed. "Not your business is what. I'm not revealing Logan's confidences to you or anyone. We're learning to put our trust in each other. It wouldn't be right."

Unconvinced, Emerson continued to press him. "But still…don't you think you should wait and see? Give it a few more months? I'm fine with you staying with me." His lips trembled and his eyes grew shiny.

There was something else going on besides Emerson's true concern for his welfare. "Hey, Emerson?" It all became clear to him, and his heart broke. "Are you worried I'm going to forget about our friendship? I hope you know that's not going to happen."

Emerson lifted a shoulder. "I-I dunno."

But Ryan did. Emerson hadn't been kidding when he said he didn't have many friends or a social life in general. And Ryan felt badly for him and wanted Emerson to regain his life, like Ryan was taking charge of his.

"It's not going to happen. Just because I won't be living here anymore doesn't mean we won't see each other. We'll still hang out."

Emerson's trembling lips pulled down. "I-I like having you here. You're my friend." He hung his head. "My best friend."

It had never occurred to Ryan that Emerson might've needed him as much as he needed Emerson. "You're my friend too. That's not going to change. We're always going to be friends. And I know it might be fast for you, but I need to see where this thing with Logan leads."

"I just don't want you to fall in love with him and get hurt."

Ryan's smile was gentle. "That's something no one can guarantee. But if we never try, can we really say we're living?"

* * *

Ryan's day passed by fast and furious, which unfortunately meant a steady stream of people with problems. He marveled at how the doctors managed to see everyone and never lose their pleasant demeanor. At five thirty, when he shut down his computer for the evening, Noah paused by his desk on his way into the call center.

"Ryan, I've been so busy, I haven't had a chance to stop and chat."

"Hi, Noah. Yeah, it's been nonstop."

"Things going well? Or do I need to ask?" Noah set his coffee cup on the counter. "I see a completely different person than the one I first met."

"I feel like a new man," Ryan agreed. "I haven't been sober and drug-free for this long since I first started using in my teens. It's still startling to me to wake up with a clear head and an appetite for food and life. It's taking some getting used to for sure, but I love it."

Noah's eyes shone with true happiness. "I'm thrilled to hear you say that. You're still seeing Tash?"

"Yes. I told him once a week would be fine, but he's sat with me whenever we both have a spare moment. He's been so patient and giving of his time. I didn't think I'd have anything to talk to him about, but once I started, I can't stop." Ryan glanced at his phone, sitting on the desk. "Matter of fact, I have a session with him in about fifteen minutes. I'm glad I listened to everyone and didn't let my insecurity and negativity talk me out of therapy with him." Aware that Noah had also offered him help, his face heated. "I-I hope you're not insulted that I ended up with him helping me and not you. It's not that I don't think you're great too, but—"

"Ryan." Laughing, Noah interrupted him. "I'm not upset you're Tash's patient. We're not in competition, and I'm thrilled you're getting help. Tash is a wonderful doctor."

"As are you, Noah." Tash appeared in the doorway leading to the rear of the clinic. "I finished my session early, Ryan, so if you're ready, we can talk now."

His answer had to wait as the door opened and Logan breezed inside. Those sparkling eyes hooked on his, and Ryan's breath caught as his heart pounded in a double-time drumbeat. Logan's commanding presence narrowed the room to the two of them. As always, Ryan felt that instantaneous tug, the connection that had sparked the first time he'd seen Logan and only burned hotter and brighter the more time they spent together.

"What're you doing here?" Ryan asked, and a wickedly charming grin crept over Logan's face.

"Hello to you, too. I had a meeting downtown with a client and decided to knock off early. I figured we could have dinner before heading home."

Tash's brows flew up in obvious surprise, and Ryan's stomach clenched. He'd planned to tell Tash that evening about his new living arrangements, but now he'd be on the defensive explaining his choice. "I, uh, have a session with Tash now."

"No problem." Unperturbed, Logan strolled into the reception area and plunked himself into a chair. "I can wait." He glanced around and acknowledged Tash and Noah. "Nice to see you both again."

"Hi, Logan." Noah's alert gaze traveled from him to

Ryan. "Good to see you too. How've you been?" Noah took a seat next to him.

"Same, Logan," Tash said and waved to Ryan. "Ready?"

Ryan left Noah and Logan chatting and followed Tash to his office, where he sat in the comfortable club chair. Tash picked up his tablet and met his eyes.

"So…home with Logan? I guess things have changed? Pretty rapidly, I'm thinking, since last I heard, you were concerned about repaying the loan and the two of you were barely speaking."

Ryan shifted. "Yeah…well, uh…we've been seeing each other. I'm sorry I didn't tell you."

"Do you know why you didn't?"

Tash always made him face the truth.

"Because I didn't think you'd approve."

Tash set his pad on the desk. "My job isn't to tell you how to live your life. Just to make you aware of your choices. I'm here to listen and offer advice, never judgment."

Ryan believed him. In all their talks, Tash never rebuked him for bad decisions he'd made, instead letting him see that he could move past them.

"We're different now—when we're together, I mean. And we've talked. Really talked. Finally. He told me things…I won't reveal them since it's his personal story, but his overbearing behavior makes sense now."

"I see." Tash took notes. "And you believe him."

Ryan narrowed his eyes. "He's not just saying it for me to pity him or to get me to sleep with him." Tash gazed at him steadily, and Ryan flushed. "I haven't…slept with him, I mean. That's not what this is about. I was an attorney. I can tell when someone's bullshitting me or trying to gain my sympathy. We've learned more about each other. I care about him. And I know he cares for me, aside from keeping me sober." Frustrated, Ryan scrubbed his face. "Look, I know it's complicated and messy. I'm not sure I understand it myself."

"Relationships often are." An enigmatic smile lightened Tash's serious expression. "I know from personal experience."

Having met Tash's younger husband, Brandon, Ryan imagined they might've received some opinions on their relationship that weren't welcome or positive. Maybe that was why he'd gravitated toward Tash. He understood the internal tug-of-war going on inside Ryan. Yet still, he'd held back the worst of his past from Tash, choosing to open his heart to Logan.

"And it's not one-sided. I revealed things to Logan I've never told anyone." He bit his lip. "Even you."

"Don't be afraid to say that. You're not going to make me angry or hurt my feelings." Tash's gentleness soothed Ryan's jittery nerves. "You're at the beginning of your journey, and it's natural to confide in different people. My concern is for you and your physical and mental well-being." He made a few more notes. "So. You and Logan talked about when you left him and why?"

Ryan stared at his clasped hands. "Yeah. I was surprised he opened up to me, but like I said, it helped me understand his mindset." His eyes flicked to Tash. "He says he wants to try and start over, work on a relationship between us. Friendship first, and then we can see where it takes us."

"Do you believe him?"

Recalling Logan's tears and devastation, Ryan had zero doubt Logan's story was a terrible truth.

"Yeah. Definitely."

Tash continued to probe. "And more importantly, is this something you want? Do you want a relationship with Logan?" At Ryan's hesitation, Tash said, "I'm not trying to dissuade you. I just want to make sure you're not being pressured into a situation because you feel like you have no alternatives. You have to know you've fit in seamlessly here and are an integral part of the clinic now. You're creating a new life, and you've done it on your own. You should feel very proud."

He didn't, but it was nice to hear Tash say that. "I'm glad, because I do like working here. I feel like I have a purpose. Maybe not as important as treating the people who come here, but helping them initially if they're nervous or a little afraid. I also went to the after-school center and got the same warm, accepting feeling there."

Tash brightened at that. "It's a wonderful place. And it has a special meaning for Brandon—he reunited with his brothers there."

"It sounds like theirs is an incredible story, but as for Logan, I don't want you to think he's pressuring me. From the first, we were attracted to each other. I know it sounds bizarre, but we have this strange connection." Revealing his sex life to a stranger, even his therapist, wasn't comfortable, but he knew it was part of the healing process. "A few years ago, when I was newly divorced, I was very drunk and high one night. Logan and I hooked up in a club, and it was the most intense experience of my life."

"Are you saying this arrangement is based on sex?" Behind his glasses, a troubled expression clouded Tash's eyes.

"No," Ryan answered with a vehement shake of his head. "There's much more between us than physical attraction. And I already said we aren't lovers."

"I didn't mean to make assumptions," Tash apologized, and took a moment before continuing. "I'm concerned for you. From what I've seen, Logan is very charming, but I don't want you to be manipulated."

"I'm not, I promise," Ryan reassured him. "But as I said, it's a complicated situation. Logan and I might've lived together once, but we never had sex during that time." At Tash's obvious surprise, a quick smile curved Ryan's lips.

"I know it sounds crazy, but it's true. Aside from that one hookup in the club years ago, we've kissed, but nothing more."

Tash took off his glasses and rubbed his eyes. "Okay. I guess saying I'm shocked is a relatively mild way of putting it."

"I know. No one can imagine two people who are attracted to each other and living together not having a sexual relationship. But it's true, and it's one of the reasons I know Logan cares. He's never pushed me to change my mind, and I don't see him doing it now." As always when he thought about Logan, a combination of desire and wonder played tug-of-war in his mind. "We've come a long way from where we started. It's not only the physical attraction between us that's growing all the time. We care about each other."

Tash steepled his fingers in front of his face. "Are you in love with him?"

Ryan's answer was immediate. "I don't know him well enough. I barely know myself enough yet to understand what love means."

"What a marvelously insightful answer." Tash studied him for a moment. "There's no right or wrong answer, but you've stated your truth. I'm seeing real progress here, Ryan. Your whole attitude has changed from our first appointment. You're less defensive and angry and more at ease. You're showing confidence in yourself and your future and making healthy choices."

"You know I wasn't a fan of therapy," Ryan acknowledged. "But I can admit I was wrong. You've helped me see that I can get clean and stay clean, and move past the disgrace of losing my career. I can have a real relationship if I tell the truth—to myself first."

"You are the most important person in your life," Tash agreed. "And once you accept that, it becomes easier to move forward. I think we can call this session a success. Keep up the good work, and I'll see you next week."

Ryan left the office, expecting Logan to be impatient and pacing the reception area. Instead, he was surprised to find him in a serious-looking conversation with Noah. Observing Logan in profile, the usually hard jaw was relaxed, firm lips trembling, and there was nothing of the suave, sophisticated, hard-as-nails dominant man Ryan knew—or thought he did. Logan's famous guard was lowered, his emotions laid bare leaving him vulnerable and fully exposed. Ryan watched as he lifted a shaky hand to brush his hair off his face.

Noah spied him, and his expression was troubled. "Ryan, hi. You're finished with your session?"

"Yep."

Logan pinched his fingers to his eyes before turning a false, bright smile to Ryan. "Ready to go?"

At his nod, Logan shook Noah's hand, and Ryan took his coat from the rack by the front door. Logan had his phone out to get a car.

"Where do you want to go for dinner?" Ryan asked.

"How about we go home and order in? Just the two of us. Nice and cozy."

Logan's teasing didn't fool him. The strain on his face was evident, and Ryan wondered about his conversation with Noah but decided he wasn't going to push. It wouldn't matter even if he did. One thing he'd learned—if Logan Silver didn't want to talk about something, he wouldn't until he was damn well ready.

CHAPTER NINETEEN

LOGAN

"You look sad, Logan. Is there anything I can do to help?" Noah had asked as Logan sat waiting for Ryan.

It was the anniversary of his brother's disappearance. Logan had marked it every year as Todd's death. And the last thing he wanted was to talk.

"No. I'm fine, thanks." He brushed off Noah with what he hoped would end all conversation. "You don't have to keep me company."

"I don't mind. My husband is working late, so there's no rush to get home." With a smile, Noah stretched out his legs and waited. Logan hadn't counted on a therapy session while waiting for Ryan, but he could hardly refuse Noah's request to sit with him. He should've called and met Ryan somewhere. Instead, here he was, in this hushed room, where the only sound was his thundering heart and his breath bursting from his lungs.

Logan was the king of no small talk, and yet for some bizarre reason, he felt he owed Noah an explanation for his silence. He released a sigh.

"I don't mean to be rude. I just don't like talking about myself. I'm a very private person."

"Sharing grief or pain isn't talking about yourself. It can be cathartic, a way to release trauma. I'm not saying that's your case, but more as a general rule."

"Trust me, you don't want to share what I've been through." Logan regretted the words as soon as he spoke. They hung in the air as if a spotlight shined on them. He darted a glance at Noah, who gazed at him with quiet expectancy. Logan laced his fingers tightly.

"You remember when we first spoke and I told you I lost someone close to me because of drugs? It was my brother. Todd. At fifteen he started using, getting in deeper and deeper until he was hooked. The last time I saw him was in the hospital on this day, twenty-eight years ago. He was only nineteen, three years older than me. He'd overdosed, and I said good night and just left him. At some point during the night, he walked out, and I never saw him again. I mark this day as his official death, since I haven't been able to find him."

"And your brother's death changed you?"

"Of course it did. How could it not? It destroyed me. I should've fought harder for him to get off the drugs. I shouldn't have cared if he called me names or yelled at me. Nothing should've mattered other than him getting clean. I wasn't tough enough."

He hadn't thought the quiet Dr. Strauss—*Noah*, as he insisted Logan address him—could soften his hardened heart, but that was probably what made him an excellent doctor. You had no idea you'd unburden yourself, but the words spilled from your lips like blood rushing from a gaping wound. For over half his life, Logan had bottled up his emotions and hidden behind either a smart-ass answer or an icy frown. Within ten minutes, Noah had him almost in tears, revealing how Todd's loss had shaped him into the man he'd become—going through the motions, unable to breathe. To love. To live.

"I see it differently."

A harsh laugh broke from Logan. "You don't know anything about me."

A sweet smile curved Noah's lips. "You're wrong. I know you were a loving brother, and that you would've done anything in your power to help him."

"Well, yeah, but anyone would do that."

Ignoring his words, Noah continued. "You were a child when he started using and when he left. It wasn't your fault. From what you've told me, Todd was hell-bent on destroying his life, no matter what you or your parents did. You cannot help someone who doesn't want to be helped."

It was all a word salad to Logan because at the end of the day, Todd was dead and he was alone. He hung his head. "I loved him, and I miss him. Every day."

Noah placed a gentle hand on his shoulder. "Of course you do. I have an older brother, and if I lost him, I'd be devastated. And now I see why you care so much about Ryan. You took him into your home, asking nothing in return, simply to help him get free of drugs. That was all because of Todd, right?"

Logan lifted a shoulder. "Yeah. I couldn't stand to see Ryan fall apart. I didn't want him to end up like Todd." Those long nights of searching for Ryan, thinking he was dead or in trouble, haunted him like a recurring nightmare, where Todd's face would change to Ryan's, both of them calling for help he couldn't give. It remained a wound that wouldn't heal.

"So you're still that same person—the same loving man who wanted to help Todd." Logan's face must've reflected his internal skepticism, as Noah leaned forward, closing the space between them, his voice urgent. "Logan, I'm serious.

Knowing that chance with Todd is lost, you helped Ryan. Don't you see it? You're a nurturer. Todd may be gone, but the spirit of love and giving inside you hasn't died." Noah reached out and squeezed his shoulder for a second. "Let yourself accept it and embrace it. That's the real Logan. I think you'll find in doing so, you'll be able to receive what you deserve."

A trembling began deep within him, as if what Noah had stated was true and all the heartbreak he'd sealed up had broken free. The sound of footsteps snapped him to reality, and he shifted away from Noah, who'd turned to greet Ryan.

Thank fucking God.

He quickly said his good night to Noah and headed outside with Ryan on his heels.

"Where do you want to go for dinner?" Ryan asked, once they were outside.

"How about we go home and order in? Just the two of us. Nice and cozy." He forced his numb lips into a smile, and to his relief, the car pulled up in front of them. He had the door open and slid into the back seat before Ryan could even respond.

Once in the car, he fidgeted until Ryan put a hand over his. "It's okay."

"Is it?" Was that ragged, broken voice coming from him? He blew out a breath and steadied his nerves. "I'm…I'm fine. Just been a long day."

"Then it's good to stay in."

"Yeah. I'd rather be alone with you."

He found himself holding Ryan's hand as they crossed into the city and continued to tangle their fingers together as they walked into his apartment. Upon entering, he wanted to continue that connection, so he stopped in the entrance and faced Ryan, who gazed at him with questioning eyes.

"What's wrong?"

Logan raised their entwined hands to his lips. "Nothing."

His mouth traveled from Ryan's fingertips to graze his jaw and cheek. "I had this overwhelming desire to kiss you."

Ryan's hands framed his face. "Funny, I feel the same."

Their mouths connected, lips soft at first, then growing firm and hungry with need. Tongue met tongue, teasing and tangling, and Logan settled his arms around Ryan's waist, gathering him closer…tighter. Ryan's firm body molded to his.

"Logan, we should stop," Ryan whispered.

He reined in his lust and placed one final kiss to Ryan's cheek. "I'm sorry I got carried away. You're very tempting, and I think you feel the same." His grin broadened at the very large bulge in Ryan's pants.

Ryan snorted. "I'm not dead, you know."

Logan's smile faded. "Yeah. And I'm thankful for that." He left Ryan and headed to the kitchen, where he took out a glass and filled it with ice cubes, then poured himself a club soda.

Ryan stood across the kitchen island. "I'm sorry. I didn't mean it like that."

Logan set the glass on the quartz countertop. "I know. But I did. Sorry. I'm a little touchy. That talk with Noah… he gave me a lot of things to think about."

Ryan took his own glass. "Noah's a damn smart guy."

"Yeah. He saw through me right away."

Ryan frowned. "Saw through you? What're you talking about?"

"Sit?" He gestured toward the sectional, and they settled into the comfortable gray suede cushions. "I had no intention of spilling my guts to Noah, but he got me at a weak moment."

Ryan snorted. "You haven't had a weak moment since you were ten years old, I'm thinking."

Logan slung an arm around Ryan. "Shows what you know. Every time I'm with you, I lose my breath and feel faint."

A cute blush rose over Ryan's face. "Stop being silly."

He wasn't, but he didn't want to get into how much truth there was to that statement. "I told him about Todd." Ryan took his hand and squeezed, but he barely felt his touch. "He said I wasn't living because I was too caught up in the past. With blaming myself for Todd's death."

"Is he right?"

A lifetime of memories buffeted him—good and bad. Todd and him at the park, riding bikes together…lying in bed, listening to their father read them stories of King Arthur…the night he came out and Todd hugging him tight, telling him he loved him no matter who he loved. And only a year later, an unrecognizable Todd, long dirty hair, sunken cheeks, and glassy eyes, screaming in his face to get out of his life…

"Logan?" Ryan touched his cheek.

He blinked away the wetness. "Yeah. He is. Which is why I took helping you so seriously. I didn't want…I couldn't stand to think of you ending up dead. Like Todd."

"To an extent, I understand it, but why me?" Ryan asked, brow furrowed, his eyes filled with questions. "We barely knew each other, yet you took me into your home, no questions, and cared, so damn much."

Logan dipped his head, unable to face Ryan. "I've told you my father's death hit me very hard, and it forced me to admit I was merely going through the motions of life. Nothing was touching me. I'd sit and watch the news, seeing all the terrible things going on in the world, and yet I remained numb. When Remi told me what happened to you, it was like a douse of ice water had been dumped over my head. Someone like you, so bright and beautiful, had fallen so far and so hard…and all I could think of was that brief encounter in the Marquee and how alive you'd made me feel." He met Ryan's eyes. "Running into you at the hotel and finding you in dire straits…it hurt to see you struggle, knowing I had so much and could help. As attracted to you as I am, I really do want to be your friend most of all, and help you, as much as you'll allow me to."

Ryan's thumb caressed his palm. "Thank you for caring. I guess I'll have to learn to accept it. It's been a long time since I had someone in my corner, or allowed someone close. And I'm sorry."

"It's okay. I've learned to live with Todd's death."

"No, that's not what I mean." Ryan released his hand. "I mean I'm so sorry I put you through this again, even though it was unintentional. You were right—I was lying to you and myself about wanting to be clean. I wasn't ready that first time. Even while I lived here with you, I wasn't off the drugs and booze. Not to the same extent as when I was married, but just enough to get me through the day. Maybe I was fooling myself into thinking I was weaning myself off, but it was mainly an excuse to keep the crutch."

"I understand. You'd been using for so long, it's where you turned to when things got rough."

"When I was disbarred, I thought the world ended for me, and I didn't care anymore, so why should I believe someone else did?"

It was a confession Logan hadn't been prepared for, but it all made sense. "I do care, I hope you know that now. But please. Tell me the truth. Are you totally sober now?"

Clear-eyed, Ryan met his gaze. "I am. I haven't touched drugs or alcohol since I went upstate with Emerson." Lines deepened in his somber face. "It was brutal as all hell, and I bet I scared off half the animals up there with my screams from withdrawal, but I needed to go through it."

"You keep saying that. Help me understand why? Why did you need to put yourself through it when I know there are other ways? Detox is never pretty, but I imagine you'd be better off monitored by an actual doctor—safety-wise, I'm thinking."

An almost wistful smile briefly touched Ryan's lips. "I didn't think it mattered to anyone if I lived or died. It sure as hell didn't matter to me. And I wanted to know and feel the torture of what it did to my head and my body, so I'd never go through it again. I wanted to get clean, but if something happened to me, it was how it was meant to be."

Ryan's simple words horrified Logan. "That's not true. I hope you understand now that you have people who care."

"I've caused so much unnecessary pain. I needed to hurt myself so I wouldn't ever again be that selfish person who used people for whatever he could take."

"Noah said something to me that I think applies to you as well. Don't you see you've already changed? Just by your words here tonight, you're showing who you really are—the person the drugs and alcohol never allowed you to be."

But Ryan's self-loathing had become so ingrained, it would take more than platitudes to drive its poison out of his system. Time and introspection would, plus friends, and maybe…a lover?

"I'm discovering a lot of things about myself."

"Such as?" Logan asked.

"That you're a very big part of this new life I'm building." To Logan's surprise, Ryan touched his face. His breath was sweet, and when their lips touched, it wasn't with desperation but rather a warm familiarity that the two of them, together, was how it was meant to be. "I care about you. And I'm so damn glad you never gave up on me."

Logan rested his forehead on Ryan's. "I couldn't. And I won't." Aching to hold Ryan but mindful of Ryan's wish to go slow, he cupped Ryan's cheek and brushed his mouth to Ryan's for a moment.

"How about we have our dinner and make it a quiet evening?"

Ryan nodded. "I could cook something. The supermarket delivers in less than an hour."

Logan brightened. "Hell, yeah. The kitchen is yours."

After the groceries were delivered, Ryan puttered around the kitchen, and Logan sniffed with appreciation. With anyone else, he'd open a nice bottle of wine to share and begin the process of seduction. Being with Ryan would put an end to all that. Did he care? Surprisingly, no.

Too many evenings had found Logan in a haze of Scotch-fueled misery, burying the pain of his losses in meaningless sex.

Now, he'd found something worth much more.

He rummaged through the bar and pulled out a bottle of ginger ale and one of club soda. Holding both aloft, he strolled into the kitchen and put them in the refrigerator.

Ryan, stirring something red and delicious-smelling on the stovetop, raised his brows high. "You know that's not necessary."

"What? That I cool the bottles? I know, but the ice cubes melt faster if it's not."

"You're really not funny." Spoon in hand, Ryan faced him. "I'm talking about the fact that you think you can't have a drink when I'm with you. I don't expect the world to change just because I have a problem."

"Maybe you should." With a frown, Logan leaned a hip against the island and crossed his arms. "If people care about you, they'll want to do what they think is in your best interests, even if they have to make sacrifices. In this instance, not having a drink is more important to me because I don't want to put the temptation in your face. It's called respect."

"Thank you. I'll have to learn to accept that." Ryan shrugged. "It'll take some time."

Logan plucked the wooden spoon from Ryan's hand and tasted the sauce. "We have all the time in the world."

CHAPTER TWENTY

RYAN

"So how's everything? Bet you're glad to have your couch back."

Emerson had agreed to meet him in a coffee shop across the street from his apartment after work. Ryan counted it as a win to get him out of his comfort zone.

"It's fine." Emerson kept his gaze fixed to the cup in his hand. "I was surprised to hear from you."

Under the booth, Ryan knocked his foot against Emerson's. "I said we'd keep in touch, and I meant it."

"I know, but…people say stuff they don't always mean."

"Not friends."

Cheeks red, Emerson ducked his head. "I-I'm glad to see you. It's quiet in the apartment now without you."

"You need to get out more than just once or twice a week for a meeting."

"I am. Really."

Dubious, Ryan had to ask, even though Emerson didn't lie. "Are you telling me the truth?"

Emerson flushed. "Yeah. I've been trying. I went to

Whole Foods the other day myself instead of getting a delivery."

"That's a great step forward."

Emerson met his eyes briefly. "I met a guy. We were waiting in line for the deli, and he started talking to me. He, uh, asked for my number."

That made Ryan stupid happy. "And? I hope you gave it to him."

Emerson lifted a shoulder. "Yeah, but…how do I tell him I'm not," he lowered his voice, "into sex?"

"I guess you don't? Why not just try being friends first?"

"Like you and Logan?"

"Yeah. Like us. One thing I've learned is, you can never have too many friends."

Emerson drank his coffee. "And things are still good with you two?"

Ryan couldn't keep the smile off his face. "Yeah. Still good."

* * *

He and Logan had fallen into a comfortable routine, where he'd cook dinner most nights and they'd talk about their day as they ate. Afterward, they'd watch a little television, with Logan stretched out on the couch, his head pillowed in Ryan's lap. It was a change from the prior months they'd lived together, with Logan watching every move he made, and Ryan occasionally getting high after work and feeling like shit at Logan's praise for conquering his struggles. He'd lie and pretend all was well, then retreat and remain mostly silent.

Instead of sneaking off with coworkers after their shifts to snort a few lines, he stayed at the clinic, talking with people, learning their stories and sharing his own. He gained strength from them, and they listened to him talk about his own personal battles. He'd returned to the after-school center and was able to help some of the kids with their homework—using his skills in writing that hadn't yet become rusty.

To his surprise, that night Logan was already in the apartment when he opened the door. Normally, he didn't get home until close to seven—sometimes later if he had to entertain a client or attend a function.

"I made reservations for dinner. And I'm not taking no for an answer."

"Okay, bossy," Ryan laughed.

Logan's eyes twinkled. "And get dressed up."

A slow wink set his stomach tumbling. For days… weeks, if he would admit it, he'd found himself watching Logan—his strong hands and the way he held his mug of coffee, the tension of the hard muscles in his thighs as he walked across the room, the slow sweep of his tongue over full lips after tasting a delicious forkful of food. At night he dreamed of what sex with Logan would be like—passionate and fiery, no doubt.

As he got naked to change for dinner, he grew slightly faint imagining Logan's capable hands on his body, coaxing him to a blinding climax with his lips…his tongue…

Stop it, you idiot. Stop dreaming.

He'd saved a few of his suits from his days at the firm, and though they were years old, they would have to do. He slid a belt around his waist, noting he'd regained most of the weight he'd lost since his recovery. When he joined Logan in the living room, he was met with an admiring gaze that scanned him from head to toe and gave him the confidence he needed.

"I'm ready."

"You sure are." Logan grinned. "I'm not kidding when I say this is the healthiest you've ever looked since I've known you."

"I certainly feel better." Ryan thought for a moment.

"Maybe it's because I never really knew who I was, aside from the person who needed to get high to make it through the day. I'm finally learning to like myself."

Logan kissed his cheek. "I like this version of you too."

At Petite Boucherie on Christopher Street, they slid into a corner table. It was a small bistro, unpretentious and charming. Ryan was more at ease in a quiet place like this than the high-powered restaurants he used to frequent.

"This is very pretty," Ryan remarked, drinking in the sights and sounds of life in the city—a life he'd almost forgotten existed. "I've been to the one uptown, which is much grander, but I prefer this."

"So do I." Logan's eyes glowed over the delicate floral arrangement in the center of the table. "It's much more intimate."

Ryan's mouth dried. Inexplicably nervous, he downed half the water from his glass. The busboy refilled it. "Yeah."

Smooth, Ryan. You're way out of your league here.

Hoping to quell his dancing nerves, he scanned the menu. "Everything looks good. What're you having?"

"Onion soup and steak *frites*."

He set his menu on the table. "Same for me."

Their server approached. "Good evening. I'm Martin. May I take your drink order?" He stood poised.

"Club soda for me," Logan said, never taking his eye off Ryan.

"Same, please."

After Martin hurried off, Logan hitched his chair closer. "I'm very proud of you. I know it hasn't been easy, but I see a tremendous change."

"You do?" Was it silly or childish to wish for praise? But Ryan knew hearing it from Logan meant more. Logan Silver wasn't a man to hand out indiscriminate compliments.

"I know how hard it is for you to trust people. But you're not the same man who came to live with me last year. You laugh more, and you're eager to talk instead of sitting silent, all dark and gloomy."

Martin returned with their drinks, and they placed their orders. Ryan buttered a piece of bread and chewed it, reveling in the salty taste of the spread and the crunchy texture of the crust. He'd learned his love of cooking as a child, watching all the shows on television. His mother had often been too tired when she came home from her shift at the local Walmart, so he'd make dinner. Once he started using, his tastebuds had numbed, food becoming nothing more than a necessity to function. Preparing dinner for himself and Logan every night was helping in his recovery.

"I'm trying. The people at the clinic have helped me so much. I wasn't sure what to expect, but certainly not how personally involved they've become in my life. And I'm glad about it. I thought I'd be pushing them away, but instead they make me want to open up."

Their soups were set in front of them, but Logan made no move to pick up his spoon. "We all want the same thing." He grinned, and his eyes danced. "Let me rephrase. We all want you well and healthy. I want something more." The smile faded. "And I'm not saying that to pressure you. I just want you to know how I feel."

God, I'd like to know how you feel. Over me…inside me. I want you to fuck me until I'm wrecked for days.

A flutter let loose deep in his belly. His blood rushed hot, and an almost painful ache swelled from within. Ryan could almost taste the heat of Logan's kisses. He must've relived their hookup that night a thousand times. He wished he had the courage to tell Logan how badly he wanted to be with him. Instead, he dipped his head.

Their meal was perfect, the steak juicy and luscious and the fries hot and crisp. They'd split a dessert between them, an apple crumble with homemade vanilla ice cream—and was there anything sexier than Logan putting their shared fork in between his lips and licking it?

Not in his life.

Buoyed by the fact that he could enjoy a dinner out without drinking, Ryan sank into the back seat of their car for the ride home with Logan beside him. Was it his imagination, or had Logan inched closer? He didn't mind it—in fact, he slanted a sideways glance, hoping to see Logan's expression, but the car was dim and Logan sat in profile. His face was unsmiling. A dichotomy of hard cuts of jaw and cheekbones softened by full lips and dark hair, frosted with silver at the temples and falling over his brow.

In his past, sex had become second to survival—he'd always tap danced on the edge of destruction, fearing that everything within his grasp could crumble at any second. Yet between Logan and him, no matter his state of mind, a current of attraction waited to bloom, from the spark always sizzling to a full-blown conflagration.

Logan put an arm around him and leaned over to whisper in his ear. "I desire you."

Not want. Logan said desire. Maybe it meant the same thing to Logan, but for Ryan, it went further. Those three words sent a thrill up his spine that blossomed into a need so great, he almost couldn't breathe.

They made it home, and Logan locked the door behind them. "I'm going to bed. See you in the morning."

They would often give each other a casual kiss good night, but this time Logan cupped his face and settled his mouth over Ryan's. Ryan sighed, pleasure washing over him in steady, pounding waves, and he slid his tongue into Logan's mouth. A needy sound escaped Logan, but instead of deepening the kiss, he broke away, chest heaving, face flushed.

"Logan? What is it?"

Shocking Ryan, instead of answering, Logan turned and fled, his footsteps fading as he put distance between them.

Ryan heard the sound of a door slamming, and he touched his kiss-swollen lips.

"Fuck," he groaned, his blood on fire, body aching. He walked slowly to his room and shed his clothes, looking at himself naked in the mirror. His dick was full, and his ass clenched tight against the pulsing throb of his hunger.

You want him.

No, you desire him.

Want was purely physical, a need that could be satisfied without anything more.

Desire transcended that. It was visceral and all-encompassing. A quest to learn more and sink into the other person until they became one. He'd never desired anyone but Logan.

If I go to him now, everything changes.

Who was he kidding? Everything had changed the moment Logan first touched him at the Marquee. He'd burrowed under his skin and into his brain, and Ryan couldn't forget him even if he'd wanted to. Which he didn't. Logan was a fever he had little desire to cure. A hunger he'd never be able to sate.

Logan will always be my greatest desire. Tonight he needs to know I'm ready.

He turned the doorknob to Logan's bedroom and heard the shower running. Steam rose from behind the glass, and he stepped inside. The cool rainwater scent that clung to Logan's skin washed over him, and a fully drenched Logan stood transfixed, his green eyes wary but focused on Ryan's face.

"Ryan…what're you doing?"

Ryan joined him under the spray. "You said you desire me. Now it's my turn. You're the only one I desire. I want you. Now. Tonight."

He reached for the body wash and soaped himself up, then rinsed off. He turned off the water, and surprised by his own boldness, pushed Logan to the tiled wall. Everything in the world settled into place when their wet bodies touched. Logan's stiff cock hit his, and the friction of all that naked skin sent him reeling. Logan's hot breath exploded in a rush, and he clung to Ryan.

"I don't understand."

"It's time. It's more than sex." Ryan nuzzled under Logan's jaw, licking the stray drops of water. "I want you to make love to me," he whispered, and at those words, Logan's cock twitched and swelled further, pressing into Ryan's belly. "I want your mouth on me, your tongue, your hands. I want to smell like you all over. I need you inside me. Logan, please. Fuck me until I can't move."

Logan groaned and kissed his neck, nipping and sucking at the skin. "Are you sure?"

"As sure as I'm alive."

Eyes locked, they dried off, and Logan took his hand and led him to his huge bed. They sank onto the mattress together, a tangle of damp limbs and wet hair. Logan spread him out beneath him.

"You are so beautiful." Heat crept up Ryan's face, and Logan grinned. "And so adorable when you blush."

"Stop talking and kiss me." Ryan grasped him around the neck and pulled him close. "I've been thinking about this all evening. What you'd feel like. How you'd taste." Logan's eyes narrowed, but not enough to mask the blaze of lust. Then his mouth claimed Ryan's and everything made sense. Lips clung, and their tongues tangled and battled. A fierce wildness rose within him. "I've thought about this for weeks. Tonight I need to know. Logan, do it. Now."

"Are you kidding? I've waited for this, and I'm going to take my time."

His face was in shadow, and yet his eyes and smile gleamed. Logan dipped his head, and a warm tongue trailed a torturous wet path over Ryan's quivering body. Every place Logan touched ached upon his departure, and Ryan squirmed.

"Please, oh God, I'm gonna lose my mind."

Logan chuckled against his belly. "I'll catch it for you, but I can't promise to give it back. I want every piece of you. Including this."

Ryan propped himself up on his elbows to see Logan's dark head at his groin, and cried out when Logan took the dripping head of his cock between his full lips and sucked.

"Oh fuck, oh God." Ryan tried to stem the rush of his orgasm. Logan squeezed the base of his dick.

"Not yet," he whispered, then mouthed along his groin, sucking the crease between his hip and thigh. "Wait for me."

The intensity subsided, and Logan slid his mouth down Ryan's throbbing shaft, his tongue performing acrobatics. Reeling with the fire pouring through his blood, Ryan closed his eyes, and a kaleidoscope of brilliant colors swirled in front of him. He was bursting with life and desire and had never felt this free.

Logan began to move in earnest, his hand joining the movements of his tongue, and this time at his cries, Logan let him climax, swallowing everything he pumped out. Ryan opened his eyes to see Logan sitting on his heels, licking his lips. A slow, deliciously thrilling grin broke across his face.

Was there ever a man so sexy? So perfect?

Logan climbed over him. "You taste like heaven." Ryan touched his face, and Logan stilled. The air crackled between them, and Ryan trembled even as his heart pounded.

"You've given me so much."

Logan's forehead touched his, his lips resting on Ryan's cheek. "Not nearly enough. I want to give you more. I want to give you everything."

His engorged cock hit Ryan's belly, and though he was sensitive from his orgasm, the nerves raw and open at the surface, he craved for Logan to take him apart again.

"Please." He clawed at Logan's shoulders to bring him closer. If Ryan had the ability, he'd take him in whole and fit him like a second skin to make Logan part of him.

Grave-faced, Logan reached for his legs, pulling them wide, and buried his face in between, lapping at his hole. A soft, wet tongue pushed in him, and he quaked as gooseflesh rose over his skin. Ryan felt pulled tight as a bow, trembling with anticipation, and his hands clutched the bedsheets as his head thrashed side to side.

"God, you taste even better than I thought." Logan's growly words vibrated against his skin. He licked him over and over, his mouth on Ryan's sac and on his now-rigid cock. Everywhere. There was no place to run. To hide. He was flayed open for the world to see.

"Logan," Ryan cried out, and his vision blurred as waves of pleasure crashed over him. He burst into a million pieces, falling apart yet made whole by Logan's touch.

The drawer slammed, and Logan's slick, cool fingers entered him. "I know it's been a while, so I'll be gentle."

"Don't," he insisted. "I want it hard. I want to feel."

Logan laughed and kissed him until they both gasped for breath. "You will. Trust me."

And he did. He trusted Logan with his heart. No one had ever kept him so safe. So cared for. Ryan gazed up at him, the man he'd tried to forget, but even through the worst of his time, the only one who'd stayed and waited on the periphery of his life, there to catch him when he fell. And when Logan pushed past his rim, sinking inch by inch, filling him up to the breaking point and beyond, he knew the truth with startling clarity.

This was love.

He loved Logan.

But he was left no time to dwell on that momentous thought. Logan began to move, thrusting deep, snapping his hips, imprinting his body to Ryan's. Ryan clutched Logan's shoulders, and Logan gathered him close, settling fully into Ryan. Never had he been so consumed, so owned, and he welcomed Logan into him, urging him on.

"Logan, more. I need you." His sweat-soaked body melted into Logan's, and they became one.

"Ryan," Logan moaned, the broken, needy sound falling from his lips like a prayer. Clamped tight in his ass, Logan's dick throbbed and pulsed as he came. They fell to the bed, Logan's weight a welcome strength on top of him, and they lay chest to chest, hearts beating in sync.

"What the hell was that?" he murmured after recovering his breath.

Logan kissed his cheek. "That was us."

CHAPTER TWENTY-ONE

LOGAN

"You're looking chipper this morning," Oliver greeted him between his office and Logan's. "I don't think I've seen you walk in with a smile for years."

"You may be right. But the warm weather always puts me in a good mood. And who the hell uses the word *chipper*?" He snickered. "I don't know if it's you being preppy or the fact that Alexandra has you watching too many British shows."

Oliver grinned. "Probably a little of both. But I am serious. Happy Logan hasn't made much of an appearance here. I've been worried about you."

"And now you see there's no need to be. I'm good."

But Oliver didn't have a reputation as one of the sharpest litigation attorneys in the city for getting easily duped, and he never backed down. He dogged Logan's steps to the coffee machine and then to his office.

"Who are you kidding? You've never given a damn about the weather. So try me again." He paused by the doorway, blocking the entrance, and crossed his arms. "What has you grinning at eight thirty in the morning? Or…" Oliver's brows rose high. "Should I say who? As in Ryan?"

"You want the truth?" He leaned in, and behind Oliver's glasses, his big brown eyes widened. "I got an extra muffin at the coffee shop because the cashier thought I was hot. Want it?" He held up the bag, and Oliver's jaw set in a stubborn tilt.

"You are such a bullshitter."

"Takes one to know one," he razzed.

"What the hell is this, junior high or a law office?" Simon stood in the reception area.

"Ask him." Logan tipped his chin toward Oliver. "He thinks I'm lying. I told him I was in a good mood because I got a free muffin for being hot." He smirked. "I still got it."

"And I said he's in a good mood because he and Ryan are hitting it off, and I don't understand why he wants to hide it from us." Oliver's expression darkened. "I'm your friend, Logan. You were best man at my wedding, and you're Haley's godfather. I've known you for twenty-five years, and if you don't think I want you to be happy, then something is drastically wrong, and maybe that friendship is really one-sided after all."

To his dismay, Oliver didn't wait for a response but stormed off, and Logan winced at the sound of his office door slamming shut. Simon raked a hand through his hair, his usual cheerful manner grim.

"Okay…that was weird. But I gotta say, Logan. Ollie's right."

Frustrated, Logan tossed the bag holding his pastries onto the small conference table. It had been a good morning—great, in fact. A night of the most incredible passion he'd ever experienced. Waking up with Ryan in his bed was an unexpected bonus, though he sensed Ryan's lingering uncertainty as to what their night together meant.

For him…he'd expected the sex to be white-hot and electric, but there was more to it than the mere physical, and that realization had shaken him. He had to restrain himself from holding Ryan and never letting go.

But Ryan had learned to mask his emotions so well, it was impossible to know what he was thinking, and it wasn't a discussion to be had as they were both rushing to get ready for work. And Logan suspected Ryan needed actions more than words.

However, the one thing he'd learned was not to ignore the people who'd been by his side throughout his life. With his parents gone, Ollie, Simon, and Denise were the only family he had left.

"I'd better talk to him." He left Simon and strode to Oliver's office, where he knocked but didn't wait for an answer and opened the door. Oliver was on the phone, so Logan stood and waited.

"I have to go. Talk to you later." Oliver replaced the handset in the cradle. "Come on in." He peered past Logan. "You too, Si. Don't think I can't see you hovering over there."

"I'm not hovering. I'm waiting."

"For what?" Logan took a seat.

"For you to pull your head out of your ass."

"Always a pleasure, Si," Logan tossed over his shoulder, then gave Oliver his full attention. "Ollie, I'm sorry. I didn't mean to upset you."

Oliver pulled off his glasses and rubbed his eyes. Were those tears he spotted? Logan was stunned, as Oliver had told him long ago he'd been taught by his parents to never show emotion and live with that stiff upper lip.

"I'm only upset because you're pretending you're okay when I can obviously see you're hurting. Like when you were looking for Ryan. Simon and I knew how painful it must've been because of what happened to Todd, yet you wouldn't let us help you. In fact, you did everything you could to basically cut us out of your life."

"You're right," he whispered, head in his hands. "Seeing the road Ryan was heading down and knowing it would lead to the same result was killing me. I'd never felt more helpless."

Simon pulled up a chair next to him. "And yet you kept pushing me away every time I made an attempt to talk to you."

"Because I couldn't stand being pitied."

"We're not pitying, you, Logan." Oliver came from around his desk to flank his other side. "We love you. And we couldn't stand seeing you literally fall apart in front of our eyes." The hard lines of his face softened. "But ever since Ryan moved back in, you've done a complete one eighty."

"Yeah." Simon elbowed him. "You're your normal snide, sarcastic self. I missed it."

"Glad to oblige. I'll make sure to send more of it your way."

Oliver, once again proving to be that trial lawyer at heart and refusing to give up without getting the answer he wanted, prodded him. "So did you and Ryan finally get together?"

His lips twitched. "We did. But." He put a hand up when Simon and Oliver both opened their mouths to speak, their faces bright with what he knew was true happiness for him. "I'm not going to go into any detail about it or what it means for the future. Mainly because I don't know."

"But it's different this time," Oliver pressed him. "All the people you've been with over the years have never left an impression. Yet Ryan has."

"It's true," Simon added. "I've never seen you so wrapped up in one particular person." His eyes twinkled. "Except yourself."

Oliver busted out laughing. "He's got you there, Logan."

This was what he'd missed—the sense of belonging

that only the people who knew you best could give. "Ha-ha. Okay, the party's over. Someone needs to be the adult here and get to work." His two friends followed him to the door, where he stopped and pulled them both in for a surprise hug. "Thank you. I don't say it often enough, but you two really mean everything to me. I couldn't have made it through without you."

"Now that's what I like to see. All my men happy together," Denise called out from the reception area.

Surreptitiously wiping his eyes, Logan waved to her as he entered his office, but he wasn't surprised to see her standing at his desk a moment later.

"Yes?" He pulled the muffin out of the bag. "Do you want a muffin? I have one extra." He took a bite and chewed.

"No, I don't want a muffin. I want to know what was going on in Oliver's office."

Any other employee would've never dared to speak to him like that, but Denise was more than that to him. He grimaced and swallowed. "I upset Oliver, so I apologized." A wry smile tipped up the corner of his mouth. "Of course that necessitated Simon sticking his nose in and giving his two cents. Or in his case, a dollar."

"You upset Oliver? How? I don't think I've ever seen him anything less than calm as a sleepy cat in the sun."

Logan leaned back in his chair. "The thing between myself and Ryan."

"Oh? There's a thing?"

"All right. I know you're dying to tell me how you feel."

Denise pursed her lips. "I'm only concerned for you. Have you two become more than roommates?"

Logan's lips twitched. "You're being so discreet." Gathering his thoughts, he drummed his fingers on his leg, debating how much to reveal. "We're working on our friendship." Suddenly shy, he licked his lips. "And maybe more."

Denise's brows shot up. "You think you can trust him?"

"I guess I'll never know unless I try."

* * *

Late in the afternoon, his phone rang. He'd finished reviewing a contract for a new client and saved the file before answering.

"Yes?"

"There's an Ash Davis here," Denise said.

"Ash? I don't recall him having an appointment—did he?"

"Well, no…" She hesitated. "He did call earlier to see if there was availability but didn't give any details, so I wasn't sure if he'd show up or not. I think you might want to see him."

Interest piqued, he glanced at his calendar. It was clear for the rest of the afternoon. "Send him in, please."

"Okay."

He straightened his tie, checking his reflection in the mirror. With someone like Ash Davis, you always wanted to be at the top of your game. The door opened, and to his surprise, an elderly lady walked in, supported by Ash's arm on one side and a cane on the other. Logan watched as Ash settled her in one of the chairs in front of his desk, took the silver cane from her, and placed it against the wall.

"Logan, thank you for seeing us without an appointment."

"You're welcome."

Ash regarded the woman with a loving smile. "This is Drew's grandmother, Esther Klein."

"Very nice to meet you, Mrs. Klein."

"Lovely to meet you too, dear." A gentle voice with a slight Eastern European accent greeted him, reminding him of his own grandmother, who'd passed away when he was eleven.

"Can I have my secretary bring you anything? Water or tea?"

"No, thank you."

"Very well." Still mystified as to the purpose of their visit, Logan took his seat behind his desk. "How may I help you?"

"Go ahead, Asher." She patted his hand. "You can tell Mr. Silver for me."

"Esther's will is out of date, and now that her granddaughter is expecting her second child, she needs to update it."

"I understand, and of course I'm happy to help, but isn't that something you could handle, Ash? Trusts and estate planning is in your wheelhouse as well."

A faint blush tinged his high cheekbones. "True, but not if I'm a beneficiary. I thought it best to keep my firm out of it entirely. Oren suggested your partners, but both are with clients at the moment." His eyes twinkled. "I think you can handle this, even though it's not your usual."

"So you'd like me to prepare a new will for Mrs. Klein? That won't be a problem. Do you have a copy of the old one? And an idea of what you'd like the new one to say?"

Ash left his chair. "That's my cue to leave you two. Esther, like I told you in the car, Logan is one of the best. He'll take good care of you." He bent to kiss her cheek. "I'll be back in a little while. Take care of her, Logan. She's a special lady to all of us."

He met Ash's eyes and nodded, signaling a mutual understanding. Esther Klein had to be well into her nineties, and Logan, who had experience with several elderly clients who loved to ramble on about the good old days or had difficulty remembering, prepared himself with an indulgent smile.

"Okay, Mrs. Klein. Do you have a list of what you'd like to bequeath?"

She opened her rather large purse, and she extracted a sheaf of neatly typed papers. "Yes. Here is everything. Not much has changed since my great-grandson, Max, was born, but now that Rachel is expecting, I've made some updates." She scanned the papers. "I'm lucky in that I have not only Drew and Asher, but all the men watching out for me. Lucas, Jordan's husband, is my financial adviser, and as you can see, my investments have done exceedingly well. That's why I'm increasing my donation to the clinic as well as the center named after Keith." She sighed. "It's been almost ten years since he passed. I still remember him well. A lovely man."

Logan blinked, impressed by her mental acuity. "He's the one the center is named after?"

"Yes. Have you been there?" Her bright eyes met his. "It's truly a worthwhile cause."

"I haven't, but a friend of mine has. He works at the clinic as well."

"Ryan? Yes, Asher mentioned you two know each other. I met him when Asher brought me to the clinic. He's very sweet. Always has a kind word for everyone."

Not wishing the appointment to go off course, Logan studied the papers and began to take notes. "Now about the will, Mrs. Klein—"

"Please. Call me Esther. Mrs. Klein sounds so stuffy. As I was saying, Ryan has been a perfect fit for the center."

"He's very happy working there. Getting back to the will—"

"Have you known Asher and Drew long?"

Sensing defeat, he set the papers on the desk. "No, I've only met your grandson once. And Ash and I know each other from meetings or sometimes being on opposite sides of a case."

"Oh, dear." Her eyes danced with mischief. "And you didn't mind losing to him?"

He chuckled. "I don't consider it losing. We've come to mutual compromises."

"That's life, isn't it? Learning to compromise and get along to achieve a mutually beneficial end? I think if the world tried more of that, we'd be in much better shape than we are right now."

"Mrs. Klein—Esther. You are a very smart woman."

"Thank you. I've always held that belief through my darkest days. That and never to give up hope."

A pang seized his heart, thinking of Todd. Would the pain of his loss ever fade? Probably not. He pinched his eyes shut.

"I'm sorry," she said. "I've upset you. I didn't mean to bring up bad memories."

"No…you didn't." But even he could hear the sadness and doubt in his voice.

"I don't know you, Mr. Silver, but you have such sadness in your eyes. You remind me of someone I love very dearly. And years ago, I told him the same thing I'm telling you. When you give up all hope, you are lost. So please. Don't ever give up hoping for whatever it is you're searching for. Because you never know what life has in store for you. One moment it might be bleak and dark as night, only to have the sun rise to shine its glory on us."

The best response he could give Esther was a halfhearted smile. It wasn't her fault she didn't know that no matter how hard he wished, nothing would bring his brother home. "I'll keep that in mind." He shuffled the papers. "About these bequests…"

CHAPTER TWENTY-TWO

RYAN

Saturday dawned bright, and normally Ryan would want to sleep late, but that morning he awoke to a very warm, wet mouth teasing his neck. He sighed and settled into Logan's arms.

"*Mmm*. That feels nice."

"Only nice?" Logan hummed against his skin. "I'd better up my game."

Ryan wiggled his ass onto Logan's thick cock, nestled in the cleft of his ass. "Your game seems pretty *up* to me."

The breath whooshed out of him when Logan flipped him underneath and took his mouth in a bruising kiss that left him gasping for air. Aching and hard, he palmed their dicks, loving the greedy sounds of Logan's moans and cries as he rubbed them up and down.

"Fuck, Ry. I need inside you."

"Want that too," he panted, and watched Logan grab for the lube and condom. He didn't take his eyes off Logan as he rolled on the rubber and slicked his shaft. A pool of saliva built up in his mouth, and desire shot through him like a bullet. "Give it to me."

Still open and slightly sore from their lovemaking the prior evening, he winced as Logan breached his hole. Logan stopped.

"Are you all right?" Concerned eyes met his.

"No, because you stopped." Ryan yanked his elbow. "I need you."

An almost feral grin curved Logan's lips, and he pressed a quick kiss to Ryan's mouth. "Hold on because here I come." He thrust hard, burying inside fully.

Ryan hissed, but that pain soon turned to groans, the pleasure so all-encompassing, he closed his eyes and let Logan's ownership of his body…his heart, carry him away.

"Open your eyes," Logan ordered, and Ryan's dick stiffened at his harsh tone. God, he loved how Logan got hot and dominant. "Look at me."

Logan's mouth slammed onto his, and he groaned, fingers digging into Logan's shoulders. "You like that, don't you?" Logan demanded as he sucked and nibbled Ryan's lips. "Tell me you want it. Want me."

"Yes, God, more," Ryan pleaded, his head thrashing on the pillow. His entire body was a single element, there solely for Logan's taking.

Their tongues probed and licked, and Ryan's toes curled as Logan continued to thrust into him hard and fast. Logan shifted to his knees and pulled Ryan closer. "So damn perfect," he murmured while rolling his hips. He grasped Ryan's cock and began to jack him off, spreading the slippery precome over the head and shaft.

"Logan," he whispered, voice shaking. A nearly violent orgasm ripped into him, and his cock pulsed and jerked out streams of come, splattering over his stomach through Logan's fingers.

A startled expression filled Logan's emerald-green eyes.

He shuddered to his climax, then dipped his head to place soft kisses on Ryan's quivering skin. "Good morning."

With Logan's cock still throbbing inside him, Ryan smiled. "It sure as hell is."

* * *

An hour later, after showering and getting dressed, they sat in the kitchen. Logan poured himself a coffee and held up the pot.

"Want another?"

"No. Two cups is all I can handle." He took a sip of coffee, debating breakfast. "What're you doing today?"

"Me?" Logan seemed curious at the question. "I don't know. Having breakfast first. What do you want to do?"

Warmth settled in his chest. "Oh, I…I wasn't sure you'd want to spend the day together."

Before answering, Logan took a sip from his mug. "I'm thinking if we're going to try this thing, the way to do it is to spend time with each other. You know, to see if we're compatible—aside from the physical." His eyes twinkled. "Which, in my opinion, is fucking amazing."

Still tingling from earlier that morning, Ryan grew hot. "Yeah. It is. And by 'thing,' you mean what exactly?" Yes, they'd discussed it, but Ryan wanted to hear Logan say it again.

Logan clasped his hands. "Exactly what you think. We did it in a roundabout way with you moving in, then us having sex, but we're still getting to know each other. So I guess we're dating? Is that still a term?" He frowned. "Are you having second thoughts about our situation, now that we've slept together?"

"No. I just want to get to know you better out of bed. We've already established we're compatible in it. The times we went out to dinner or to the Broadway show were more fun than I've had in years. I want more of those moments with you."

Logan rinsed out his now-empty mug. "I might be more fun in the sheets. But sure. Let's spend the day together. Any ideas?"

Ryan thought. "We could just walk around the city. Maybe go to a museum and have lunch."

"I haven't done that in years," Logan mused.

"I remember you used to work from home on the weekends. Was that because you wanted to keep an eye on me?" Ryan challenged him.

It was Logan's turn to blush. "Well…yeah. But also…it kept me busy, since I had nothing else to look forward to."

Those words hit Ryan like a knife to the heart. Here Logan sat in his beautiful penthouse apartment, all the money and success he could want, and yet he was as lonely and isolated as Ryan, who had virtually nothing.

"Now we do. Let's go to the Met, then Central Park, and maybe the zoo."

But Logan didn't answer him and instead stared off into the distance.

"We used to go to the park every weekend. My father had to work—the bakery's busiest days were Saturday and Sunday. Our mom would meet her friends, and Todd and I would spend the whole day there. When it got too cold, we'd go to the Brooklyn Museum or the library."

The utter desolation in Logan's eyes hurt Ryan's heart. Logan wasn't thinking about their plans for the day. He was trapped in the past. "I've never been to either. Maybe we should go there instead."

Logan blinked and turned an astonished face to him. "To Brooklyn? Why?"

Because you're hurting and you need closure.

But Ryan couldn't say that, so he attempted to keep it light. "Why not? I hear it's the cool place to be these days."

Logan's stare was unreadable, but then he nodded. "All right. Why not? But let's eat first. I know a little diner that has great pie."

"Pie? It's barely eleven in the morning."

Logan winked. "I already had my cake. We can have brunch."

He shrugged. "Okay, sure."

* * *

Logan remained mostly silent on their walk to what turned out to be a slightly grungy diner.

"Here it is."

Puzzled that they'd passed much nicer restaurants, Ryan hesitated before entering. "This is where you want to eat?"

"Don't be a snob," Logan teased, then pointed to a booth in the corner. "Let's sit there." They slid in, Logan across from him, just as the waitress strolled over.

"Coffee, folks?" Her blue-shadowed eyes grew wide when she saw Logan. "Hey, I know you. How you doin', honey?" She poured them each a cup, though neither had answered. A busboy appeared from behind her and slapped down two glasses of water. "You're looking a heck of a lot better than last time, that's for sure. This the boyfriend you were mooning over?" She cackled. "He's a cutie."

His cheeks red, Logan darted a quick glance his way.

Mooning over?

Ryan's heart gave a funny twist.

"I didn't think you'd remember me," Logan said, and Ryan watched in fascination as Logan chatted with her. Logan's earlier, contemplative mood had evaporated, replaced by his charming personality.

"Are you kidding? How could I forget you? Best looking guy to come into this godforsaken joint. Plus, I remember everyone." She tapped her frosted blond head. "Mind like a steel trap.”

“Donna, pick up,” a voice yelled out, and she rolled her eyes. “Be back to take your order. Don’t get the chili. Frank put in too much garlic, and it don’t make for good kissing breath, if you know what I mean.” She left with a wink, and Logan snickered.

“She’s a trip.”

Ryan sipped his water. “There has to be a story behind how Logan Silver ended up here.”

“I grew up going to diners like this.” He drummed his fingers on the speckled Formica tabletop. “The truth is, one night when you were missing, I’d gone to the police station to see if they had any new leads on you. I wandered in here afterward because I didn’t want to go home, and this was the only place open. And as you can see, Donna is the talkative type.”

“And you talked back?”

Logan studied the menu for a moment before setting it on the slightly sticky table. “Let me set you straight. I wasn’t born with a silver spoon in my mouth. Everything I have today is because I worked my ass off to get it, and I make zero apologies for how I live now. But that doesn’t mean I forgot where I came from.”

Embarrassed by his assumptions, Ryan met Logan’s annoyed gaze. “I’m sorry. I guess it’s good we’re doing this, so we can learn about each other. I just figured you came from money.”

“Yeah,” Logan said bitterly. “I get it. And you know what the worst thing is? Now that I do have more than I know what to do with, none of it matters. I’d give it all up to have my family with me.”

“I’m sorry,” Ryan whispered, chastened by Logan’s revelation.

Logan sighed. “It’s not your fault. Forget it. Let’s get something to eat and then have a good day.”

Donna returned. "So, whaddya want? The burgers are good, and Frank makes a mean tuna melt."

"I'll have a cheeseburger with fries, and I hear your pies are something special." Ryan's stomach growled.

Donna turned pink. "Aw, ain't you sweet. Yeah, lemme bring you something just for you." She wrote his order. "And you, honey?" She cocked her head at Logan.

"I'll have that tuna melt and lemon meringue."

"You got it."

Their orders came quickly, and they both demolished their lunches.

"You're right. The food is good—those fries were perfect." Ryan wiped his face, and his eyes widened as Donna approached. She carried two plates, one with Logan's lemon meringue and then his, with an assortment of three pies: peach, cherry, and banana cream.

"I figured why not a little of each. Lemme know which one you like best. Here's the check, but take your time."

Ryan figured she'd leave, but when she stayed by the table, he glanced over at Logan, who winked and grinned, before proceeding to eat his pie. Realizing Donna wasn't going anywhere until he tasted them all, he tried a forkful of each.

"I can't pick. They're all delicious."

Donna smirked. "You're as smooth a talker as your boyfriend." Hips swinging, Donna strolled away.

"They really are good," Ryan remarked, then finished all three slices. He realized Logan was staring and stopped licking his fork. "What's wrong?"

A strange smile flirted on Logan's lips. "Nothing. I'd like to take you somewhere."

His heart pounded. "Where?"

Logan picked up the check and left double the amount. Ryan always felt you could tell the character of a person by how they treated their servers, and Logan was extremely generous.

"Trust me?"

Ryan nodded, and they waved good-bye to Donna, who winked and blew them a kiss. An idea popped into Ryan's head as they walked down the block. "Would you want to see the center Jordan started? They're open on the weekends to help parents who have to work."

"If you'd like."

"I know you're not into it, but I promise it won't take up too much time. We'll go to Brooklyn afterward. I think it'd be nice if you saw it, and I should be going more—"

Logan's mouth hit his, stemming the flow of words. "You're babbling. I'm fine with it. Really." He took Ryan's hand. "Lead the way."

It took less than fifteen minutes to walk to the center, and when Ryan pushed in the doors, he spotted Jordan and his husband in the library area. They looked up and waved, said something to the two children they were speaking with, and headed their way.

"There are Jordan and Luke." He nudged Logan, who stood a few steps away from him and was scanning the large, airy space.

"This is very nice. I'm impressed."

Jordan reached them first. "Thanks, Logan. Ryan, you didn't say you were coming today."

"We were close by, and I wanted to show Logan what you've done here for the neighborhood."

Jordan took Luke's hand in his. "Not only me. It's a joint effort. Wanda, the head of the center, has accomplished more than I even dreamed, and Luke has kept up the fundraising to cover the ongoing expenses." He frowned. "It's a never-ending battle, but we're determined to succeed. We want to make sure we can continue to stay open on the weekends."

"Let me have your info, and I'll get my firm on board." Logan took the card Luke handed him. "We're always in the market for worthy causes, and this one certainly qualifies."

Jordan's brows rose. "Thanks, Logan. I appreciate it."

Inexplicably, pride swelled in Ryan's chest, but then he laughed to himself.

Look at me, acting like a proud boyfriend.

"Daddy, Papa, listen to my story." A curly-haired little girl clutching a book ran up to Jordan and Luke. She didn't wait for a response and began to read to them. Face beaming, she finished. "TJ and Brandon helped me practice all week."

Jordan scooped her up and kissed her. "That was great, Ellie-belly."

Ryan spied TJ at the back of the center, gathering up the scattered books and papers, and then he disappeared into one of the offices. Seeing him reminded Ryan of his story and how far he'd come after being hooked on drugs. Knowing TJ made it encouraged him to think more positively about his own recovery.

"Eww, don't call me that." The little girl made a face and wriggled out of his arms. "Grandma's here," she yelled and ran to the door, where Ash and Drew approached with Esther, whom he'd met several times at the center. Ellie hugged and kissed Esther.

"Your daughter calls Esther her grandmother?" Logan asked, sounding confused. "Isn't she related to Drew?"

Jordan chuckled. "Yes, but Esther is a surrogate grandmother to everyone. My parents are Nanny and Pop-Pop to her." His brow wrinkled. "How do you know Esther?"

Ryan wondered the same thing and listened to Logan's explanation of how he'd come to update her will. The group approached, and Jordan and Luke hugged Esther gently before she faced him and Logan with her inquisitive gaze.

"So nice to see you both again."

"You as well, Esther," Ryan said. "Logan and I just stopped by because I wanted to show him the center, but we'll be on our way."

"I understand." Her eyes twinkled. "I'm sure you two have plans for the rest of the day."

About to deny Esther's obvious matchmaking, Ryan received the biggest surprise of his life when Logan took his hand.

"We do. It was great to see you all, but we have to get going. Jordan, Luke, I'll be in touch."

They left, and halfway down the block, Ryan slanted a glance to Logan, who had his phone out to call for a car. "That was smooth."

"I try," Logan deadpanned, then squeezed his hand. "I know they're your friends, but I'd really rather spend the day with you. Alone."

"Can't argue with that logic." Ryan kissed Logan's cheek. "Especially since I agree with you. Where are you taking me?"

Logan's face grew grave. "Someplace very special to me."

It was apparent no more information was forthcoming, and Ryan had to be content with Logan holding his hand as they waited for their ride.

CHAPTER TWENTY-THREE

LOGAN

The closer the car drew to Prospect Park, the more nervous Logan grew. Silly, he knew, but exposing this part of himself to Ryan, a part he'd never allowed anyone to see, not even his closest friends, raised his anxiety to a fever pitch. In business he sequestered his emotions, focusing on the cold facts of his cases, but here, memories crowded out any rationality, rendering him unexpectedly, *incredibly* needy to hang on to Ryan for support.

Hand in hand, they walked into the park, along the trails he used to run with Todd. The well-worn path in the grass he remembered still remained. He tugged Ryan's fingers.

"This way."

Ryan remained silent, for which he was grateful, and together they passed children playing until they reached the familiar clearing. He stopped by the small jumble of rocks and sat on them instead of the grass. Ryan remained standing, and after a minute or so, Logan felt capable of speaking.

"This is the spot Todd and I would come to when my

mother would take us to the park every weekend." At his hesitant words, Ryan joined him, and it was natural to wrap an arm around his shoulders. "I come here when I need to take a break from everything. And take a breath." Ryan settled in closer, and the tightness in Logan's chest loosened for the first time in years.

"I can see why. It's very peaceful." Ryan's lips were soft against his cheek. "When I was upstate, detoxing, I'd leave the cabin and disappear into the woods, finding a spot much like this." His mouth pulled down in a frown. "Thinking of disappearing. That my life didn't matter."

Logan pulled him tight. "Don't say that." His voice shook. "Don't ever think that. You do."

"I know that now, but then? My mind was in a bad place, and all I knew was to remove myself from the people I was hurting. I figured they'd be better off without me."

"I hope you know that's not the case."

"In some respects."

Not liking where the conversation was heading, Logan cupped Ryan's cheek, forcing their eyes to meet. "In my case, I'm better off *with you*." His lips touched Ryan's briefly. "Much better off."

Ryan's face softened. "Did you ever think that maybe Todd felt the same way I did? That he was only being a burden and that's why he left?"

He ducked his head. "No way. He knew how much we loved him. I—"

"Logan," Ryan interrupted him with a quiet voice that stopped him cold. "Todd's problems had nothing to do with you." A quicksilver smile came and went. "As hard as it might be to understand, not everything revolves around you. Todd's problems were his to work out, and at that point, he wasn't ready to accept help. I understand where he was coming from."

"Because you felt the same way when you left?"

"Yeah. It's a hopelessness you can't fathom unless you've reached rock bottom. Plus the guilt of knowing I lied to you, along with losing my career."

"And now?"

"Now I'm just glad to be alive."

The simplicity of Ryan's statement was devastating, and Logan's breath caught. Looking at a now-healthy Ryan, skin fresh and clear, blue eyes bright, golden hair gleaming in the sun, it was so easy to forget the hollow, beaten man he'd been months earlier.

"I'm glad you are too."

An overwhelming desire to kiss Ryan welled up inside Logan, and he acted on it, feeling Ryan's lips soften against his. Gentle and sweet, as opposed to the hungry intensity their kisses usually brought. They clung to one another, and Logan rested his cheek to Ryan's. "Look up."

Ryan squinted at the bright sky. "Okay?"

"What do you see?"

Ryan's brow furrowed. "The sky," he answered slowly. "And some clouds."

Logan tilted his face to the warmth of the sun. "When Todd and I were young, we'd come here and lie in the grass, making up stories about them."

Ryan's gaze grew distant. "I'd do that as a kid. I'd pretend the clouds were animals, trees, or faces. And when I was older, I wished I were a bird and could fly far away."

"Because you were gay?" Ryan rarely spoke of his family or growing up in a small town, and Logan was anxious to discover as much as he could.

Ryan nodded. "It was awful. Early on, I was attracted to men, and at the same time, I knew I'd have to keep it a secret. At school, if you weren't good at sports, or if you liked theater or were simply too quiet, you were called queer boy, or worse. I made the track team and managed to keep out of their line of fire, but some kids weren't so lucky.

Bullying went on all the time, especially in the locker rooms after gym class or walking home from school."

Of course Logan had heard stories, but they'd remained that—stories he was told in college or read about or watched on the news, but never personally experienced. Ashamed, he had to admit that even after all the evidence he'd seen, he still found it hard to believe things like that happened. "You had no one to talk to?"

"About kids getting beaten up 'cause they might be gay?" Ryan snorted, rolling his eyes in disbelief. "No one would dare say anything at home about it because the last thing you wanted was for your parents to ask why you cared, if you were friends with those kids. And I had to worry about my father. His favorite saying was 'Man's gotta be a real man.' We went to church every Sunday and were indoctrinated with some truly awful preaching. Gays, Black people, Jews, immigrants…everyone was blamed for the problems of the world."

"I'm beginning to understand why you left and never wanted to talk about it." Logan rubbed Ryan's back. "You know you're safe here, I hope."

A skeptical expression settled over Ryan's face. "Am I? I'm not so sure we're really safe anywhere."

About to dispute what Ryan said, Logan hesitated. He'd walked through life with impunity, never paying much attention to those who didn't feel so free. Did he have a right to counter argue? "I'm ashamed to say I've never believed I'd have to worry. Like I said, my family accepted me, and I have my small circle of friends. Frankly, I don't make my private life public." He grinned. "What I do in the bedroom is my business. And now yours."

Ryan cast his eyes downward. "I said something pretty awful to Garrett about Jewish people, which I deeply regret. I was in a bad way."

"You were high?"

A flush rose on Ryan's cheeks. "I was high all the time."

Logan admired his honesty and wasn't surprised, as he'd heard the same from both Remi and Garrett. "I'm glad you realize it's wrong and that you took the initiative to apologize to him directly. Garrett's an easygoing person, plus he's happy now. It's time you learned to forgive yourself."

"Not so easy, I'm thinking," Ryan answered, facing him with a wry smile. His voice gentled. "Have you thought of taking your own advice?"

"What're you talking about?" His jaw hardened.

"Logan. Come on," Ryan chided, and it was Logan's turn to get red. "You know what I'm talking about."

This peeling away of the scar tissue around his heart was as painful as a freshly inflicted wound. "Even after all these years, I still don't understand why. Why did Todd turn to drugs in the first place? You had no one to lean on—I can understand the utter hopelessness you must've felt. But Todd wasn't alone. He had our parents, friends… me…dammit, he had everyone in his corner. We could've helped him. I could've…" Tears threatened, and he hung his head to hide them.

But Ryan wouldn't let him and pushed his face into Logan's space. "No, Logan. You couldn't. You tried with me, and it didn't work. It never will, unless the person wants the help and is ready to be healed." Ryan squeezed his shoulder. "Todd wasn't. You need to come to grips with it."

Startled, Logan wiped at his eyes. "You're right. Maybe it's time to finally put the past to bed." He ran his knuckles over Ryan's jaw, feeling him quiver beneath his touch. "Speaking of bed…"

Ryan's blue eyes glowed. "Less talk and more action, Mr. Silver."

* * *

Logan took Ryan's thick shaft past his lips, the bitter precome filling his mouth. He swallowed, his heart pounding. Nothing had ever tasted as good as this man. The tension sitting like a hundred-pound weight on his shoulders melted away until it was simply him and Ryan. He swirled his tongue over the crown, mouthing the silky skin, tickling the slit. "Sweet, so damn sweet," he murmured before licking and sucking his way down the full length of Ryan's dick to bury his face in the wiry groin hair.

"I want to make you mine. Prove to you how much I want you." Their eyes locked as his fingers delved deep inside Ryan.

"Don't you know I already am? You don't have to prove yourself to me."

Logan covered Ryan's mouth with his, falling into a spiral of pleasure he never wanted to unwind from. He sucked Ryan's tongue, and Ryan's dick jerked, trapped between their sweating bodies.

"Fuck, Logan. Oh, my God." Ryan moaned and shook as Logan nuzzled his neck, moving over his chest to nip and tease his nipples. The smell of Ryan's desire rose around him, and Logan couldn't wait.

He rolled on a condom, slicked himself up, then breached Ryan's tight hole, the muscled walls clasping him. So tight. So hot. Logan pushed all the way in and began to thrust. Faster. Deeper. Ryan's eyes locked with his, and Logan was blinded by the blaze of desire. They sucked him into the fiery blue depths, and he surrendered willingly. Ryan squeezed him tighter. He was inside him, but it wasn't close enough. Blood to blood, marrow to marrow, Logan willed his body to become one with Ryan's.

"I want you. I've always wanted you."

"You have me. Now. Forever." Ryan clutched his shoulders.

Insatiable hunger broke through the last vestiges of his

loneliness, and Logan knew for certain he could never live without Ryan anymore.

"You're mine." His hips snapped harder as he moved at a punishing pace. The bed creaked and groaned, but Logan didn't give a damn if it broke. Everything in his life narrowed to this point. This moment where he knew.

He was falling to pieces, and only Ryan could make him whole.

"Don't leave me," he managed to whisper.

His heart thundered at a painful pace. The absolute necessity to hold on to Ryan was raw. Powerful. The way Logan wanted to consume him was as necessary as breathing.

Ryan's fingers tangled in his damp hair. "Never."

Shattered by that one word, his climax tore through him, every nerve ending focused at the point where their bodies were joined. At the same time, Ryan came, his cock throbbing and pulsing out streams of come between them.

His face buried in Ryan's neck, Logan sought to regain his equilibrium, unable to move. Ryan remained motionless under him, and Logan greedily drew in his scent and mouthed his collarbone. Even now, drained and spent from their lovemaking, Logan couldn't get enough of him. Couldn't stop touching him.

"I meant what I said."

"Which is what?" Ryan's lips moved against his hair. "You said a lot of things."

Logan felt the smile in his words, and his heart sang with a freedom he hadn't known in years. "You're mine. For good. Forever, if you want. I…I love you."

Ryan stiffened. "What?"

"I'm in awe of your strength, of your courage to start over, more than once. You've helped me learn to appreciate my life again. If you're not with me, I count the time until you are. I can't stop thinking about you, and I don't want to be without you anymore."

Ryan didn't respond, and Logan rolled off him and stared at the ceiling. Maybe he'd come on too strong, too fast, and Ryan was having second thoughts. Ryan shifted closer and threw an arm across his chest and a hairy leg over his own.

"You have no idea what you mean to me. The person who believed in me even though I didn't believe in myself. I think I fell in love with you because I never believed I could love myself, but I love the person I am when I'm with you. The man who made me feel like I could do anything because I was worth something."

Logan cupped his cheek. "You are. To me, you're worth everything."

CHAPTER TWENTY-FOUR

RYAN

He set the phone on the desk and opened the tab on his computer screen. It was nearing five thirty and time for him to leave, but he had a few things to look at before closing up. He read and took notes, his pulse quickening. An idea had been simmering in his mind for several weeks, but seeing it in black and white made it more real.

"A master's in social work?" Jordan spoke over his shoulder, and he jumped.

"Jesus, Jordan." Hand to pounding heart, Ryan spun the chair around to face the man's dancing blue eyes. "Warn a guy, why don't you?"

Ignoring him, Jordan peered closer at the computer. "Are you thinking of going back to school?"

"Maybe." His answer was guarded, but he couldn't help but be curious as to Jordan's thoughts. "What do you think?"

Jordan plopped himself in a chair and laced his fingers in front of him. "Well, I think it could be a great idea. What would you plan to do with the degree?"

Ryan chewed his lip. "I really enjoy working here, but I feel like I want to do more. Spending time helping the kids at the after-school center made me realize I could give back that way. Lots of kids have issues at home or at school, and they might feel more comfortable talking about it at the center because it's a neutral place. I never thought I'd enjoy spending time with children, but shockingly, I do." He paused. "I feel like this is a fork-in-the-road moment for me."

"And why's that, do you think?"

Normally sarcastic and somewhat arrogant, Jordan was deadly serious now as he listened to Ryan, which he appreciated—and it also made him emotional to know that this life-changing idea was something achievable.

"I-I think I'm healing. I'm truly clean for the first time in decades, and I'm happy with who I am. With me."

"*Mmm*. I think you are. Happy, that is. And healing from what?"

Ryan glanced down at his hands. "The first part of my life. The failure of my marriage. Pretending to be someone I'm not. I almost lost the person I am, but the funny thing is, I'm not sure I would've known who that was to find."

"And now?"

Ryan's lips twitched. "You're very good at asking questions, aren't you? Sure you're an orthopedic surgeon and not a psychiatrist?"

Jordan's smile was wry. "I've been in therapy for a decade. Trust me, I've picked up a few pointers from Tash along the way."

Jordan was a friend—his friend, not Logan's—and had made no secret he thought their relationship had progressed too fast for his liking. But Ryan had wasted enough of his life being someone he wasn't to hide who he'd become.

"I finally know where I'm going, and equally as important, I know who I want to be with."

"Logan," Jordan stated flatly, his distaste obvious.

"Why do you dislike him so much?" Ryan was not only curious but determined to get it all out in the open.

"It's not that I don't like him, but I'm not sure I trust him."

"For what reason?"

"That whole setup he'd arranged—you living at his place and him acting like your savior by taking care of everything you needed. No questions. It's a very self-righteous way of thinking. My concern is you having enough independence not to allow him to sway you to his way only."

"That's a lot of word salad, Dr. Peterson, to say you think I'm a manipulative bastard and Ryan's a patsy." Logan's sarcastic drawl sent Ryan spinning in his chair, and he rushed to prevent an argument between the two men.

"Hey…hi. I didn't know you were coming."

Logan stood in the doorway of the clinic, his tie loosened and collar unbuttoned, a sign, Ryan had learned in their time together, that it had been a rough day. "I spent the entire day negotiating a contract. I just finished with the client at the Barclays Center, and figured we could go out to dinner."

"I'd like that."

The blaze of anger in Logan's eyes dimmed as he crossed the reception area to give Ryan a kiss. Ryan could feel Jordan's eyes on them, and Logan's lips thinned as he faced off with him.

"If you have something to say to me, Jordan, tell it to my face."

Unperturbed, Jordan shrugged. "You said it, not me. Are you a manipulative bastard? And for the record"—his gaze shifted to Ryan for a moment—"I don't for a second think you're a patsy, Ryan. But some people have an ability to make black seem white."

"Thank you for making me more powerful than I imagined myself," Logan sneered. "I've never once thought of Ryan as easy to manipulate—for Christ's sake, I don't need to fucking manipulate *anyone* to get them into my bed."

Those words hit Ryan like a dagger to his heart, and he froze.

Jordan, perceptive as always, homed right in. "So is that all it is for you—physical?"

"Trying to put words in my mouth? That sounds pretty manipulative to me." Ryan watched as a light broke out over Logan's face. "Don't be a fool, Doctor. I love Ryan." Logan met his eyes. "Are you ready to go?"

Said out loud to someone else, Logan's words shook Ryan to his core. "Give me a sec," Ryan murmured and powered off his computer. He grabbed his jacket and backpack. "See you tomorrow, Jordan."

"I'm sorry if I was out of line. Talk to you tomorrow."

Ryan didn't answer and followed Logan, who'd called for a car. They waited outside the clinic, Ryan stealing glances at Logan's unyielding profile until he could no longer stand the silence.

"I'm sorry Jordan poked and forced you to have to say it."

Logan expelled a harsh breath. "Is that what you think? That I was forced to say I love you? No one forces me to say or do anything." And then Logan lifted Ryan's hand and kissed his knuckles. "I'm sorry if I was short. It's been a fucking day."

The car pulled up, and they got inside. "Where are we going? We could stay home."

"No. It's okay. I made a reservation at Tribeca Grill."

Ryan hadn't been there in years, not since his days at the law firm, and it conjured up old memories, most of which he would rather forget. Nights out there would start with numerous cocktails, then more drinks with dinner. He'd move on to the harder stuff when they'd go out clubbing. But Ryan was reluctant to ask Logan to change his plans.

"I used to go there often."

"With your firm?"

"Yeah. We'd entertain clients and have our weekly Friday roundups there. The dinners were merely a prelude to the partying after."

Logan stared long and hard into his eyes. "Okay. We can change plans and go home instead. We can order in."

"Why?" He lifted his chin. "You think I'll be tempted?" Suddenly he wanted to walk through those doors and kill those demons dogging his footsteps.

"I'm hoping I'm your only temptation." Logan smiled and played with his fingers. "And I didn't say that. But maybe you don't want to relive the past."

"I don't plan on it. I have too much to look forward to."

Admiration rose in Logan's eyes, and he kissed Ryan. "I do love you. Even if you have questionable taste in friends."

They arrived at the restaurant and were seated immediately. And again, even though he'd told Logan he wasn't bothered if he ordered a drink, Logan chose club soda, as did he.

"I'm not unhappy about joining you on your sobriety journey. Too many nights I drank my pain away, but it sat waiting for me when I sobered up in the morning."

"Does that include all the people you slept with?" Ryan asked unflinchingly. "Or hooked up with?"

Logan's brows shot high. "I wasn't drunk the night we hooked up at the Marquee. I wanted you with a clear mind." He peered closer. "What's going on? Something's bothering you."

"Earlier at the clinic, you were so casual about not needing to manipulate people to get them into your bed."

"And you think I'm including you in that group?" Logan's husky growl surprised him. "You can't be serious. Not after the other night."

"I didn't think so, but—"

"But Jordan made you think twice about me." Logan leaned forward. "I thought we'd put this to rest, but I guess not."

"It's not that I don't trust you. But I still struggle with why me."

Ryan appreciated that Logan took the time to answer and didn't just brush him off.

"Because my head and my heart tell me so, and I'm listening to them. My partner Oliver fell for his wife, Alexandra, who's the polar opposite of him, at a college party. First weekend of freshman year. They were inseparable from that point on. No one would've ever put them together, yet they're disgustingly happy." He grinned. "His words, not mine. I might not know much about relationships, but I do know what I want. And that's you. With me." He held out his hand, and Ryan took it, entwining their fingers. "Only me. Don't let people who don't know us ever make you question who we are."

There was no reason to doubt Logan's words, so Ryan accepted them and enjoyed their meal. The steak was delicious, his mashed potatoes creamy and garlicky, and the brussels sprouts bright and crispy. Logan had truffled fries, and Ryan, having finished his plate, picked a fry off Logan's. Logan's hand grabbed his wrist.

"I don't recall giving you permission."

"What else do I need to ask you for? Is there a list?"

"I'll make you one when we get home." Those green eyes radiated heat and the promise of a continuation of the passion they'd only begun to explore.

A heavy hand on Ryan's shoulder interrupted their moment.

"Well, damn. Look who's alive. Ryan, dude."

He blinked and gazed upward to the flushed face of Denny Wallace, an attorney he used to work and party with. At one of his lowest points, he'd reached out to Denny, hoping for some friendly words and help, but Denny never returned his call. Ryan twisted away from his grasping fingers.

"Hello, Denny."

"What're you doing here?"

"Eating dinner."

Logan had returned to eating his steak, a tiny smile quirking the corner of his lips.

"Guess you landed on your feet. You always were a cat with nine lives, though I thought you used them all up when you got disbarred." He guffawed and downed the amber liquid in his glass. "Murph," he called out to the table filled with suits and raised his glass. "Another one. You want, Ry? Or is that a dumb question?" he cackled.

"Sounds like your specialty," Logan said mildly, having finished his food.

Denny's sandy brows pulled together. "What the fuck does that mean?" he bristled. "And who the hell are you?"

"A good lawyer never asks a question he doesn't know the answer to." Logan smirked. "Should we get the check? I'd rather have my dessert at home."

Ryan nodded, and Logan signaled for their server.

Denny's hazy eyes grew wide, then crafty. "Ohhh, I get it. This your new sugar daddy? You dumped that schoolteacher for a newer model?" he sniggered and leered. "Guess it doesn't matter if you don't have your law license anymore—I heard you do your best work on your back… and your knees."

"The fucking hell you say that to him." Logan got to his feet, but Ryan stepped in front of him.

"Logan, don't." Curiously, none of Denny's degrading words hurt. Maybe because people could only hurt you if you let them, and Ryan was done with allowing that. "He's nothing. Not worth anything, and neither are his words. Let's go home."

Without taking his eyes off Ryan, Logan took the bill from the server, scribbled on it, and set it on the table. They walked out and grabbed a taxi discharging passengers at the curb. The ride to the apartment was quick, and in no time, they were upstairs and undressed in the bedroom. He'd finished before Logan, who'd sat on the edge of the bed, watching him.

"What?" Ryan asked. "You're looking at me funny."

"Who was he? The jerk in the restaurant."

"Someone I used to work with." Ryan made a face. "Good thing I'd already finished my dinner. Any reminder of someone like Denny Wallace is enough to make me sick to my stomach."

"Don't let him upset you."

Ryan lowered himself next to Logan and slipped an arm around his waist. "I'm not. Are you?"

"I don't like what he insinuated. That you're nothing more than a user."

"What he insinuated was that I'm no better than a whore. But I don't really care what he thinks. I care about you. And me. I don't think I'm that person."

"I know you're not. You put that dick in his place tonight, though I still think you let him off too lightly."

"What should I have done? Punched him in the face at the restaurant? I meant what I said. His words mean nothing to me. I would've felt more like they did, had I still been using and staying here, dependent on you for every single damn thing, but I'm not."

"No, you're not," Logan agreed. "You're sober, you've got a job, friends—"

"I want to go to school to get a social work degree," he declared, chest heaving, his words echoing loudly in the bedroom. "I want to help people who are struggling. People who've lost hope because they don't believe life can ever get better."

"I think that's a terrific idea." Logan took his face between his hands and kissed him. "You're living proof that it can."

"And I'm not going to take any money from you."

"Did I offer?" Logan murmured against his cheek. "I don't remember saying anything of the sort."

"You're such a jerk," Ryan muttered, yet unable to control his grin as Logan shook with laughter. "I just mean I want to find a way to make it on my own—scholarships or working extra hours. I can't depend on a safety net forever."

"I'm sure you can make it work because I think you can do anything you want."

"How about anyone?" This time he grabbed Logan and kissed him, pushing him onto the bed. "I'm ready to do you."

"Not anyone." Logan met his tongue and sucked it. "Only me."

"Only you. You're the only one I want."

CHAPTER TWENTY-FIVE

LOGAN

"So things still going well with you and Ryan?"

It was early morning, and he and Oliver were in Oliver's office, waiting for Simon to arrive so they could begin their monthly recap. Logan sipped his coffee.

"They are."

Oliver took off his glasses. "But?"

"I didn't say but."

Oliver stretched out his long legs. "You don't have to. For the first time, you're in a relationship, and I'm sure it's different being with the same person day after day."

"Different, yes, but not unenjoyable. In fact, I'm beginning to understand the benefits."

"I'm sure you are." Oliver's eyes twinkled. "There's a lot to be said about taking the time to learn your partner's needs and wants."

"I know exactly what Ryan needs and wants. Me," Logan responded with a smirk. "He wants to go to school for social work. It's a good choice for I him, I think."

"I agree." Oliver was thoughtful. "His life experience will certainly help him relate to people."

"Exactly what I said."

"Exactly what you said about what?" Simon breezed into the office and sat opposite him. "Fill me in."

Logan didn't have the chance, as Ollie recapped their conversation for him. Simon nodded.

"He sounds like a man with a plan. That's a good thing. He's doing the right thing otherwise?"

Logan bristled. "Meaning?"

Simon wasn't the least put off by his warning growl.

"Meaning, is he keeping off the drugs and booze?"

"Yes, of course he is." Irritated, Logan snapped at his friend. "You sound as if you're waiting for him to fail, and I'm not liking that, Si."

Atypically solemn, Simon shook his head. "No, that's the last thing I want. But you also know how easy it is to relapse, and I'm concerned for him and for you."

"There's no need to be. Ryan isn't the same person he was the last time. He's driven and focused, and most importantly, he's taken full responsibility for his choices—good and bad. From the beginning you've doubted him, and it's pissing me off that no matter what he does, it's not good enough for you."

"I didn't say that. I want the best for him."

"And like I told Ollie, he's got that. Me." Logan's anger faded. "Look. I know what he's up against. But I learned my lesson from last time. I'm not his savior, and he's not hiding anything from me. Ryan's not Todd. He's stronger than I thought, and we're going to see this out to the end. Together."

"All I want is for you to be happy," Simon said, and Logan could finally answer him without a doubt.

"I am. Ryan getting a degree is the structure he needs. He really enjoys helping at the after-school center. You two ought to check it out. I plan on the firm making donations to its operations. And Ollie, I bet Alex would love to bring the kids there. It's not far from your apartment."

"Oh, yeah? I'll let her know to check it out. Maybe she can help out as well. Now that the girls are in school full-time, she's itching to use her degree again."

"I'm sure they could use a high-school teacher to help tutor. Ryan's become friendly with someone who's a school guidance counselor, and I think that's part of the reason he decided to take this course of action. I like that he wants to do more with his life."

"He's a go-getter," Simon agreed.

"I'll be there today to meet Ryan. Maybe Alex could come over, and we'll introduce her to Wanda, the director."

"Give me the address, and I'll text her," Oliver stated. "She can pick the kids up from school and go there after."

Logan repeated it and checked his watch. "I need to get going. I have a will to get out and some contracts to revise. How about we go over the monthly figures now?"

After they finished, he left but found Simon trailing after him. When they entered Logan's office, Simon shut the door behind him, and Logan faced him with an inquiring raise of his brows.

"Something wrong?"

"I feel like I need to apologize again. I'm sorry if you think I'm not being supportive of your relationship."

Logan took a seat behind his desk. "I'm not angry with you. I understand where you're coming from. In the beginning you were right to be cautious, and I appreciate you being a friend. But like I've said, Ryan's not the same person he was then."

"Neither are you. I never knew who you were before your brother died. We met so soon after you lost him, I've only known you grieving."

"That person *was* me. I lost who I was once Todd died,

and I was content to be that way. Speaking to Noah at the clinic, and having Ryan, helped ease the suffocating darkness that losing Todd sucked me into. It's taken me twenty-eight years to get over his death, and despite knowing I'll never be the same without him, I'm finally enjoying my life."

"That's all we ever wanted to hear."

Logan gazed at Simon speculatively. "You know, everyone's so wrapped up in my life, I never asked about yours."

Simon made a face. "Mine?"

"Yes. Are you seeing anyone?" Logan watched his friend shift from foot to foot, uncharacteristically nervous, and he wondered why. Simon had always stated he had no desire to settle down. Ever. His parents' nasty divorce had turned him off monogamy, and he'd always appeared at any event with a different socialite on his arm.

"I'd better let you get to that work you said you had to get to."

Now he was convinced Simon was hiding something. "Don't be silly. Come on, Si. I've laid it on the line for you. So…?"

"No. I'm not seeing anyone. And I can't believe you're turning into one of those people who, now that you're coupled up, thinks everyone needs to be."

Logan put up his hands. "Whoa, hold up. I did *not* say that. Why are you so touchy?"

Simon huffed out a sigh. "Sorry. I spoke to my father last night, and he was getting on my case about not being married and carrying on the family name, blah, blah, blah."

Logan winced. "Ouch. That's unpleasant. I know your father is very opinionated."

"He's a bastard who only cares about his money."

"What're you going to do?" Logan asked. "Is he threatening you if you don't get married?"

Simon shrugged. "Our relationship is a series of

continuous threats. I told him that he and my mother had set such a great example, I couldn't possibly ruin some poor woman's life, knowing that it would all turn to shit in the end."

It hurt Logan to see his friend so bitter. "It doesn't have to be that way. And no, I'm not talking about myself and Ryan because it's new, but Ollie and Alex have been together since college and married for almost fifteen years, and they still love each other."

But Simon ignored that. "I've got my own work to do, so I'll see you later. And maybe I'll come check out the after-school center with you. I could use another worthwhile place to give my money to that isn't my father's choice."

Simon didn't speak to his family often, but when he did, it took him several days to recover from the bitterness those conversations always brought to light. Spending time with the kids at the center would help him. Even Logan, who wasn't at all interested in children, except for Oliver's daughters, found it impossible not to feel good seeing their smiling faces. And Ryan was in his element, which made him happy.

His intercom buzzed.

"Yes?"

"Maverick Wilson is here with his agent about his contract."

"Send him in."

Time to get to work.

* * *

At nearly six that night, he pushed open the door to the center with Simon on his heels. Logan immediately spotted Ryan at a table with a boy around fourteen. Books lay spread out in front of them, and Ryan was talking and pointing to something on the page. The young boy nodded and wrote in his notebook. Logan spied Wanda and waved, and she bustled over with a beaming face.

"How are you? So nice to see you again."

"Same here." He took off his coat and hung it on the rack. "This is my friend and law partner, Simon Brown. Simon, this is Wanda, who runs this place."

"Good to meet you. Any friend of Logan and Ryan is a friend of ours."

"Simon is always looking for worthwhile causes to give his family money to, and I told him there's none better than what you're doing here. Keeping kids off the streets and away from guns and helping them with schoolwork."

"Why don't I give you a little tour?" She tucked her arm in Simon's, and Logan chuckled to himself as he left them to make his way across the center to Ryan.

"Hi, there. Doing some schoolwork?"

Ryan gazed up at him. "Yeah. Jack here is learning about the Industrial Revolution."

Logan made a face. "Not the most pleasant topic."

Jack shrugged. "We have a test next week. I've been coming here to study every day after school 'cause my mom has to work late at the store and doesn't want me home alone."

Ryan met Logan's eyes and nodded. "I told Wanda I'd stay until Jack could go home. I promised him pizza, and TJ was nice enough to offer to pick the pies up, so we're waiting for him. Do you mind? You can meet him, finally."

"Mind what? I love pizza."

The door opened, and Alex walked in. "Alex," he called out. "Over here."

She waved to him, and with the two girls in tow, crossed the room. "Hi, honey. Sorry I'm so late, but Haley had piano after school and then Jilly couldn't find her headband. But we're all sorted now."

He kissed her cool cheek. "Good. This is Ryan," he

introduced them, and Alex gave him an effusive hug and kiss.

"I can't tell you how thrilled I am to finally meet you."

"I think you just did," Logan said dryly, and snickered when she swatted him.

"You be quiet. You'll have to tell me your schedule so we can all get together for dinner soon and really get to know each other." Her attention fell to Jack. "Hello. This is Haley and Jilly."

"Uh, I'm Jack."

"What grade are you in, Jack?"

"Tenth. I go to Beacon."

"Haley's in tenth grade too. I was a high-school teacher. What're you studying there?" Alex peered at his book. "Oh, the Industrial Revolution. You just finished that, didn't you, Haley?"

Logan hid a grin as Haley rolled her eyes. "Yes, Mom." She sat next to Jack. "We have the same textbook at Brearley. I can tell you what my teacher tested us on." Soon she and Jack were chatting away, and Jilly had found the arts-and-crafts section and was coloring. Alex took off her coat.

"What a wonderful place. I can't believe I've never heard of it."

Ryan explained its origins and purpose, and Simon returned with Wanda. He introduced Alex to Wanda, and they walked off, heads together in deep discussion.

"Logan was singing the praises of this center, and now I see why," Simon said, his gaze sweeping over the interior. "I told Wanda I'm happy to contribute, and I'm going to have a meeting with my financial adviser to set up something monthly for them, aside from the firm's donation."

"That's great. Thanks, Simon."

"And I hear you're going back to school. I think that's a good career choice for you. Congratulations, Ryan. You've really come a long way. You should be proud."

Logan slipped his arm around Ryan. "I agree."

"Pizza's here," a voice called out. "Sorry I'm late. I stopped and bought myself some soda. Can't have pizza without it."

Ryan took his hand. "Come on. TJ, I want you to meet my boyfriend, Logan, and his law partner Simon."

Logan turned…and his heart stopped. TJ's smile faded, and he stood motionless, holding pizzas and a bag with the six-packs of soda. The bag fell to the floor, and several soda cans opened and began to spray at TJ's feet, but he made no move to step out of the way. As if in slow motion, TJ set the pizzas on the table. Logan couldn't breathe or move.

Thick hair, totally gray, a face weathered and worn, but the eyes…the *eyes*. Logan had known those eyes his whole life. He saw them in his dreams every night.

"Todd?" His voice broke. Was that wobbly voice his? "TJ…Todd Jacob. I'm right, aren't I?"

Simon grabbed his shoulder. "Logan, what the hell are you saying?"

"What? TJ is Todd? Are you sure?" Ryan asked.

He didn't answer. Couldn't. Instead, he dropped Ryan's hand and closed the distance between them. TJ—Todd—stayed rooted in place, and their eyes locked. Logan's heart pounded so hard his chest hurt.

"Todd," he breathed. "Is it…it's you." He reached out and touched the scar on his cheek. "This. You got this when we played swordfights in the park and you fell off the rock."

"I didn't fall. I slipped." A sob broke free, and Todd covered his eyes.

Logan gripped the back of a chair. Alex had ushered the children away, and it was only the two of them, with a worried Ryan hovering in his periphery. This had to be a dream. But if it was, he didn't want to wake up. Todd wasn't dead. He was alive. *Alive.*

He and Todd continued to stare at each other. Logan wanted to hug him tight and yet hurt him for all the pain he'd caused.

"Why?" he pleaded. "Where were you all these years? Why did you leave and never come home?" A thousand other questions awaited on the tip of his tongue.

"I couldn't make my problems yours anymore. I wasn't worth a damn, so I ran away and let you think I was dead. It was better for everyone. The drugs…at first it was cool and exciting. I got tired of always being the good kid and wanted to break free of the monotony—go to school, do homework, spend time with the family. It was boredom… stupid, stupid boredom, and I guess I thought I was being a rebel. But the more drugs I did, the unhappier I got." He rubbed his face. "It was a rapidly accelerating treadmill I couldn't get off, and the faster I ran, the more out of control my life became."

Recalling what Ryan had told him, Logan could understand, but it didn't stop him from questioning Todd. "But letting us think you were dead? How could you think that was okay? All we wanted was to help you."

Grief settled in every line on his face. "I didn't see it that way. I knew I was being a burden and draining the life out of everyone. I thought if I left, it would be easier. You could forget about me…I couldn't keep hurting you and Mom and Dad." Agony clouded his eyes. "Are they…"

"They're gone," he said flatly. "Mom passed years ago—her heart. It's been two years since Dad. They never stopped grieving you."

Tears streamed down Todd's face. "And I didn't help their suffering. God, I missed you all so much. But I didn't think I was worthy of your love. Time after time, I kept screwing up. The only way I saw out of all the pain I caused was to leave. I changed my name from Todd to just TJ and got a fake ID—you can get anything in New York. I didn't want you all to find me and bail me out again. I was a screw-up. I was prepared to die."

A too-familiar story. Logan couldn't help but dart a glance at Ryan, who gave him a hesitant smile, but he knew it was too far for him to have heard what Todd had said. Logan focused on Todd and struggled to remember what Ryan had taught him about listening and hearing what people had to say. Instead of lashing out, he tempered his words.

"But you didn't. You just let us think that's what happened." He couldn't help his accusatory tone.

"I thought it was for the best. I got on a bus and went west. Still getting high. I stopped in several states, got odd jobs to keep up my habit, then ended up in Arizona. One night I was dying for something, anything, but I didn't have enough cash. I tried to rob someone. I didn't know it was a member of a gang. He shot me and left me on the street to die. It was the lowest point of my life. I lay there, my face pressed to the cold concrete, feeling the blood pour out of me, and all of a sudden I wanted to live. I thought it was too late, but an ambulance came and took me to the hospital. They stitched me up and saved my life. While I recovered, an addiction counselor visited and asked me if I wanted to go to rehab. I figured why the hell not? I had nothing—no place to stay, no family. Whether I lived or died was solely up to me. It took two years and a couple of relapses along the way, but I did it. I credit Ariella."

"Who's that?"

The hard lines of Todd's face softened. "My wife. She knows my whole story—knows I'm Todd. You also have a nephew. I named him Charlie, after Grandpa Chaim." He pulled out his phone and brought up a photo of a brown-haired woman with soft eyes, holding the hand of a boy around ten. "Remember King Arthur of the Round Table? I've started reading the stories to Charlie, and he loves them as much as we did."

Logan's vision blurred, and he blinked. "He looks just like you did at that age."

"Before I screwed up my life." Todd's shoulders slumped.

"How could you think it was better to let us think you were dead?" Logan had to ask because none of it made sense. "Do you know Mom cried every night? I swear she died of a broken heart." Todd paled, and the tears trickled down his face, but Logan couldn't stop. "Even a card… just to let us know you were alive." It was unfathomable to him that Todd had simply walked out of their lives without imagining the devastation he left behind.

"I thought it would be better—for you especially. Mom and Dad were so wrapped up in my problems, they were ignoring you. Once I disappeared, they could concentrate on you."

"They never ignored me. But I missed you. I loved you so damn much, and you just forgot about me," he whispered.

Did he sound like that wounded, broken little boy left behind? Perhaps he was because the pain in his chest was almost too great to bear. Maybe it was his heart breaking again, when it had finally begun to heal.

"I didn't forget about you. I left because I didn't love myself enough and couldn't love you the right way. Going to rehab, getting clean and making a new life…it all had to be done to find myself again. But at the time, I didn't know anything else except wanting to get high."

"How long have you been in the city?"

Todd's gaze dropped. "About six months. After rehab I went to college, got my master's, and Ariella and I got married. We had Charlie about two years later. I was a school guidance counselor. Ariella is originally from New Jersey and missed the East Coast, so we talked about it, and she thought it was time I came back. She has a great job in a hospital, and I'm working for the city."

Logan had to ask. "Were you ever going to get in touch with me? Or just continue to let me think you were dead?"

"I looked you up every year to see how you were doing. I saw you became a successful lawyer." Todd's mouth drooped. "I figured you didn't need a former drug-addict brother weighing you down. You were better off without me."

"You had no right to make that decision for me. I wasn't better off. I wanted my big brother. I was lonely, miserable. After you left, I'd come home from school and walk around the neighborhood, thinking maybe I'd find you. When I went to college and law school, I'd look for you in the crowds I'd pass on the street. For years, every single place I'd go, I'd search strangers' faces, thinking maybe, *maybe* that day would be the one where I'd find you. I even hired a detective to look for you. You're my brother. I never stopped loving you."

"And you and Ryan? He said you're his boyfriend."

For the first time, Logan smiled. "Yeah. But I almost screwed that up because at first I smothered him. I didn't trust him. All I could think of was you. I thought if I could give him everything and make it easy for him, maybe he'd stay."

Ryan came to him and held him close. "All I want is you. Everything is nothing without you at my side."

True happiness brightened Todd's face. "I'm glad you have someone. From working with Ryan, I can tell he's a caring, loving person."

"He is." Logan held him tighter. "I just had to allow myself to be happy. It's not easy. I blamed myself for your death, thinking I should've tried harder."

"I'm sorry." Anguish clouded Todd's eyes, and he pressed his hands to his face. "I'm so sorry, Logan. I understand it might be too early to think of reconciliation, but maybe… maybe you can forgive me?"

"I'm not sure I can give you an answer right now. I'm a little overwhelmed." Shoulders slumped, he let Ryan lead him to the side. Simon waited there with anxious eyes.

"Are you okay?" Simon took him by the shoulders.

"I don't know," he said honestly. "I want to grab him and hug him, but also…I want to scream and yell at him that he caused us all so much pain."

He watched Todd bend to pick up the ruined soda cans and place them on the table.

"Ryan, Logan."

Ash Davis came over with his husband, Drew, and their grandmother. Logan's stomach clenched. The last thing he needed was a cheery group chat.

"I'm not in the mood right now. I'm sorry."

"Is everything all right, Mr. Silver?" Esther asked. "You look like you've seen a ghost."

"I did. TJ who works here…he's Todd. My brother." He shook his head and gave a short explanation of what happened. Oddly, Ash paled, and Drew took his hand. Esther put her hand to her mouth.

"Oh, dear God."

"I know it sounds unbelievable, but…" He shrugged.

"It doesn't." Ash looked grim. "Trust me."

"It wouldn't be the first time this center has seen miracles," Esther declared. "How wonderful for you."

"I'm not sure I can forgive him for leaving us the way he did. He hurt my parents, me…it's complicated." Logan sneaked a quick peek at Todd, who was on his phone, shoulders hunched. Probably talking to his wife. He wondered what Todd had told her.

"Imagine how your brother felt, knowing he had a family left behind, but didn't feel he had the right to see them."

"But he made that choice. He could've stayed, and we would've helped him."

Ryan put a hand on his arm. "I think you know by now the truth isn't so simple. Not as Todd saw it. I imagine he's lived with tons of regret all these years, thinking he had no choice at all. Not in his mind."

Esther placed herself in front of him. "Mr. Silver, I've

lived a very long time and seen many, many things. Some terrible, but many more wonderful. One of the joys of my life was when Asher found his brothers here, in this very space, after searching for many years. It was something none of them believed possible. Their healing took time and a lot of hard work, but they're a family now."

He opened his mouth to speak, but she continued.

"You had everything—your home, parents, friends. Love and stability. Todd gave it all up, choosing to live alone rather than put you through hell and back over his addiction. Yes, he hurt you, but you have the chance to regain the joy you lost and never thought you'd find again."

"My grandmother is a very wise woman, Logan. You should listen to her." Ash's demeanor was somber.

"I'm an old woman. He doesn't have to listen to me."

Logan recognized the hope in her eyes and chuckled. "Esther, I think those who don't, soon discover how foolish they are."

Her smile was sweet. "I can only imagine that if your parents were still alive, they'd be beside themselves with joy to know their beloved son was alive and had come home."

It was so overwhelming, Logan could barely stand on his feet. He wanted to sink to the floor, curl up in a ball, and wish the world away.

"What're you going to do?" Ryan touched his arm.

Todd had finished his phone call but remained at the table, head in his hands. Without answering, Logan left the small group and sat next to his brother. Todd met his gaze.

"I spent my whole life since you disappeared thinking you were dead, wishing there was something I could've done differently, dreaming up scenarios in my head of what I'd say to you if I ever found you. Now you're here, and I'm at a loss to express how I feel. It's a tragedy that we lost so much time, but there are only two choices as I see it: either I hold a grudge that you left and send you away, *or* I try to understand the crisis you were in and get my brother back."

Todd wiped his eyes. "I know which one I'd choose."

"There's so much joy inside me that you're alive, yet sadness that Mom and Dad aren't here to share it. But do you remember what they always said when we were young? We have to stick together. Because we're family. I love you, Todd."

They hugged, and Todd murmured in his shoulder, "I love you too."

Those castles in the air were no longer a dream, but reality. A foundation he could build the rest of his life on. A life now filled with love.

EPILOGUE
RYAN

One year later

"Tell me again," Logan insisted in the car ride over to the center, and Ryan laughed.

"I got straight As in all my classes. And I've been given a dean's scholarship for the rest of the program, as long as I keep my grades up."

Logan leaned over and kissed him. "I have no doubt. You never have trouble keeping me up."

Ryan's lips curved against Logan's. "You're cute. And you have a dirty mind."

"And you love it." Logan smirked. "But seriously, Ry. I am so fucking proud of you, I could burst." His eyes glowed. "And I love you. So damn much."

"I love you too. And you know how much of this is because of your support." Ryan stopped at Logan shaking his head. "What?"

"Don't think that. Yeah, I supported you, but this is your hard work. All those late nights studying and working full-time…you're an inspiration."

His throat closed up. "I just wanted to do something better."

The car pulled up in front of the Keith Hart Community Center, where they were all meeting to have a little celebration for Ryan completing his first year. Before they walked inside, Logan put a hand on his shoulder.

"I'm so in awe of what you've accomplished for yourself. Do you know how strong you are? I look at you and think, how am I so lucky that someone who has so much to give, chose me to share his life with?"

Ryan hugged him. "I know you don't like hearing it, but your faith in me gave me that strength. It was knowing I had your love that pushed me through the long nights. You holding me every night, telling me I could do it, made me believe it."

Logan cupped his face. "So what you're saying is we're a good team."

Ryan kissed him. "The best."

Once inside, Wanda rushed up to greet him with a hug and kiss. "I knew you could do it. And you'll have a place here once you graduate. You and Todd can do such good things for the kids."

"Speaking of my brother," Logan said, scanning the room. "Is he here?"

"Right behind you, little bro."

They turned, and Ryan's heart still sang with happiness as Todd and Logan hugged. Ryan greeted Ariella with a kiss.

"How're you doing?"

"I'm great. Congratulations. And you should really think about getting into the school system and becoming a guidance counselor. Talk to Todd about it."

He'd been giving it some thought. "I might. But first I have to graduate."

"Uncle Logan, Uncle Logan." Charlie tapped his arm.

"They're going to do a play at school, and it's all about knights, and I'm playing King Arthur."

"You are, huh?" Logan picked up the little boy and swung him until he shrieked. "I think I should show you how I used to beat your father at sword fighting."

"All lies," Todd insisted. "Prepare to be beaten."

Ryan watched Logan and Todd pretend-fight for a moment, then spotted Simon, Oliver, and Alexandra. "Hi. Thanks for coming."

"Wouldn't miss it." Simon clapped his shoulder. "Congratulations."

Alexandra hugged him, and Oliver shook his hand. "What a great year you've had," Oliver said, his normally solemn expression bright. "Doing so well your first year while working full-time at the clinic and helping here." A burst of laughter from Todd and Logan as they played with Charlie drew their attention. "And thank you for saving Logan."

His brow furrowed. "Saving him? I thought I caused him trouble."

"At first you did," Simon stated. Ryan had always appreciated his blunt honesty and his unwavering friendship with Logan. "But Logan always had your back, and even when we weren't quite sure if he was doing the right thing, he was. I owe you an apology. I'm sorry I doubted you. I thought you were only out to take from Logan." Simon's smile warmed his eyes. "But I see you've given him so much."

"I'd give him the world."

"Give who the world?" Strong arms slipped around his waist.

Ryan leaned into his broad chest. "Who do you think?"

"I have you in my arms. That's my world."

Simon groaned. "God, I think I liked you better when you were obnoxious."

"Don't worry, Si." Ryan snickered. "Logan hasn't lost his touch."

"Thank you." Logan's voice dropped to a murmur. "Especially when I'm touching you."

"Oh brother, maybe Simon is right."

Logan chuckled. "Why is everyone so serious? This is a celebration." Logan kissed his ear. "I have some sparkling apple juice for the toast."

"The truth is, I was apologizing to Ryan," Simon confessed, and Logan's grip tightened.

"For what?" Logan demanded.

"I realized all this time had passed and I'd yet to say I was sorry for being so negative toward him and your relationship in the beginning. I've never seen you so happy, and that's all we ever wanted for you."

"I appreciate that, Si," Logan said quietly.

"I do as well." Ryan held out his hand, and Simon gripped it. "We're not the same people we were even a year ago. People can change."

More people entered, and Ryan waved to Jordan and Luke, Tash and Brandon, and Ash and Drew. Everyone swarmed him with their congratulations. His circle became complete when Emerson showed up with his boyfriend, Harvey. They waved to him but waited near the door.

"I'll be right back." He joined his friends. "Hey, guys, thanks for coming."

They each gave him a quick hug. Harvey had called Emerson after they'd met at Whole Foods, and after a few dates, they'd discovered neither was interested in a sexual relationship. After six months, Harvey moved into Emerson's apartment, and they were crazy in love. Ryan liked Harvey and thought the two made a great couple.

"We wouldn't miss it." Emerson's obvious happiness made Ryan happy.

Harvey nodded and squeezed Emerson's hand. "Yeah. I

think it's great, Ryan. Congratulations. I know it's not easy to return to school after so many years. I see lots of people try and fail. But Emerson knew you wouldn't." Harvey was a professor of Human Sexual Behavior, and the first time the four of them met, Logan had asked why an asexual person would teach a course on sexuality. Harvey's eyes had twinkled. *"Those who can, do. Those who can't—or have no desire to—teach."*

Ryan pointed at the tables filled with food. "Please have something to eat and drink. Everyone from the clinic is here."

He watched as the two men greeted Jordan and Luke.

Tash drew him aside. "How are you feeling? It can be a little overwhelming, I imagine."

"It is, but in a good way. I'm feeling so positive these days, and it took me some time to realize that's normal and not an aberration."

"It's an incredible accomplishment when you look at where you were only a few short years ago. I'm very proud of you, and I'm so happy you're continuing therapy."

Ryan had decided that being in therapy wasn't weak but a sign of strength. "I know this is only the beginning. I'm ready to see it through."

From the corner of his eye, he watched as Noah and his husband spoke to Logan and Todd. "Excuse me, I want to say hi to Noah and Oren."

"There's the man of the hour. Congratulations, Ryan. I never doubted you for a moment. You are the most determined person I've ever met."

"Speaking of fresh starts," Logan interrupted. "I was wondering, Noah, if you had time in your schedule to fit Todd and myself in." He gazed at Todd, who nodded and put a hand on his shoulder. "I think we need some healing of our own."

Noah's eyes grew tender. "I was so thrilled when you found Todd, but I can only imagine the trauma you've both endured since then. I was hoping you'd reach out, and whenever you want me, I'm available. Evenings are good, since Oren has been drafted to uncle duty."

Noah's husband, Oren, took his hand. "I've been helping my sister and her husband with their babies. Ilana and Yair just had twins, and my parents aren't up to helping much—although you didn't hear me say that—so I've been doing what I can."

Noah kissed his cheek. "They're adorable, and it's only made us more excited to start a family of our own."

Ryan noticed Logan's thoughtful face and his quick glance at Charlie, who was hanging out with his mother and Alexandra. Was Logan thinking of children? That was a step Ryan had never contemplated, and he decided to broach the subject later that night when they returned home.

* * *

It wasn't until they'd undressed for bed and lay wrapped in each other's arms, Logan stroking his back, that he decided to bring it up again.

"Can I ask you something?"

Logan kissed his ear. "Ask away, but I can't promise I'll answer. I'm dying for you." He nipped at the dip where Ryan's neck met his shoulder. "I want to make love to my hot grad student."

Ryan wiggled away from him. "I'm serious."

Logan sat up, face flushed but eyes wary. "Oookay. What's wrong?"

"Nothing, just…" He took a deep breath. "Do you want kids?"

Logan blinked. "What? Kids? Where is this coming from?"

Ryan pushed the hair out of his eyes. "Tonight, when Noah and Oren talked about their niece and nephew, and then seeing you and Charlie…you're so good with him, and he adores you."

Logan's eyes grew soft. "He's a great boy, isn't he?" His brow furrowed. "But kids? I-I don't know. I never thought about it. I'm in my midforties, Ry. I honestly don't know if I can handle a baby." Logan reached out and stroked his face. "I'm also a selfish bastard and don't think I want to take time away from us."

All things Ryan had considered. And yet…

"What if it wasn't a baby? There are so many older children who need parents. Gay teens whose parents turned them out, or kids who think they don't fit in. Maybe—"

"Maybe we could help them?" Logan scooted closer and took his mouth in a bruising kiss. "I always knew you were brilliant."

Ryan wound his arms around Logan's neck. "So you think it's a good idea?"

Logan kissed him again, his lips smiling. "I think that's a terrific idea. You're such a good person. I'm sure Wanda would know how to help us. We can talk about it with her tomorrow." He sucked Ryan's earlobe and pulled him close. "But right now I want you."

As always when Logan touched him, the fire simmering between them exploded into an inferno, and Ryan gave in to his hunger for the one man who understood him.

Needed him.

Loved him.

"I'll always want you."

He was finally free.

Finally home.

* * *

Thank you for reading *Castles in the Air*. I hope
you enjoyed Logan and Ryan's journey. And what a
journey it was! If you're interested in the other couples
who made up a big part of their lives, you can find
their stories in the Through Hell and Back Collection:
A Walk Through Fire, *After the Fire*, *Embrace the Fire*
and *The Miracle*. Dr. Noah's story is *One Call Away*.
As always, I would appreciate a review. Reviews are
lifeblood for indie authors.

FELICE STEVENS writes romance because what is better than people falling in love? Her favorite part of a romance novel is that first kiss…sigh. She loves creating stories of hopes and dreams and happily ever afters. Her stories are character-driven, rich with the sights, sounds and flavors of New York City and filled with men who are sometimes deeply flawed but always real.

Felice writes gay romance because she believes that everyone deserves a happily ever after. Having traveled all over the world, she can safely say that the universal language that unites people is love. Felice has written in a variety of sub-genres, including contemporary, paranormal, and she has a mystery series as well. You can find all her book listed on her website.

Felice is a two-time Lambda Literary Award nominee and the Lambda award-winner in Gay Romance for her book, *The Ghost and Charlie Muir*.

BOOKBUB
https://www.bookbub.com/profile/felice-stevens

NEWSLETTER
https://tinyurl.com/y85e69ab

READER GROUP
https://www.facebook.com/groups/FelicesBreakfastClub/

FACEBOOK AUTHOR PAGE
https://www.facebook.com/felicestevensauthor/

INSTAGRAM
https://www.instagram.com/felicestevens

GOODREADS
https://www.goodreads.com/author/show/8432880.Felice_
Stevens

WEBSITE
felicestevens.com

PAYHIP STORE
https://payhip.com/FeliceStevensAuthor